THE Y CHROMOSOME

THE Y CHROMOSOME

by

Leona Gom

to Rolf,
read this in
good health,
Leona

SECOND
STORY
Press

CANADIAN CATALOGUING IN PUBLICATION DATA
Gom, Leona, 1946–
The Y chromosome

ISBN 0-929005-16-3

I. Title.

PS8563.05Y2 1990   C813'.54   C90-095068-4
PR9199.3G65Y2 1990

With thanks for their support to the Canada Council, the University of Alberta, the University of Winnipeg, and the University of Lethbridge; and to Dale Evoy, Denise Bukowski, Aritha van Herk, and Bill Shermbrucker.

Excerpts from "Goodbye to Beef" and "Gorgeous" by Erin Mouré, from *Furious* (Toronto: House of Anansi Press, 1988). Reprinted by permission.

Printed and bound in Canada

Second Story Press gratefully acknowledges
the assistance of the Ontario Arts Council and the Canada Council.

Published by
SECOND STORY PRESS
760 Bathurst Street
Toronto, Canada M5S 2R6

CONTENTS

CHAPTER ONE

DANIEL

HE HEARD THE HORSES BEFORE HE SAW THEM. And the voices: two people at least. He dropped the pail of raspberries and hunched down beside it. He could feel his heart begin to bang at his chest, the sudden pulse of sweat in his armpits. He peered through the canes, relieved that he could see nothing, that he must be reasonably well hidden from the road.

They were directly opposite him now. The beat of hooves on the road was so loud it felt as though someone were clapping in his ear.

"My ass is *aching*," exclaimed a voice. A stranger. "How much farther?"

"A kilometre or so. Not long." It was Doctor. He knew her voice. But she sounded nervous, afraid almost.

"You were right," sighed the other voice. "I didn't know I was so out of shape."

Doctor made some reply, but they were past the raspberry field now, into the bush again, and Daniel couldn't make out her words.

He left the pail of berries where it had fallen and ran. The branches beat at him, and twice he fell as the underbrush tangled his feet, but he leaped up and kept running. He had to reach the farm before the stranger did. He slid down the gully into the dry creek bed, looking anxiously to his right, although he knew the crossing that the road took was a quarter of a kilometre to the north, where the incline was less steep, and he was fairly certain Doctor would keep to the road. He clambered up the other side, his feet knocking loose rocks and earth, but he grabbed at the birch-tree root he knew would be there and pulled himself up. He hadn't used the shortcut since he was a small child, but his body remembered the route as though he had just come this way this morning. A prairie chicken fluttered up at his feet. He jumped over it without slowing his pace. He could feel the burning in his side, but he couldn't stop; he was almost there, just through the clearing and past the last fringe of poplar. He could see his aunt's house now, flickering among the branches, and then he was through.

His aunt, Highlands, was in the garden, hilling the potatoes, the hoe clanging down on the hard, dry soil as though it were metal. He leaped carelessly over the rows of peas and cabbage. Highlands's hoe stopped in mid-air.

"What's wrong?" she demanded.

He stopped three rows down from her and bent over, his hands on his knees. "Stranger," he gasped. "Coming with Doctor." He gestured feebly at the road where it entered the farmyard.

Highlands had already dropped her hoe and was running to her house, her shirt flapping behind her like a torn wing. He watched her go, his breath raking his chest. He saw her pull the bell twice, the danger signal, and then he made himself hobble to the longhouse. When he reached it, his father was already opening the door, and his cousin, Montney, Highlands's son, ran up from where he had been working on the other side of the garden.

"What's happened?" Montney asked, excited. It had been

a long time since the danger bell had sounded.

"Stranger coming," Daniel said. "On horseback. She's with Doctor."

His father took his arm. "Come on," he said. "Don't stand around out here." Then he dropped his hand quickly, as though he remembered that Daniel was eighteen now and could no longer be ordered about like a child. Daniel gave him a little smile, acknowledging both the mistake and his tolerance of it. He enjoyed being eighteen, the sudden new respect, something Montney would have to wait a few more years for.

Once inside, his father closed the door and bolted it.

"They're here!" Montney shouted from the window, dropping below the sill and pulling out the loose piece of plaster between the third and fourth logs. Daniel joined him, squinting into the sunlight.

They were there, all right, dismounting now. The stranger, a middle-aged person with long grey hair pulled into a braid on one side of her head, grimaced as she slid down. Highlands came up to them, and Daniel could see them exchange greetings, the funny formal gripping of the shoulders, the dipping of the head, he'd had to learn. When he'd protested, his mother had insisted, "It's better they think us odd than that they should find out about you." And so he had learned the peculiar mannerisms he would be expected to exhibit around strangers, if he ever had to meet any. But it was rare for visitors to come here. An ancestor had made up a name for the inhabitants of the four farms with others like him — *Isolists* — so that outsiders would consider them a religious cult and leave them alone. It had worked well. When strangers did come, what they noted as unusual was not what was *really* unusual. Misdirection, Highlands called it, a magician's trick.

More of the farm people were coming up to Doctor and her

companion now, all of them sombrely greeting the stranger in the same mannered way. The children, he saw, all wanted to try it, most of them not yet having had a chance to practise on a real stranger. Daniel could see Highlands exhanging an anxious look with their mothers.

"Go back to work now!" shouted someone, and the children backed off, suddenly reminded this was no game. Only Bluesky and her sister, Shaw, stayed, confident in their new status as adults. Shaw, he remembered, had taken advantage of her option of choosing a second name and insisted on being called Shaw-Ellen now. But it was Bluesky he watched. She was tall and muscular, her thick pale hair pulled back from her face with two red pins. He remembered the way she had been yesterday, in this very room, naked above him, her eyes squeezed shut and her lips pulled back as though she were in pain. He had to close his eyes to stop seeing her, but still the erection pushed warmly at his thigh.

"They're going into our house, I think," his father said.

Daniel snapped open his eyes. Highlands and Daniel's mother had already gone inside, and Doctor and the stranger were following them in. Two of the others went in, as well, and the rest waited outside for a few minutes, whispering nervously, and then went back to their own houses. He thought he saw Bluesky throw a quick look at the longhouse.

His father turned and leaned back against the wall, his legs thrust out in front of him like two long thick logs. He ran his callused thumb absently around the head of a nail starting to work itself loose from the floorboard beside him.

Daniel turned, too, sat with one leg pulled up against the inside of the other. He didn't resemble his father at all; small-boned and blonde, he looked more like his mother. It was his sister, Mitchell, who looked like their father, heavy and dark, with the large mouth and brows like two hedges overhanging the eyes.

"I wonder why Doctor would bring her," his father said.

"I don't think she wanted to," Daniel said. "I heard them on the road. I think the stranger insisted on coming."

"She must suspect something. Merde." There was a frightened edge to his voice, and Daniel looked at him, catching his fear. His father rubbed his hand up and down one cheek, and the sound of stubble rasped against his fingers.

"You didn't cut your face hair," Daniel accused.

"I know," his father said. "I forgot."

"You said it was the most important thing," Daniel insisted. "How could you forget?"

"I *know*," his father said. "I just forgot, that's all."

"They're coming out," Montney said. "Now they're going into Mother's house."

Daniel turned again to look. He could see Highlands opening the door to her house, inviting the stranger in.

"It's like some kind of inspection," Daniel said.

"She won't come in *here,* will she?" Montney asked.

"No," Daniel's father said, sounding firm and confident again. "Of course not. Your mother won't let her. No one can enter the longhouse without the Leader's consent."

And the thought of Highlands seemed to reassure them all. She was the one they could count on; she would protect them. When Daniel was young he had sometimes been afraid of her temper, the fights she would have with his father, not the way a brother and sister were supposed to behave at all, but the older he got the more he liked and admired her, her quickness and self-assurance. Once he told his father he wished Highlands were his mother, and his father, looking at his mother across the yard taking down the clothes from the line, slowly, her placid face upturned to the sky like a cup filling with sunshine, said, "There are skills just as important as intelligence, Daniel. Intelligence can let you down. But love doesn't." It didn't make much sense to Daniel, but it sounded like something that might one day, so he knew he should probably remember it.

Still, it was Highlands Daniel would go to when he wanted to talk, choosing her over both his mother and father, even though the things she told him were often not the things he wanted to hear. It was Highlands whose approval he wanted most of all, perhaps because it was not easily given.

"What if they want to stay overnight?" Montney asked suddenly. "It's late for them to make it back to Fairview."

"I don't think they'll want to stay," Daniel's father said. "They haven't unsaddled the horses. Doctor would have told the other one that hospitality is not one of our virtues. And your mother will show her the shed with Cayley's old broken bed and imply that's where they'd have to sleep." He laughed, and so did Daniel and Montney, giggling at the thought of the way Highlands would handle it, enjoying herself.

"Still," Daniel's father said, "I don't like it that she came with Doctor. She may be a doctor, too."

"Maybe she's the one Doctor told us about," Montney said. "The new one she was going to train and tell about us."

"I don't think so," Daniel said. "She's too old."

Montney got up, began to prowl restlessly around the room, idly picking up the school-books stacked in small neat piles on the shelves. Daniel had read them all, some more than once, and he was always the first to pounce on the person who came back from town with the boxes of new library books. Now that he was eighteen, he could go into town himself if the farm gave its permission — he could spend a whole day, if he wanted, in the library, a building, they told him, full of a thousand books.

The thought of it filled him with excitement. He would have to be careful, of course, and dress in the special townclothes that were made of heavier cloth than what he usually wore on the farm in summer. But his father went into town sometimes, and Kit from East Farm had gone to Leth for a whole week. Leth: where the university was, where Daniel had dreamed of going, before he had to accept that it was forbidden, too dangerous for a male.

Male. He had looked it up in the dictionary once, that same dictionary that Montney was pounding lightly with his fist. *Male*, it said, *from French "mal" and Latin "male". 1. bad, abnormal, inadequate; 2. sub-species of human extinct in 21st century.*

"They're coming out of Mother's house," Montney said suddenly.

Daniel and his father turned, crouched at the crack between the logs, and peered out. Doctor and the stranger were coming out first, followed by the others, who remained standing together on the porch while Doctor and the stranger walked a few steps farther, then turned back. Everyone on the porch, in almost perfect, graceful unison, bowed.

Doctor bowed, too, and the stranger, hesitating a moment, bowed as well, awkwardly, holding her head up to keep everyone in sight. Then the two of them untied the reins of their horses from the post by Highlands's house, mounted, and rode off. Doctor gave a quick look behind her and waved, furtively perhaps. Daniel felt his hand go up, too, without thinking, to wave back. He liked Doctor. He wished he could have talked to her. Daniel, she was always fond of remembering, was the first male she had ever delivered. Until then, she'd confessed to his mother, she'd never quite believed what the doctor who was training her told her about the existence of the males; she'd thought it was just some bizarre story to test her gullibility. Now, of course, the farm could not imagine being without her, and they were as anxious about the new doctor she would have to tell and trust as they first had been about her.

"Let's go," Montney said, heading for the door. Daniel followed him, his thoughts turning already to the raspberry field and his dropped pail, into which the ants might have gotten by now.

"Wait," his father said. "We have to make sure it's not a trick."

Through the window Daniel could see Highlands approaching the longhouse. "Your mother's coming," he said to Montney. "Let her in."

Montney unbolted the door, and Highlands stepped inside. She was so tall she had to bend to keep from hitting her head.

She was smiling. "I especially liked the way we bowed," she said. "Weren't we good?"

"Wonderful," Daniel's father said. "Well, what did she want?"

"It's okay. It was Doctor's supervisor. She just decided to come out and do a work-load check on Doctor. Nothing to worry about." She rested her forearm on Montney's shoulder, let her hand with its long thin fingers dangle in the air.

"Did she ask about those of us who weren't with you?" Daniel asked.

"I said three of our farm were out in the fields. It seemed to satisfy her. I think she was just curious about us. But it went all right. Doctor winked at me when she left."

"I told you it was nothing to worry about," Montney said to Daniel's father.

"You can't be too careful," he said.

"You didn't cut your face hairs," Montney accused. He turned to his mother, a triumphant excitement on his face. "He didn't cut his face hairs," he repeated.

Highlands looked at them both coldly. "I can see that," she

said. "We'll have to bring it up at next Meeting, Christoph."

"That's not right!" Daniel's voice shivered with the effort of standing up to Highlands. He'd never done it before, not really. But he was eighteen now, an adult, even if he was a male. "Father had early work-load today. He doesn't usually forget. You don't know what it's like, every morning —"

"No, Daniel," his father said quietly. "Highlands is right. It's too important to forget."

He hated seeing his father give in so easily, let her win without even trying. He didn't used to be like that. Daniel was suddenly angry at all of them, his father for his meekness and deference, Montney for telling, Highlands for using her postion as Leader to humilate his father. He could feel his cheek muscles tightening, his lips squeezing themselves thin as though his whole face were under pressure. His madface, his mother used to call it affectionately when he was a child — but he was an adult now: his anger would no longer be amusing. He made himself relax, drop his eyes to the floor.

Highlands said nothing for a moment, only looked from one to the other of them. Finally her gaze settled on Daniel's father. "Well, no harm done, I guess," she said. "You're only human."

His father smiled wryly at her. "Nice of you to think so."

She looked at Daniel then, and perhaps because she said nothing to him he knew suddenly and to his surprise that she was pleased at the way he had defended his father, even though she shouldn't be — she shouldn't allow such a challenge to her authority, not even from an adult. He felt confused and uncomfortable. And something else, too, something he would think about later, when he was alone. He felt powerful.

CHAPTER TWO

BOWDEN

"I CAN'T DECIDE WHICH OF THESE VIDSPOOLS TO USE," Delacour said. "What do you think?"

Bowden put down the book on geriatrics she was reading and walked across the centreroom to where Delacour sat, her desk scattered with more than a dozen spools of film. The player built into the back of the desk was showing one of them, pictures of a male, late twentieth century, judging by the clothes; he was jumping from a high building and as he fell he was being transformed into something else, an animal of some kind, a wolf perhaps, which then pursued and caught two other males running from him. It all took only a few seconds, as though Delacour had the spool on "accelerate," but Bowden knew it was how the film was supposed to look.

"Is this still your male empowerment series?" she asked.

Delacour groaned, pressing the fingers of her right hand rigidly against her forehead. Bowden noticed, a little alarmed, that she had been biting her nails again.

"Yes," Delacour said. "Archive keeps sending over more." She gestured at her desk. "Most of these came in yesterday. Even if I eliminate the animal conversions, like this one — " she reached over and snapped off the player; the wolf was just changing back to a male " — and the robotics and machine enhancements, there still seem to be dozens of the self-activateds." She picked up a spool labelled *Incredible Hulk*. "This one for instance. How do I classify it? Do you know it?"

"No, of course not." Why should Delacour think Bowden would know about things like that, things that probably nobody in the world aside from Delacour and Archive had ever heard of?

"It's about a male contaminated in some lab accident that turns him, at implicitly convenient times, into a powerful green humanoid monster."

"A powerful green humanoid monster?"

"That's right. A hero-quest subgenre, the male searching for normalcy. But the monster, of course, is aggression idealized, self unambivalent as perfect weapon, so it's the usual paradox. Anyway — " She tapped the spool lightly on the desk. "Do I consider this a true self-activated, like *Kung-Fu* and *The Mandrake*, or is the lab accident interventionism?"

"I don't know," Bowden said. "Why do you bother with all this, anyway? Who really cares about all that ancient stuff?" She knew it was a mistake, saying that, but she couldn't erase the careless words.

Delacour looked up. "It's my work," she said, speaking slowly, the way that made Bowden feel patronized, simple-minded. "I'm a historian. I teach history. It's important."

"I know it is. It's just — all this stuff about the male. The Change was more than three hundred years ago. You can't assume everyone is interested in those times."

Perhaps Delacour heard the pleading in Bowden's voice, because she sighed and said vaguely, "I suppose," but the way her voice came down hard on the last syllable, sup*pose*, still spoke more of irritation than conciliation.

They were silent for a moment, not looking at each other. They seemed to be arguing more and more lately, stupid little hurtful arguments, and it always left Bowden feeling helpless and inadequate, as though their lives were an untidy room, an unmade bed, dirty dishes in the sink, which could be cleaned and straightened if only they cared enough.

Impulsively, she went over to Delacour's chair and sat down at her feet, resting her head in Delacour's lap. She ran her hand lightly up and down Delacour's bare leg, felt the soft static in her skin. Delacour's hand settled on Bowden's head, sifted through the thick red hair, which, she'd said, had drawn her to Bowden like a flame by which to warm herself when they first met eight years ago. Bowden could still remember the day: she had been working in Hospital, as usual, as a helper for old people, and she had gone down to Medical Archive with Shawna, another helper, to look for genetics records on one of their patients. And there they had seen Delacour, grumbling over misfiled vidspools. When Shawna had offered to help, she had said impatiently, "No, no, I'll figure it out."

But Bowden could feel Delacour's eyes following her as she walked away down the aisle toward the genetics section, and she wasn't quite as surprised as she pretended to be when Shawna, raising an eyebrow, told her next day a message had come in on the ward computer asking for the name of the red-haired person who had been in Medical Archive yesterday.

"How did she know which ward we were on?" Shawna asked.

"She must be more resourceful than she seemed," Bowden said.

She smiled now, thinking of it, and looked up. She liked it when Delacour played with her hair, the way it made her scalp tingle, goose bumps run warmly up her back. She could feel her whole body responding. She pushed her hand farther up Delacour's leg, parting the loose teacher's-robe, touching thigh, the prickle of pubic hair.

Delacour's hand grew still on Bowden's head. "I have to teach," she said softly. "We haven't time." But she didn't draw away.

"That's too bad," Bowden said. She pulled her hand back, not too quickly.

They sat as they were for a few minutes, Delacour's fingers tightening, relaxing, in Bowden's hair. Finally Delacour sighed, took her hand away.

"I really have to go," she said. She stood up, began pulling together her papers and books and vidspools for her class.

Bowden stood up, too. "Shall we eat with the others tonight?" she asked. "Or I could make us something." Their apartment, like the others in their complex, had a small food-preparation area, but most people preferred to eat in the common dining-room. Bowden still owed a few hours of work in the kitchen this month, and she'd thought she would make them up this afternoon, after Delacour left; there were always leftovers she could bring home and reheat.

"Whatever you think. Don't go to any extra work for me."

"It's no extra work."

"Why don't you come to class with me?" Delacour said suddenly. "You have the whole day off work, don't you?"

"Well, yes — "

"So come. You might enjoy it. My best student is discussing compensation theory."

"But — would she mind, somebody new coming in?"

"No, of course not. People are encouraged to drop in whenever they want. There are always a few there I haven't seen before."

"Well, all right. If you're sure it's okay." She didn't really want to go, but she was glad Delacour had asked her. And it would be more interesting than working in the kitchen.

She changed into a new pair of pants and pulled on the sweater

Delacour had bought for her birthday. It was really too warm outside for something so heavy, but she thought it might be the kind of thing the students wore. She didn't want to look like an outsider. She pulled a comb through her hair and pinned it back, watching her face in the mirror. She was attractive; it was no vanity to see that. But she was no longer young; she was almost forty, and Delacour was ten years younger, surrounded by people even younger than that. She pulled her lips back into a tight rectangle of smile; it made her cheeks hurt. When she relaxed her lips she noticed the way the skin around her mouth still held the tension lines, and she reached up and rubbed at them as though they were smudges of dirt.

Delacour was waiting for her at the door to the hallway. "It's such nice weather," she said. "Let's walk outside."

Surprised, Bowden agreed. Most of the time Delacour insisted on taking the moveways because they were faster; she had no patience with the wandering pathways outside. For her, the destination was usually more important than the journey.

They left their unit and took the stairs to the ground floor, then pushed open the heavy main door that led outside from Residential. The hot summer air rushed at them. They walked through the garden, Bowden stopping to exclaim at the tall gladioli and sensual orange roses that she bent to smell even though she knew they had no scent. Delacour broke a small fistful of needles from a pine tree beside the path and rubbed them between her fingers. Then she handed the cluster to Bowden. Not wanting to waste it now that it had been picked, and not knowing what else to do with it, she put it in the pocket of her pants.

At the end of the garden they turned onto the main walkway that paralled their apartment section and led, to the east, to University and, to the north, to Hospital. It felt odd to take the east walkway; Bowden rarely had reason to go to University, and whenever she did she got lost. Of course, people who weren't familiar with Hospital complained about how confusing it was, too, yet its corridors and rooms and units felt as familiar to her as her own hand; the map of it turned in her head like a globe, like a huge and beautiful atom.

The entire Hospital-University-Commercial-Residential complex was really one enormous building, more than three square kilometres in area, and up to ten storeys high in places, built along the east bank of the deepcoulee that loped down to Oldman River. Hospital still dominated the structure, since it was there that the whole complex began, when, after the Change, the country (although there were still two countries then) poured its wealth into frantic research; some of the old twenty-first-century structure was still standing, and the medical museum kept most of Dr. Kostash's six labs intact.

It was an impressive building, no doubt about it, Bowden thought as they turned into University and she looked behind her, the sun wrinkling the air as it bounced off concrete and bondglass and sunsavers and metal. The building seemed to go on until it dropped below the curvature of the earth. Some of the oldcity still existed to the north and across the deepcoulee, but, as in most cities now, individual structures tended to be impractical and wasteful, and it had become easier just to replace them as needed by expanding the existing complex. The population had been more or less stable for the past century, of course, so there had been little new building of any kind; it had mostly been a matter of updating and replacing and maintenance.

A tour group wearing badges saying "LosAngels Hospital" passed them on the right, and Bowden felt a little nudge of pride, as she always did, to see people from so far south here to tour Hospital. Leth Hospital was the second largest on the continent. Of course, some people were coming just as tourists, too, to see the Kostash labs.

They entered University. Bowden felt out of place here, intimidated by the rooms full of books and vidspools, by the students, by the ideas she chose long ago not to pursue. The place smelled faintly dusty and stale, and she realized she was expecting it to smell like Hospital, with its priority-one air control. She felt her pace slowing, and twice Delacour had to stop and wait for her to catch up. By the time they came to the History branch, Bowden felt utterly lost in the chaos of hallways.

The walls in the corridor they had just entered were painted a bright orange, and she knew this was a coding of some kind, probably for a subcategory of History. In apparently random collage-clusters on the walls were pinned notices by students: meetings, intellectual arguments, sketches, poems, advertisements, unashamedly personal confessions or appeals for advice. Certainly these seemed more interesting to Bowden than the computyped infonotes put up by the teachers on the display boards around the busier intersections they had passed. But perhaps if she saw such student notices every day, as Delacour did, she would walk past them, too, without a glance.

Then Delacour was slowing down, and people were greeting her, sometimes pausing to ask about meetings or research projects or just to make conversation. Bowden knew she had met some of these people at the monthly gatherings, but she couldn't remember their names, so she stood beside Delacour with a vacant smile on her face, and nobody bothered her. She found it interesting to watch Delacour's colleagues talk to her — it was something Bowden had gotten good at in her own work, hearing what people were saying by not listening to the words themselves. She heard respect in their voices now, sycophancy sometimes, and sometimes a trace of fear. It didn't surprise her. If she worked with Delacour she could imagine feeling all these things about her.

As they got closer to the department centre, people seemed to be moving faster, buzzing around the hive with their pollen of papers and books. One large person about Bowden's age, who walked by means of throwing herself from side to side, huffed her way toward them.

"Delacour," she said, not smiling. "Archive sent over more spools for you."

Delacour groaned. "I can't keep up with what I have already."

The person nodded her several chins. "Do less," she said, nodding again at her words. "Do less." She flicked her eyes at Bowden, ran them like a scanner down her body, up again to her face. "Bowden," she said. Then she lurched on past down the hall.

"Who was that?" Bowden whispered, alarmed. "How does she know me?"

"She's the centre co-ordinator. You met her once. One of the gatherings. She has a rather formidable memory."

"She's the co-ordinator, and she wants you to do *less*?"

Delacour laughed dismissively. "I don't expect she means it."

They turned a corner, and Bowden recognized the library centre where Delacour worked. It wasn't a large room, and more than half of it was filled with shelf-rows of books and vidspools. Three of the walls were stacked to the ceiling with them, and the fourth was lined with small computer screens and fiche-readers. One corner of this wall held Delacour's desk, around which about a dozen people were sitting, some on the floor, in a loose semicircle. By the way they looked up and cut their conversation to trailing murmurs Bowden knew they must be Delacour's students. She glanced at Delacour, saw her face eager, excited.

Bowden walked to the back of the group, trying to appear

inconspicuous, and sat down in one of the few vacant chairs. No one paid her any attention.

"All right, then," Delacour said, striding to the front, her teacher's-robe belling out behind her. "Male compensation theory today. Your presentation, isn't it, Hythe?" She smiled at someone near the front, who stood up, turned casually, and, propping an elbow on one of the shelf-rows, began to talk, without notes, in a fragmented and jumpy but almost bored way. Bowden didn't listen to what she was saying; she could only stare at her. She was beautiful — flawless skin the colour of almonds, large blue eyes with brows arching smoothly above them, blonde hair done in the fashionable four braids and attached with a red clip to the shoulder of a white cotton shift so thin it was almost transparent. She made Bowden feel old and foolish in her heavy sweater, and Bowden wished Delacour had told her to dress more appropriately.

" — the revisionist-structuralists. Redundancy anticipation. If the male-defining phallus had really been pride-stimulus, it would not have been so determinedly hidden. Photographs. Film. Art. We are commonly depicted naked. Not males. The phallus: obviously an attribute of shame. Furthermore — " She tapped the forefinger of her right hand on that of her left. Bowden noticed she had a tiny and delicate transfer-tattoo on the back of her right hand. "Transvestism. On one hand, males dressing secretly in clothing of people. Or 'fe-males,' as we were called then. Other hand: identifying with fe-males of other species by choosing dowdy dress. Basic confusion-compensation. Then — " she tapped her forefinger again " — popularization of male-childbirth technology. Early twenty-first century. Self-repudiation."

She smiled languidly at Delacour, who nodded in apparent agreement and encouragement. "Challenge?" Hythe asked, gazing around the group. Bowden hunched down in her seat.

"But if the male was envious of us and felt inferior," asked someone, "how do you explain their oppression of us, their war-making and aggression?"

Hythe shrugged. "Antithesis compensation. When one cannot emulate, one emphasizes difference. Elevate deficiency to superiority."

"There was a saying before the Change," Delacour said, propping her foot up on a chair behind Hythe. " 'To make a virtue of necessity.' "

Hythe turned, gave her a smile that almost seemed patronizing. "I suppose so. But more like another old saying, 'If you can't join them, beat them.' "

Bowden sat up. The phrase was wrong, she was sure of it. It was supposed to be the other way around. Eagerly she looked at Delacour, waiting for her correction, but Delacour only smiled vaguely and nodded. Surely she must know, Bowden thought — why didn't she say so?

"Challenge?" Hythe said again, looking around the room and opening her hands in front of her as though she were holding a globe of air.

For one alarming moment Bowden felt her mouth opening and the words shaping in her throat, and then she sank back in her seat. She had never spoken out in a class, had always been the one to sit in the back and hope to go unnoticed. And this was Delacour's class, and she only a visitor, and her point, after all, was a very trivial one. She looked down at her hands.

No one spoke, and the room was silent except for the person beside Bowden who was writing something down, her pencil sounding as though its lead were made of gritty sand.

"Well," Delacour said finally, "let's have a short break, and then we can discuss the application of this approach in the Adam

Markov journal. Hythe, thank you."

She put her hand on Hythe's shoulder, and something in Bowden went cold, afraid.

The students got up and, in little groups of twos and threes, left the room, talking excitedly to each other. Bowden had no idea if it was about the presentation or not. She was still watching Delacour and Hythe, who stood at the front of the room, close to each other, talking in low voices.

Slowly she got up and approached them. She saw that Hythe's braids, although obviously done with considerable care, were tied with pieces of string. Just the sort of touch Delacour might think was charming.

"Hythe, this is my mate, Bowden," Delacour said, putting her hand on Bowden's shoulder, in exactly the same way she had put it on Hythe's, the thumb dropping forward and nesting under her collarbone, "Bowden, this is Hythe."

"I'm happy to meet you," Hythe said.

Bowden nodded, her throat dry. "Hello," she said.

"How did you like Hythe's presentation?" Delacour asked. Her hand was still on Bowden's shoulder. It didn't feel reassuring; it felt only like pressure.

"It was ... very interesting." She tried desperately to think of something less banal to say. "Was it your own research?"

Hythe stared at her with her beautiful large eyes, and her perfectly arched eyebrows arched even higher. She laughed. "Oh, of *course* not. I was just the presenter. It's basically a revisionist-essentialist position."

Bowden could feel a blush, an absurd betraying blush, pressing at her cheeks, and she looked at the floor, nodded stupidly at her feet. She saw Hythe wasn't wearing shoes, another current fashion, and it made her feel even worse.

Delacour took her hand from Bowden's shoulder. "Well, the

essentialists approach it a bit differently, you know."

"Only in respect to antithesis compensation — "

Bowden stopped listening. She stood there like the child in the classroom who hadn't known the right answer, who would have to stand there until Teacher dismissed her.

Some of the other students were coming back into the room, taking their seats.

"I think I'll go home," Bowden said. She'd interrupted something Hythe was saying.

"Don't you want to stay for the second half?" Delacour asked.

Bowden fixed her gaze on the shelf of vidspools behind Delacour's left ear. Delacour's face separated into two, transparent. "I've got things to do at home."

"All right. I'll see you later then."

Bowden nodded. Then she made herself look at Hythe, that calm, confident face with the smile ornamenting her lips, and she said, "I'm happy to have met you." She turned, not waiting for an answer, and walked out of the room. She had to ask twice for directions out of the building.

When Delacour came home, Bowden was washing the floor in the hallway between their sleeprooms. Delacour set her things on the entranceway table and walked over to her.

"Why are you doing that? I washed the floors just last week."

"I felt like doing something physical," Bowden said. She squeezed the sponge out, her hand turning into a hard red knot. She ran the sponge along the curled board that became part of the wall, and was childishly pleased to see it come away grey with dirt.

"Are you hungry?" Delacour asked. "We could go down now

and eat."

"You go if you want to. I had some fruit when I came home."

Delacour sat down on the floor and took hold of Bowden's hand as it moved toward her on the wallboard. Water drizzled out of the sponge from the pressure of their clenched fingers.

"What's the matter?" Delacour said.

"Nothing's the matter."

Delacour pulled the sponge from Bowden's hand and tossed it in the bucket. "Tell me," she said.

Bowden sat back on her heels and pushed the hair from her eyes with the back of her hand. Her face felt greasy and damp with sweat. "You and that student," she said.

"Hythe? Whatever do you mean?" She sounded convincingly bewildered.

"I could see there was something between you. Is that why you wanted me to come to class with you? So I could see? So she could humiliate me in front of you?"

Delacour leaned her head back against the wall and closed her eyes. "Bowden, Bowden," she said softly.

Bowden could feel the impotent tears pushing at her eyes. She stood up, but Delacour remained where she was, leaning against the wall, her legs pulled up slightly and her forearms draped on her knees, her hands dangling loose and relaxed as though she had disconnected the tendons. Her choosing to remain on the floor gave her even more authority somehow, and as Bowden looked down at her she felt clumsy and irresolute.

"I asked you to come to the class," Delacour said, her eyes turned up to Bowden, "because I really thought you'd find it interesting. Hythe is my best student, and I thought she'd give an entertaining presentation. I was actually rather disappointed." She sighed. "And the class didn't seem very well prepared to challenge. Compensation theory can be amusing to discuss."

"I've never even heard of it before," Bowden said. She walked into the centreroom and dropped down so hard into the armchair at the entrance to the hallway that it sent a wince of pain up her spine. The upholstery sighed at the sudden weight. I'm *sick* of this arguing, she thought. Still she heard her voice ask, "And Hythe? Won't you admit you're attracted to her?"

Delacour lifted her hands, capped them carefully over her knees. "She's lovely. Of course I'm attracted to her."

The admission took Bowden by surprise. "And is that all?" Her voice wobbled, like that of someone ill pressing Doctor for the cruelest diagnosis. "Have you made love with her?"

"For heaven's sake," Delacour cried, her composure snapping. "Why are you going on like this?" She got to her feet. "You agreed you didn't want a monogamy-bond."

"I know." Bowden sank back in her chair. It was true, she told herself miserably. She was being jealous and possessive, everything she had promised herself she would not be. Why was she behaving like this, she, Bowden, the one everyone at work said was so tranquil she would smile through an earthquake? It was true she had dismissed, cavalierly and even laughing a little, the idea of a monogamy-bond when she and Delacour had first met; she had, after all, had one with Enilda, with whom she had lived for five years, and it had been no deterrent to her leaving Bowden for someone else. But still — knowing Delacour made love to others pressed in her some primal pain, and again and again she would berate herself: *She is all I desire; why am I not enough for her?*

"If you want our promises made legal," Delacour said, "well, you know the law. We can have a child."

"A *child?*" The word stuttered from Bowden's lips in an astonished laugh. "Delacour. We agreed — I'm too old. And you — you'd make a terrible mother. You told me so yourself.

A baby might entertain you at first, and then you'd leave her for me to raise."

Delacour's brows pulled themselves straight and tense on her face, scooping a small trench on the bridge of her nose into which Bowden had the sudden absurd desire to lay her finger. And then Delacour laughed. "Of course you're right," she said. She dropped her hand on Bowden's head, sifted her fingers through her hair, lifting, dropping, like a winnower. Bowden could feel her scalp shiver, could feel the tightness in her shoulders ease. She reached up, took Delacour's other hand and pressed it to her cheek.

"I wish our holiday began tomorrow," Delacour sighed. "August is so far away."

"It'll be worth waiting for," Bowden said. But she wasn't really convinced. They — or rather Delacour — had planned a rather ambitious camping trip. Still, Bowden had been pleased that Delacour would want to spend so much time with her, so she had readily agreed. And it *would* be nice, she assured herself — it was what they needed.

Outside, it began to rain, a warm summer rain smelling of settling dust and wet leaves. They watched it, soft as feathers, brush against the west windows that looked out over the deep-coulee, watched it push in through the screen and darken the clay pot full of parsley sitting on the sill.

"Let's make love," Bowden said.

"Yes."

They went into Delacour's sleeproom and got undressed and lay down on the bed. They stroked each other in the places they knew the other liked, kissed breasts and lips and the soft insides of knees and elbows, ran their fingers down the delicate beads of vertebrae. There was a gentleness to them that ground down the edges of their passion, but Bowden didn't care; it made

31

her remember the caring there was between them.

Delacour got up first and went into the bathroom; Bowden could hear her running the shower, although they had used up their quota this morning and she would have to be content with tepid water. Bowden got up, too, at last, and dressed, and went into the hallway, where she picked up the bucket and sponge and put them away. Then she sat down on the sofa in the centreroom and opened the book on geriatrics she had been reading. She knew two of the other helpers wanted to discuss it with her tomorrow, but she couldn't concentrate, her eyes like binoculars out of focus, set for the distance between her and the door to the bathroom. But when Delacour opened the door Bowden quickly pulled her eyes down to the book, turning a page with apparent thoughtfulness. She realized two of the pages, printed on thin and often-recycled paper, had stuck together, but she didn't go back and separate them.

"I'm going out," Delacour said. She was wearing her white pants with the red embroidery, a project she had begun with enthusiasm, but as soon as she had mastered the intricate stitching she tired of it, and Bowden had hired someone at Hospital to finish it for her. "I have some work to do at the library centre."

"It's so late," Bowden said, looking at the time-chip in the wall. It was past six. "I thought you wanted to go for supper."

"I'll get something on the way. You said you weren't hungry."

"I am now, a bit."

Delacour fidgeted, scratching at her upper arm. Her nails were so short they didn't dent the skin, but the pressure of her fingers left four red rows. "I really can't come. I have to get this done."

"All right." She watched Delacour walk to the door, the long strides she took, the way she carried one shoulder a little higher than the other, the way her short black hair curled at her neck, and she was wrenched with such love for her she almost cried out.

32

"I might be late," Delacour said, her hand on the door. "You don't need to wait up."

After she had gone, Bowden wandered around the apartment, picking things up and then setting them down again. She would decide on little chores, but by the time she went to do them she would find herself in a room with no idea what it was she was there to do. Finally, although she really had no appetite, she left the apartment and went down to the dining room, a large room on the main floor, which served the Red South section.

Not many people were left in the room, but two of the doctors she worked with and who lived in her section called her over to their table, so she ate with them, trying to become interested in their conversation about the new thermal machines. She kept thinking about Delacour, the way she'd looked when she put her hand on Hythe's shoulder.

She refused the doctors' offer of a game of springball after supper and headed to her apartment. She walked outside, inhaling deeply the fresh wet air. It was still raining a bit, a thin misty rain so fine it seemed almost to be falling up from the ground.

Back inside, she went into the bathroom and shook her head over the tub. Flecks of water flew against the tiled walls. She took off her clothes, watching herself in the mirror. I don't look old, she told herself, not really. I look the way I am supposed to look. She ran her hands down her body, the heavy breasts with the large brown nipples, the right breast slightly larger than the other; the waist still slim; the hips and thighs that flared out too generously, perhaps, with too much dimpling flesh .... Annoyed, she turned from the mirror — why was she evaluating herself like this, against what standards? I look the way I am supposed to. I am not supposed to look twenty.

As she tossed her damp clothes over the shower rail, some-thing fell from her pants pocket. She jumped back, alarmed, seeing a large leggy insect, a spider; but then she remembered: it was the clump of pine needles. She picked it up from the floor, the needles limp but, with the damp, releasing a sharp clean smell into the room. She set it on the counter.

She finished hanging up her clothes on the rail, pulling down Delacour's teacher's-robe, which for some reason was hanging there. Impulsively, she put it on. It hung almost to her ankles, but otherwise it was surprisingly comfortable, loose and light. It must, Bowden thought wistfully, make the wearer feel safe and confident, concealing all trembling flesh, deflecting the phys-ical judgements of the world. She took it off and hung it in its usual place by the front door and put on her own robe, an old red one with the elbows nearly worn through but of which she had grown too fond to replace.

In the centreroom she turned on the entertainments guide, but nothing that scrolled past her on the screen particularly in-terested her, although she paused on the news runner about the Middle East droughts that were turning the region into the same huge desert Africa had become. The birth rate there, the runner noted, had, unlike in most countries, dropped to con-siderably under replacement, whether by choice or because of the difficulty of reaching Cairo Hospital it didn't say. Tomor-row, Bowden decided, she would go to Management and tell them to raise her world-welfare tithe above the obligatory twenty-five per cent.

Perhaps she could persuade Delacour to do the same — her basepay assessment was higher than Bowden's, after all, and it was time she became as involved in the future as she was in the past. Well, that was hardly fair — granted, Delacour found the local government consensus meetings tiresome and gave her proxy vote to Bowden more often than she should, but she had also been one of Leth's world-government representatives for five years. She had worked harder than anyone to resolve the Argent-Brazil disputes.

"In the good old days," she'd told Bowden cheerfully, "the males would just have had a war and killed each other off. Presto."

"Don't joke about it," Bowden said, shuddering.

"I know, I know," Delacour sighed. "Peace just takes so damned much time, that's all."

Bowden programmed in some audio and left it playing on low and went to pick up her book. As she walked past the table at the entranceway she glanced at the books and papers and vidspools Delacour had left there when she came home. She noticed two large, odd-shaped binders, their pages plasti-proofed, that she hadn't seen before. Curious, she picked one up. Stamped in large letters on the cover were the words, *Warning. Pre-Change Original. Do not remove from Archive.* She set it down, alarmed. She had learned even as a child the importance of preserving ancient documents, since so few survived the Change. But that was Delacour for you, she thought with a flare of anger, treating the rules as though they were made for someone else. There was no reason Delacour couldn't be using a copy instead of the original.

She picked up the heavy binder again, her fingers trembling. She'd never actually held a Pre-Change Original before. But if the pages were plasti-proofed, perhaps it wouldn't matter as much if she looked, so long as she was careful. Delacour would be pleased, she thought wryly, my taking an interest in history. She opened the cover. *The Journal of Adam Markov. Volume 12*, it said on the front page.

The Journal of Adam Markov. She'd heard of it before, when she was in school; they'd read excerpts of it, but she couldn't remember much, only that it was kept by someone who had lived in this city, across the deepcoulee, and that it was one of the few journals still in existence that chronicled the Change, and from the point of view of a male. A male: she felt an old and unexpected shudder run through her. *The male will get you, the male will get you.* She could still hear the giggly cries of her playmates when she began her kilometre-long walk home alone from kindergarten, through the woods made suddenly sinister by their echoing voices. And behind every tree, around every bend in the path there he would be, the male, the monster, and even if she evaded him he would follow her home and climb into her dreams and she would awaken screaming, unable to tell her mothers the nightmare, so terrifying was it, so beyond description.

She took the journal with her to the armchair and sat down. She looked at it for several moments, lying there in her lap, and then, hesitantly, and with great care, she lifted the cover. She noticed that Delacour had, starting at about the middle of the binder, stuck pieces of orange paper in at different places. Bowden opened the journal at the place the first orange paper was inserted.

The handwriting was clear and strong, with a pronounced right-hand slant and unusually large loops to the upper letters. Bowden ran her finger along one line, tried to imagine Adam Markov himself writing those words, on this same page she was holding.

She began to read. Then she turned to the next marked page and the next, although sometimes there were whole years between the markers.

THE JOURNAL OF ADAM MARKOV
Volume 12

Sept. 4, 2053:

Even worse than last year. I should have been prepared for it, but how can you be? Ten years ago the Grade Twos alone were enough to split into two classes. And to see the ones who were missing — I was nearly goddamned crying when I read the Grade Three roll and kept seeing the names that were gone since I had them in Grade Two just last spring — Jeffrey Lukas, deleted between Christine Engels and Jason Markowski; Johnny Pivato, deleted between Owens and Reimer; and at the end, Paul Wolski, his name not even removed, just crossed out by the secretary this morning because he died last week. Not even from a real sickness, but from some infection in his knee, which he'd scraped playing football and which never got better. A scraped knee — what sort of a thing is that to die from? I felt like throwing the roll book across the damned room.

But, no, I am the teacher; I am the one who's supposed to be strong and to give them answers, to prepare them for a future we've corrupted for them.

The boys all look so listless. Wan, that's the word — wan, something sucking the life out of them, their immune systems just shrugging and not kicking in. Little Eric looks like a skeleton. He'll probably be dead by the end of the year. My god — how can any of us stay sane and watch the children dying?

The girls are different, too — they huddle together at noon hour like a cageful of frightened rabbits. When I come in and find them playing normally they stop and look at me guiltily, as though they'd been caught laughing at a funeral.

So I was drunk when Elizabeth came home. I had a

right. I was pissed; she was pissed off. Ha, ha.

"*Dad,*" she said, her most irritating voice, sounding twelve instead of twenty-two. She picked up the sherry glass and set it down hard in front of me, as though I hadn't see it.

"And how was *your* day?" I smiled at her avuncularly. What a nice word. Avuncularly.

"Oh," she said, dropping her briefcase on the table and sitting down in front of me. "It was bad, was it?"

"Only five boys. That's in all three grades that are in my room now, only twenty-one altogether, and only five boys."

I think I may have started to cry then, and she came and massaged my shoulders, and I must have stopped, because I remember peeling the potatoes and cracking the eggs for the omelette and I wasn't crying then.

Over supper she told me something about Jenny, but I didn't really listen. There was a silence and I realized she'd asked me a question. I said I was sorry.

She sighed, crossed her knife over her fork in that meticulous way she'd learned from Linda, like someone carefully crossing her legs. "You never listen to me, Daddy," she said.

"That's not fair. Merde. Of course I listen to you." Oh, my, yes, didn't I sound righteously indignant, though? When she's right — I don't listen to her. I don't understand her life, so I don't want to hear about it. I'm a selfish bloody bastard. I don't know how she can stand to live with me.

She picked up her plate and took it to the sink. "Jenny's coming over later," she said, her voice neutral. "We're going out to play a game of tennis."

I'll bet that's not all you're going to do, I almost said, but I didn't, thank god, I had that much bloody sense.

It's late. To bed. I'll be hung over in the morning. But I keep writing and writing, my words slithering their pathetic story across the page, thoughts looking for a way out, and I give them only scribbles on a goddamned paper.

Sept. 5, 2053:
I just felt such rage at Bill in the staff room today I could have smashed his damn head onto the table. He sits there and tells us that the boys are dying because it's all in God's Great Plan, and the righteous ones will meet again in heaven, and we should rejoice, all that bullshit, it's God's Will. And the others all roll their eyes and make jokes, Clara exclaiming, "God's Will! I didn't know he left one! Am I in it? Can my lawyer get a copy? Must be public domain by now, right?" and so on, and usually I'd have been right in there, adding my bit of smut, but something in me just snapped today, and I stood up and started screaming at him; I really felt like grinding his face into his fucking lunch bag. Prince came over and took my arm and said, "Now, now, Adam, that's not very nice, come on, calm down now."

So everybody sat there looking embarrassed and/or terrified, and then they tiptoed out of the room as though I were a land mine they might step on.

"We have to respect each other's opinions," Prince said, patting at my arm.

So now we have two lunatics on staff. Three if you count Prince.

I didn't even see Elizabeth tonight. Just a note saying she wouldn't be home for supper, and it's almost eleven now and she's still not back. I hope she's at her lab. I hope she's finding a cure for everything.

Sept. 6, 2053:

I just tried to read one of Elizabeth's reports she brought home from work. "Sexlinked Immunodysfunction Syndrome." What a pretty name they've given death. I couldn't understand a damned word: even the grammar seemed alien, not just a separate vocabulary but a whole new syntax. It amazes me Elizabeth can understand all this, can write like this. The amazement of every parent when what used to chew at your pant cuff and call you Dada grows up smarter than you.

The parents of the Reynolds boy in Grade Five with the bad bronchitis are taking him to some faith healer in Tucson. Well, why not?

Sept. 7, 2053:

Robert asked me at recess, "Am I going to die, Mr. Markov?"

So I made myself laugh and answer, "No, of course not. Not for a very long time."

And he looked at me with his old man's eyes and said, "I think I am, Mr. Markov. My brother says we're all contaminated. From the bombs and the dead ozone and things. He says human beings are finished."

Robert, Robert. What did I answer? Some lie, some placebo. *Human beings are finished.* When I was his age the big secret older brothers told to disillusion us was that there was no Santa Claus. No Santa Claus, no human beings.

At the staff meeting after school Prince had an item on the agenda that was about how would we please not call him Prince any more, his name was Douglas, and Prince for Principal was a cute joke, but really the board might think it was disrespectful and wasn't it becoming just a little —

"Oh, for god's sake," Clara snapped. "I'll call you any damned thing you want, let's just get this fucking meeting over with."

"That's not very nice," Prince said.

"I'm sorry," Clara said. She leaned over and put her head between her knees and sat that way for about ten minutes. Four lunatics on staff.

Oct. 23, 2053:
I was right about Eric. His mother came to me after school today, crying, and said she was taking him out of school. "What's the point?" she kept saying. She cleaned out his desk, and when I came to help her she hit at me, as though I were responsible. I went and sat in the staff room. A little while later she came and knocked at the door. I told Clara to tell her I'd gone home. I can see I actually have a bruise on my arm from where she hit me, a round, fist-sized purpling stain spreading under my skin.

I showed it to Elizabeth. "Look," I said. "One of the mothers hit me today."

She thought I was making a joke. "Oh, you probably deserved it," she said.

Oct. 24, 2053:

Elizabeth brought home the latest annual birth-rate figures.

"Look at this," she said.

"What?"

She pointed to the male birth-rate. "This."

"It looks fine to me." It was in the hundreds of thousands somewhere.

"It's *not* fine. It should be a hundred times that."

"You're kidding."

She shook her head grimly. "Look." She pointed at a graph on one of the scrolls of paper she'd strewn on the kitchen table. Her finger traced the monthly drops in the past year. I watched the locus move down, down, to where it hovered an almost invisible distance from the x-axis, at the bottom, the zero mark, the flat line on the cardiograph that meant death. Extinction.

"Why?" I said finally. "What's happening?"

"Your little spermies just aren't making boy babies any more," she said, with something she must have intended as a laugh.

"Maybe your little eggies just don't want us," I said.

"They want twenty-year-old frozen sperm, apparently." She rummaged around the printouts and pointed at some other graph. "They just don't want this modern stuff."

"Why not? What's wrong with it?"

Elizabeth sighed and picked at the paper. "I don't know. But whatever is causing this must be the same thing that's making the boys die. And that involves basic and Y-specific chromosome damage, Dr. Kostash has proven that. But we don't know how, or why. And now it looks as if it's killing them even earlier. At conception. Or at least by the fourth month."

"The secretary at school had a miscarriage last week."

Elizabeth lifted her hands slightly in the air, then let them drop onto the table as though they were too heavy for her arms to hold. "I knew miscarriages were up again, but I didn't know they were so male-concentrated. It seems to be on such a huge scale now — "

"Hard to believe that fifty years ago we were desperate about how to control overpopulation."

"Be careful what you wish for. You might get it."

We were quiet for a while, staring at the papers again, the masses of numbers, written by machines indifferent to interpretation, implication. I turned the pages over, trying to understand, to not understand, I don't know.

"Look at this," I said finally, pausing at a page that listed the sex ratio. "Live births, female: 98.7%. Live births, male: 1.2%. Live births, other: 0.1%. What the hell is 'other'?"

"Someone like me, maybe," she said. She folded up her papers abruptly and took them to her room.

I should have said something. But merde, what the hell does she want me to do? If I say something about her and Jenny, it sounds critical. If I don't, it sounds critical.

But what's there to say about anything any more? The future grips us like a vise. In every path/Man treads down that which doth befriend him.

Oct. 25, 2053:
In the papers today, big headlines: *Male birth-rate plummets*. But Elizabeth came home all excited because her lab has had a big chunk of money diverted to genetics from nephrology because of it.

"They were stinking mad over at nephrology, I can tell you," she said, biting eagerly into her vegetable-crisp. I didn't like seeing her gloat like that.

"So what are you supposed to do with all that money?"

"Research," she said. "Research, research! Into what's gone wrong with spermatogenesis."

I almost said, "Maybe it's God's Will," but I managed to restrain myself; who knows if she'd have thought I was kidding. It does, after all, make as much sense as anything, God the old Malthusian Fart-in-the-Sky saying, Lo/Ho/Yo! People — it's been a *tranche*, really it has, but game's over, time to let something else have a turn at wrecking the playground, something more purposeful than intelligence — how about, oh, let's see, Rodentia?

I pick up the photograph of Linda on my night table and stare and stare into her eyes. Last week I put the photo away in the drawer, but last night I took it out again. Not ready. What a short sweet time we had together, not even ten years. I still turn my head because I hear her step behind my chair, see her walk by me on the street wearing a stranger's face —

Report cards. I have to finish my damned report cards. "Jane is a hard-working and intelligent girl and she has a bright future ahead of her especially since she will probably be the only one in it by then."

❖

Sept. 9, 2064:
Elizabeth and Jenny came by after school. Well, I was glad, of course, to see Elizabeth. Jenny went into the kitchen

to make herself a sandwich and Elizabeth sat down in the chair opposite me, like a guest, someone paying a formal visit. Well, that's how it is now. I could tell she was alarmed about the new plants, but she didn't say anything. Not to my face. But I can imagine her now, telling Jenny, "The old merdehead is definitely over the edge. Did you *see* the size of that fig? There's hardly any room to move in there." Well, maybe that's the point.

She wanted to know about school. So I told her: one boy in Grade One this year and he's —

"An Artificial?" she said.

"You know how I hate that word," I said.

She sighed. She looked tired. Her hair was greasy and needed to be cut; it hung down over her eyebrows, and I thought it must be like trying to look out from under a fringed cloth. "I'm sorry," she said. "It's just lab shorthand. If we'd known it was going to become a significant phenomenon we'd have invented a less offensive term."

"No one made a big deal about artificial insemination before. You don't need a goddamned new word now."

"It's just a way for us to keep track. In case some come along who aren't Artificials." She sighed. "Unlikely as that may be."

Jenny came in and sat at Elizabeth's feet. I could hear the noises her throat made as she swallowed the sandwich. Fig kept poking her in the neck; it pleased me, sour old man that I am.

"At least the boys who are left aren't dying any more," Jenny said. "Not the way they were ten years ago. That's got to be a good sign."

I almost had to laugh. "A good sign. Sure. They're turning out to be sterile — that's a good sign? Soon there'll be no babies at all any more, of any sex."

"We're making progress," Elizabeth said, scratching her

head and then looking sadly at the flakes of dandruff she'd scraped up under her fingernail. "We've isolated the problem to one gene. At least now we know where to look. We just need time — "

"Time's running out." Cynics are never original.

"It's not Elizabeth's fault you men can't reproduce," Jenny snapped, and, oh, maybe I deserved that, sounding so cranky, but I couldn't let her win, not after the way she'd said "you men," so I shouted back something nasty and then so did she, it had the phrase "malfunctioning sperm" in it, I remember that, my abstracted diarist mind always taking notes for later. I suppose we were getting ready to resort to our usual arguments about the parasitic patriarchy when suddenly Elizabeth got up and walked out. We sat there feeling ashamed.

"We shouldn't do this to her," I said, finally.

Jenny nodded, looking fixedly at the hibiscus, which had taken over the south corner of the living-room. "She's been so overworked. She comes home exhausted. Everybody at the lab is working twelve-hour shifts, or more. And she's worried about the press conference tomorrow. When they have to reveal that the male Artificials are sterile."

"That still doesn't make any sense to me. Why should *they* be sterile, if they start out without the gene damage?"

"I don't know," Jenny sighed. "I don't know. The damage must occur later. No one really knows all the effects of the kind of UV we're getting now. And the air is so full of crap, just breathing makes your cells mutate. I know damned well they didn't tell us the truth about Hanford. Or Kalistan twenty years ago. Or the war in Ukraine. Or ... it just goes on and on and on." She picked off a leaf turning pale on Fig and rubbed it between her fingers.

"Yeah," I said. "Ignorance was bliss."

"They knew what they were doing. It wasn't ignorance."

"But was it bliss?"

Jenny looked at me coldly, thinking I was being a smart-ass, but I was serious, in a way, wanting to think that people, perhaps even ourselves, had once known a joy, however selfish and hedonistic, that our misery now might be paying at least for that.

"I bloody well hope not," Jenny said. She dropped the leaf into the pot.

The fridge kicked in, spewing out god knows what new toxins for the next generation to discover. We sat there in moody silence for a while, and then Jenny slapped her hands down onto her thighs so hard it made me jump and said, "Well, merde, it's not the end of the world, yet. We've still got the sperm banks."

"They won't last forever," Elizabeth said. She stood leaning against the door into the kitchen, and her face looked so old and full of pain I almost cried out — she seemed so much like Linda at the end, before she stopped fighting and took my hand and said, "I guess it's time," and I told the nurse and she came and took off the bag on the IV and put on the one with the large red stripe across the top.

I sit here writing and writing. For whom, whose eyes but mine own? There is delight in singing, though none hear/Beside the singer. Sure. Journal writers, I read somewhere, are people lacking in social skills. Yes, yes. I become more hermetic by the day. I should have been a pair of ragged claws; my pencil scuttles across the floors of silent paper. Addiction, compulsion. A nightly ablution, cleansing me of the day's horrors, of the dark gathering its dirty drawstring around my race.

I didn't like the way Jenny picked that leaf off my fig.

Sept. 10, 2064:
Some of the children were crying today after recess, and I had to give them my little Reassurance Sermon, which is so threadbare a wrong tug one of these days will disintegrate it entirely, let the Naked Truth shine forth. And what's that? That the world is going mad with despair, that there is no future.

I saw Elizabeth on the television, standing beside Dr. Kostash. He stared into the camera like someone under hypnosis. When he read his statement his voice was shaking. Elizabeth stayed beside him, still as a photograph, one hand arrested in pulling off the rubber glove on her other hand.

I had a shower, and then I stood in front of the mirror in the hallway, looking at myself. I touched my penis, watched it flutter like a fibrillating heart. I cupped my testicles in my hands and just stood there, hunched over like a moron, looking at myself. An ordinary man, the last of his kind. I let go of my testicles; suddenly they disgusted me. Failures. Incapable of their one simple function. And then I began to masturbate, until the useless sperm flew at the mirror.

Well. What a thing to confess. Pepys never did anything like that.

Before I go to bed I will clean the mirror. Some concessions still to civilization.

Sept. 11, 2064:
Ron just walked out today, left his coat and everything in the staff room. It's what we all want to do, just walk out. I don't know why more of us haven't, why we come

in every day with our dutiful lesson plans and teach the children, the last of the children, the lessons of history and culture and science, all the things that have brought us to where we are today.

I phoned Elizabeth. She said they'd been instructed to release a report saying there'd been a breakthough, in hopes it might ease people's depression. "Of course, it's not true," she said. Of course, I said.

I talk to my plants. Good, kind, reassuring things. They hold their leaves out to me like cups to be filled with my words. Thou shalt inherit the earth, I tell them. But they know that. They've always known that.

Sept. 12, 2064:
Ron wasn't in school. His wife phoned to say he was sick. Aren't we all? What would I do if I had the courage to walk out like that? Go home, the gun to the head, the slit wrists? And let my plants, hunger-crazed, devour me. The woods avenge themselves.

But the breakthrough news seems to have helped; Clara was actually humming as she made the coffee. I wish Elizabeth hadn't told me the truth. I alone am escaped to tell thee.

Sept. 13, 2064:
I finally had to throw out Ivy One today. Couldn't pretend she'd recover. Euthanasia. The spider mites, I suppose, and old age. She had only two green leaves left. But it was still life. I cried. I actually cried. I murdered your mom today, I told Ivy Two. She just shrugged, callous bitch.

❖

Nov. 20, 2066:
Elizabeth and Jenny, bursting with news. A breakthrough, a real one this time, they said. Let's see if I can remember how it goes:

"Dr. Kostash had been working on it, but nobody really thought he'd do it," Elizabeth said excitedly, biting into her apple so enthusiastically juice squirted in the air. "Even *he* wasn't sure, that's why he threatened to lobotomize us if we talked about it outside the lab. But his first child has just been delivered, so there's absolutely no doubt. Laura Anderson. She'll probably be showing up in your Grade One class in six years. What he's done, you see, is combine two haploid eggs to produce a viable diploid zygote, with its full complement of forty-six chromosomes. But of course there are only two X chromosomes, no Y, so the offspring has to be female."

"Wouldn't that produce Turner's syndrome?" I asked, struggling to follow her.

"No, no — that's an XO chromosome constitution. A normal female requires two X chromosomes, even though only one is transcriptionally active in each cell."

"Is this like parthenogenesis? Or cloning, something like that?"

"No, not at all. There are two genetically-separate parents involved here. It's not asexual reproduction, as genetics defines it. And the process is a lot simpler than cloning. In nuclear transplantation, embryogenesis gets started but tends to stop at the blastula stage, so serial transfers are necessary — we're still a long way from cloning humans. But this, ova-fusion, Dr. Kostash calls it, requires only the initial implant into the mother. *One* of the mothers. Dr. Kostash says he could train doctors in the process in a matter of weeks."

"Forgive my obtuseness," I said, "but I don't see how this is a real breakthrough. I mean, we don't exactly need more female children. You still haven't solved the problems with spermatogenesis."

They looked at me, coldly, I thought. Then Jenny said, carefully, "What this *means* is that there's now the possibility of a future for the human race once the sperm banks are exhausted."

"I see," I said. "And this future would consist only of women."

"Isn't that better than goddamned extinction? Jesus, Dad." Elizabeth tossed her apple core angrily at the sink. It rolled down the counter and confronted the sugar canister.

"Yes," I said meekly. "It's better than extinction." I picked up her apple core and dropped it carefully down the organics shute.

"Maybe it's just evolution," Jenny said, forcing a grin at me. "You know. Another one of the big steps, the first fish crawling up onto land."

"Evolution. I see." I took a deep breath, trying it out, mutating, air instead of water in the lungs. It hurt, but it seemed to work. I turned to Elizabeth. "I don't suppose this ova-fusion business could be used with sperm — some kind of sperm-fusion?"

Elizabeth smiled. Avuncularly, I thought. "No, Daddy. The sperm is what has the genetic damage. And in any case the males are the heterogametic sex. It — well, it make it a whole lot more complicated. Now, if you were a silk moth, for instance, you'd be the homogametic sex."

"Well, it's a shame I'm not," I said. Fish out of water.

"Look," she said, impatiently. "Its not as though we're stopping our other research. We know ova-fusion isn't the whole answer. But, Christ, it gives us some *time*. It gives us at least another generation, more if we ration the sperm bank supplies carefully. There's such a feeling of renewed *energy* in everybody at the lab. And we've consolidated the viable sperm banks into only the four safest major research centres in the world — including ours — so we can intensify the research and provide better security — "

"That's confidential," Jenny protested.

"He's my *father*," Elizabeth said. "He won't tell if he knows it's privileged."

"He won't tell if he isn't talked about in the fucking third person," I snapped.

"Ah, Daddy," Elizabeth said. "What would I do without you?" And she came over and hugged me. I was so startled I just sat there stiff as a stick, and before I could hug her back she'd pulled away.

So there it is. I have seen the future and it is women. Well. Quite a concept. The garden, going on without us. This is the way the world ends. T.S., Eliot.

Nov. 21, 2066:

At school the kids were all so hypered. They'd heard the news even if they didn't really understand it. I gave up trying to teach. In the middle of Arithmetic I told them all just to scream and run around like crazy people. They did. It was rather fun.

    Place: the staff room
    Time: 12:05

Bill: I don't like the sound of it. If God had intended blah, blah, blah.

Clara: Oh, get fucked.

Rob: Okay, okay — it's good news. I guess. But even if by some miracle they can still fix the Y damage, by then women will be running everything. Jesus.

Eleanor: Sounds good to me.

Patrick: Will whoever took the printer out of my classroom get it back *right now*?

Rob: No, really. Far be it for me to agree with Bill, but there *is* something rather disturbing about this —

Bill: *Thank* you, Rob. Another sane voice at last.

Rob: It's meddling in something we really have no right to —

Clara: Oh, merde! You don't complain when they're meddling to try to fix the Y damage.

Rob: I know. But this is different. It's creating, I don't know, a new kind of life.

Clara: Oh, pifflepoop. Admit it — your objection is just plain old misogyny.

Rob: Well, think about it for a minute, will you? A world full of nothing but women. Who would seriously want that? You can't expect us to be thrilled.

Patrick: I mean it. I want that printer back on my desk by one o'clock.

Bill: If God had intended women to —

Clara and Eleanor: Oh, get fucked!

Prince: Now, now, let's not get carried away.

(Where was Adam during this discussion? Why did he sit there like a chunk of cheese and say nothing? Did he have no opinion? Answer in twenty-five words or less.)

Nov. 22, 2066:

School still the proverbial animal farm today, like supervising eight hours of recess on a rainy day, nobody wanting to concentrate on work. Those little hands waving in the air did not want to say "gravity" or "fourteen" or "frog," the answers teacher expected — no, they were twitching with, "So the world isn't going to end, after all, Mr. Markov?" and, "My mom says no more babies are going to die now," and, "But there's going to be only *girls* from now on? Yuck." And the funny way the girls responded to that last one, giggling a little and looking, I don't know, embarrassed? ashamed? smug? afraid? Kind of the way the woman in the bar looked —

Yeah, right, the bar. Found Clara and Rob arguing in the staff room after school and they'd reached the ususal impasse of two intelligent opinions ("Will, too!" "Will not!" "Oh, yeah?" "Yeah.") so I dragged them off to Bar None for a drink. We had to wander around for five minutes until we found seats, the place was so crowded, mostly men, a few women, everybody arguing about the breakthrough news.

"The din of inequity," Clara shouted at me over the noise. Even Rob conceded her a smile.

We gave up trying to talk, just sucked on our drinks and listened to the people at the next table, two men and one woman who sat there fiddling with her coaster and saying nothing.

"I still think it's got to be a joke, somebody's sick idea of a joke."

"It's no joke, they've really done it."

"So that's it, then? Men are just supposed to accept this?"

"Well, we've got no bloody choice, do we?"

"Yes, we've got a bloody choice! I didn't work my ass off at Hardy's for twenty years so a bunch of goddamned women can come in and take over. No offense, Susan."

The woman shrugged, didn't look up.

"It goes beyond your job, Dave, you know. It means no more men, ever. Quite a prospect, eh?"

"Jesus." Dave banged his glass down on the table so hard we all jumped. "They did this on purpose, somehow. I know they did, it's some goddamned plot by those god-damned dykes to get rid of us."

"What a pile of shit," Clara said loudly. She was on her third glass of wine.

"Shh. He'll hear you." Rob looked nervously over at their table.

"I don't care! He wants us to hear *him*! Well, here's to all the goddamned dykes, Dave!" She dipped her glass at the air, took a big swallow of wine. The men at the next table glanced at her, flat, hostile looks. I don't think they realized she was talking to them; she was just a fat middle-aged woman behaving badly in public.

"Let's leave," Rob said. He pushed back his chair.

"Yeah," said Clara, "the reek of testosterone is making me nauseous," and then we were all standing up and shuf-fling to the door.

" ... show them who's boss," Dave's voice pursued us. Rob took hold of Clara's arm.

Outside, we all began to laugh, but uneasily, and proba-bly for different reasons. "What a cretin," Clara said. "What an asshole."

The noise of the bar followed us to the bus stop. The din of inequity.

Only girls from now on. Yuck. What did I answer the boy? I can't remember. Nothing that mattered/matters/will matter. Go to bed, Adam. The future doesn't want your help.

❖

Feb. 17, 2067:

"I just don't understand," Elizabeth kept saying, sobs cutting into her voice. "Why are they doing this? Why do they hate us so much?"

I don't know. I don't know.

We watched the television, little moaning sounds breaking from our throats as we saw another women's centre in — where? — London? — in flames, the crowd of men around it shouting, frenzied, the police seemingly incapable of control. Then the scene that made us both cry out in horror — a group of women caught on the street and the crazed mob falling on them, beating and kicking — the camera fell or was pushed away, or we covered our eyes, or turned off the set, I can't remember.

Elizabeth was almost out of her mind, "Oh god, oh Jesus, oh god," she said, her voice a strange keening I'd never heard before. I went over to put my arms around her but she pushed me away, wildly, as though I were trying to attack her.

"I have to find Jenny," she said frantically, stumbling to the door.

"She's okay," I insisted. "There're no riots here." But she pulled away from my hand and ran out to the street. "She's okay," I called after her. "There's no trouble here."

Not yet.

Feb. 18, 2067:

The riots continue. Worse than yesterday or last week. The attacks are getting more generalized. It's still mostly women's centres, but now the rioters seem to be taking on places like libraries, museums, universities. Hospitals. Anyplace, it seems, where they think there'll be women. Maybe anyplace that represents to them culture, civilization. And the police and armies just ineffectual, even joining in sometimes, on the news tonight a soldier emptying his rifle into the windows of a bookstore. Insanity. I'm numb, watching it. How did we come to this?

We were all supposed to stay home again, with our doors locked, but except for a few teenage boys throwing stones through the windows of the high school everything seemed quiet. Thank god for living in what that Toronto journalist called the most boring city in Canada.

Looking out over my calm backyard, the caragana bushes with their hats of snow, old Mrs. Melmann next door ignoring the warning and starting her daily walk, it seemed impossible that there could be such chaos as we have heard, mere anarchy loosed upon the world. *Mere* —what the hell is mere about it?

Elizabeth phoned me, asked me again, "Why are they doing this? Why do they hate us so much?"

So I had to give her, us, an answer. "Because they see it as some war that they've lost and the women have won. Because they want to destroy as much as they can so that it won't fall into enemy hands."

"My god. War. Enemies. We're all just people. Would they rather nobody survived at all?"

"I remember one of those old *Planet of the Apes* movies — at the end the main character activates the atomic bomb, knowing it will destroy everything — himself, the apes, the remaining humans, rather than have the apes win. Just pure rage, I guess, and hate, and despair."

"That was made a whole century ago. We don't think that way now. Do we? Do we?"

We must, some of us must.

Feb. 19, 2067:
The rioting as bad as yesterday, some in Toronto now, too, and Winnipeg, I couldn't watch, sat here huddled in my house with the curtains drawn listening to Vivaldi, trying to read, the same page over and over and over.

I phoned Elizabeth. Jenny answered, said she was at the hospital. "Well, she shouldn't be," I said, and I suppose it sounded like an accusation, because she snapped, "She insisted on going. I can't stop her." And so I grunted something and she snarled something and we hung up.

I shouldn't be surprised Elizabeth would be at the hospital, warnings or not, helping Dr. Kostash train the German doctors. "They won't be able to stop us," she'd said last night. "Too many doctors know the procedure now." Of course that was before we'd turned on the television.

Feb. 20, 2067:
I can hardly bring myself to write this. But I have to. I have to try to understand.

I was watching television. A sea of men, somewhere in the U.S., shouting their impotent rage at the skies. I watched, unable to pull my eyes from the ugliness, the violence. For more than an hour, I watched.

And somewhere in me, in some evil black space between my bones, I felt a kinship with them, with them as men, the screen a mirror of my own face, and I felt my hands clench around the bricks they threw, my throat form the words of their rage, my heart turn black and bitter and vengeful against the women, wanting to hurt them and punish them, the ones who had beaten us at last.

It repels me to write this.

Feb. 21, 2067:
The riots subsided a little today. The films were mostly of smoky ruins, gutted buildings, crying women holding their beaten and raped and murdered sisters. Behind the shaken man reading the news I saw unreeling film clip after film clip of the destruction: a women's clinic in London, bombed into rubble, more than a hundred dead; the Louvre, part of its collection shredded; half of Trinity University still in flames; Montreal General closed down indefinitely — How long will we be spared here, especially now that we have the co-ordinating hospital for the west?

When I think of how I felt last night in front of the TV, that grotesque exhilaration, some part of me participating, endorsing — I can feel nausea cramp my gut. But I have to face it. I was part of the mob. I wanted to destroy. I wanted revenge.

I talk to Fern on my desk. "What do you think, Fern?" I say. She doesn't answer. She used to, once. She's ashamed of me, now. They flee from me that once did etc. I take another drink. I drink too much. It doesn't matter. I'm starting to write like Hemingway.

Feb. 22, 2067:

Prince brought over some homework some of the parents had given him that he wanted me to mark. Honestly. On the last day of the bloody world some teacher will be sitting there, marking.

I made coffee and we tsk-tsked in a kind of surreal way about the state of the world. He's not a bad guy, I guess, Prince; I've worked for worse.

Then we turned on the news. Awful, awful. We saw them blow up Bryn Mawr. The camera followed two women running, screaming, on fire. When they fell, the camera turned away, looking for something else. I wanted to shut it off but Prince said, no, we have to watch, we have to know. There was some feed from Argentina, I think, a reporter moving his lips in Spanish and an English voice saying that the building behind him was a nurses' residence, and in it two hundred women had been massacred. Then some jumpy footage inside, carnage, blood everywhere, most of the women stripped naked.

But maybe even worse was the talk show that came on after. The Pat Van Horn Hour. Van Horn's guests were four guys calling themselves part of the Men's Defense League. "We know," said one of them sincerely, leaning his young face forward, "there's a conspiracy. There's no question about that. We know boy babies are being born. And killed."

"It's happened before," said the lumpy older man to his left, who looked enough like the first man to be his father. "Just read your Bible. Why was Moses in the bullrushes? And why did the baby Jesus have to flee to Egypt?" He shook his finger into the screen. "What are they afraid of out there, the boy-baby killers? Ask yourselves that!"

"Holy Moses," Prince said, and began to laugh, hysterically.

"Lunatics," I said. "Religious warp-heads."

As though the younger man had heard me, he leaned forward again and continued earnestly, "We're not fanatics. We know what's happening. The boy killers and man haters have to be stopped."

"And how do you intend to stop them?" Van Horn asked, his face serious, the slight practised frown not disapproval as much as simulated concentration.

"How do you think?" The third man spoke for the first time. He gave a little woof of laughter. "Don't you watch the news?"

"We're just fighting back," the first man said hurriedly. "It's self-defense."

"Why don't they arrest the bastards?" I heard myself shouting. "God, they're as good as admitting they've murdered people! Why aren't the police there arresting them?"

"It's TV," Prince said. "The police have no jurisdiction. Like the Vatican. A separate country. It makes its own laws." He gave his weird whinnying laugh again.

The third man was speaking now, his voice hard. "We didn't start this. We were forced into it. But we're fighting for survival. For *your* future." His finger jabbed at us. "We have to stop them. We have no choice."

Finally Prince let me turn it off, and then he got up to leave. At the door I almost grabbed his arm and said, "Don't go yet." Afraid suddenly to be alone.

The house is so quiet. The TV squats there like some dirty window I'm afraid to look through.

I sit here marking the kids' homework. Mary, her neat handwriting filling a whole new scribbler, answering the Language questions right to the end of the book. "When Timothy came home, he found his uncle had brought him a pony." "Karen was unhappy because her friend Wendy was moving to England." To the end of the goddamned book, as though she thinks, she knows, she'll never be able to come to school again.

Feb. 23, 2067:
Quieter today, the news just catching its breath, catching up. "Maybe it's over," Elizabeth said, when I finally got her on the phone. I could tell she didn't believe it, either.

Feb. 24, 2067:
They tried to open the schools again, but by eleven they called in the buses and sent us all home. They'd bombed Emily Murphy College in Calgary — almost a hundred killed, they think. And another bomb thrown into the Othervoices Bookstore but it didn't go off. Closer, it's getting closer, the rough beast, its hour come round at last, slouches toward Lethbridge to be born.

"We should spraypaint *dy* at the end of *Ann*," Clara said, pointing to the big "Ann Rogers Elementary" sign above the school door as she was climbing on the bus. I don't think she was joking.

When I got off the bus Mrs. Melmann gave me a sour look and shook her head. "You men," she said. "You boys." I nodded. Yes.

Feb. 25, 2067:
The riots intensified again. A school in Whitehorse, for god's sake, levelled by an explosion. Some part of Buenos Aires looking like a giagantic rubbish dump. Another bomb-

ing in Calgary. Hard to tell if it's organized or just random. Surely those loonies we saw on TV don't have an international network. Or maybe they do; maybe it's been there for a long time, waiting for an excuse.

TV coverage is getting pretty spotty — some of the stations have been attacked. One of the reporters just started to cry in the middle of the broadcast, and they left it in.

No school here. Everything closed. Two women beaten up at the drugstore just a few kilometres away, and some windows broken downtown. I feel as though we're all holding our breaths and waiting, like plants through the winter, waiting for the sun to warm us again, tell us it's safe to unbolt our doors and unfold our arms and come out into the free air.

❖

Mar. 5, 2067:
Jenny came to tell me.

They broke into the hospital. She's dead.

I can hardly see, my eyes so swollen. My Elizabeth, my sweet little girl.

❖

Mar. 30, 2067:
I found the communiqué in my mailbox this morning. I'm not sure who left it, Jenny probably. It says this, exactly:

CONFIDENTIAL:
KIEV, SALZBURG, LETHBRIDGE, CAIRNS.
VIABLE SPERM BANK SUPPLIES DESTROYED,
1500 HRS M.S.T.
WOMEN'S FRONT

So that's it, I thought calmly, holding the note in my hand for a long time. The last human male on this earth has been conceived. There will be no more.

❖

Bowden had a hard time struggling awake.

"Come to bed," Delacour was saying, shaking her shoulder lightly.

"Ah," Bowden said, sitting up, looking around the room, alarmed, confused. "I guess I was dreaming. About the riots." But it wasn't just the riots; it was her childhood nightmare of running, terrified, through the woods, pursued by something monstrous. *The male will get you.* Delacour would laugh if she knew.

"You've been reading the journals, I see."

"I hope you don't mind," Bowden said, trying to be casual, to push away the lingering images. She picked at a grain of sleep in her right eye. "It was fascinating. All the detail. Funny how reading about something can seem so vivid. More in some ways than seeing the vidspools." She stood up, placed her hands at the back of her neck and stretched her arms up.

"His writing is good for that. Every single day he made an entry. Some of them were up to ten pages long. How much

64

did you read?"

"Only the pages with your orange markers."

"Well then. You've missed things. I was just concerned with the history. The journals offer more than that."

"He was likeable, actually. For a male. Still, it was males that brought all that violence at the end." Bowden shuddered. "I still find it incredible. That they would do that. We're so fortunate, to be living so long after they disappeared."

"I suppose so," Delacour said, picking up the journal and opening it at her first orange marker, as though she had to check something. "It wasn't all like that, of course. It wasn't always as bad as during the Change. There were other males like Adam Markov. You should read the journal to the end sometime."

"What happens at the end?"

"Oh, nothing that important, I suppose. He's old; he dies."

"They all died. Thank god."

CHAPTER THREE
DANIEL

"I CAN'T BELIEVE YOU'D TREAT ME THIS WAY," Daniel said. "Don't you think I've any feelings at all?" He wiped his hand quickly across his eyes.

"I'm sorry," Bluesky kept saying, not looking at him. "I didn't mean to hurt you." She stopped buttoning her tunic, and let her hands fumble to her lap, where she picked up a straw and poked it repeatedly into her palm. He could still see her breasts, and that upset him even more, as though she expected him to feel nothing at the sight of her nakedness, as though he were no more than a barn animal.

"Why did you make love with me at all," he said, "if you feel repulsed by me?"

"I didn't say you repulsed me," she said miserably.

"You said it was unnatural. It's the same thing."

She shook her head. "I like you, Daniel, I do, I *do* — " She clenched her hand on the straw, cracking it like a small bone. "But I don't feel right about this. I want a, well, a normal relationship."

"Is my mother and father's relationship unnatural? Is Vargas and Lawrence-Paul's on North Farm unnatural? And the cows and the horses, even the plants — are they all unnatural?"

"You know what I mean. Maybe your mother and Vargas and the others had more courage than I have, to choose someone so — different."

"So different," he echoed bitterly. "A freak, that's what you mean, isn't it? I've heard people say the word. I didn't think you'd be like them."

"Well, I'm *not*," she insisted, looking up at him at last. She held her head carefully, delicately, as though it were a glass of liquid she had to be cautious not to spill. Tiny specks of dust from the hay swam in the air between them. "I never used that word. Never." She lifted her hand to touch his arm.

He pulled away from her. "But it's what you think."

Her hand slid through the empty air where his arm had been and hovered briefly a few centimetres above the hay before she let it fall, palm up.

"Besides — " She paused. "Mary-Redwillow from North Farm. She says she desires me."

"And you — do you desire her?" The thought of her with someone else was like a vise in his chest.

She hunched one shoulder, twisted her head a little to that side, an evasive gesture he'd seen her use with her parents. "I suppose so. Maybe."

And she's *normal*, of course. Not like me."

"Please don't be angry. You'll find someone else." The sunlight slitting through a crack in the boards drew a thin white bisecting line through her.

He had to get away. He stood up and stumbled over to the ladder that led down from the hayloft.

"Are you coming to Meeting tonight?" she asked brightly, as though nothing had happened, as though they were simply co-workers on the farm again.

And he realized that that was how it would have to be, that

there was no escape from her, that he would have to see her every day, a cruel reminder. It seemed unbearable.

He swung himself onto the ladder without answering her and, his feet missing half the rungs, slid to the ground. Then he began to run, pieces of straw dripping from him, past his own house, around Johnson-Dene's, around the longhouse where he heard Huallen's voice saying to the children, "And the q is always followed by u." It intensified his misery, hearing himself forever beyond those childhood lessons, knowing there was no learning that could educate away this pain.

He ran past the chicken coop, brown wings with a memory of flight beating away from his careless feet. Only when he reached the woods did he stop running, his breath hammering at his chest. He found the thick fir at whose base he'd often sat, reading and rereading the books he'd borrowed from the longhouse, and he sank down there again. But it offered him no comfort. Everything familiar around him seemed to be changed and turned against him, an external world he could no longer trust. He put his face against the rough chapped trunk and cried.

It was how Highlands found him, later.

She sat down beside him, her long muscular legs stretched out in front of her, and she put her hand on his knee and said softly, "Ah, Daniel."

He didn't answer, only pressed his forehead harder into the bark of the tree. He wished she would go away.

"She wasn't fair to you, Daniel. But you *will* find someone else."

"I don't want someone else. I want Bluesky."

She sighed. "Sometimes it's best not to get what you want." Daniel knew she was thinking about Montney's father, Rossiter, the male she had mated with for two tumultuous years before he left her for someone at East Farm. When she talked about him she referred to him only as "that piss-head."

"That's hindsight," he said, unable even now to resist arguing with her.

She smiled, darkening the little pale pleats at the corners of her eyes. "You're right," she said. "While it's happening, your life has a certain sense of — " she waved her hand vaguely in the air " — being out of control. Especially when it comes to mating desires."

"She said it was unnatural. To make love with me." He slapped harder than was necessary at a bloated mosquito on his wrist. The blood splattered up his arm like a small explosion.

Highlands sat for several moments, squinting at the sky, where a hawk was circling on the thermals. The sun coming through the leaves fell along the scar on her cheek from where the cultivator blade had come loose and flown up to cut her five years ago, only one of several scars she had accumulated in farm accidents. She reached up and brushed back her greying brown hair from her forehead, which was wide and corrugated.

At last she said, "I don't know how to answer you, Daniel. Bluesky has the right to make her choices, for whatever reasons."

"I'm a freak," he said.

"You're rare. It's not the same thing."

"I wish I'd lived before the Change! Things would have been different then. Bluesky wouldn't have rejected me."

Immediately he knew he shouldn't have said it. But it was too late to pull back the words. He could feel Highlands go tense beside him. She took her hand away from his knee, and its absence made the spot feel suddenly cold and bare. She stood up, blotting the sun. When he dared to look up at her, her face was a black circle cut in the sky.

"Tell me First Law," she said.

"Before the Change was Chaos, and it was Male. Male is Danger and Death. Male must be Hidden." First Law, what everyone on the farms had to learn almost as soon as they learned to speak. He knew he had challenged it. Nervously he twisted a fallen leaf around his fingers.

"I'm glad you remember," she said, her voice hard.

"I didn't mean to challenge," he said. "I was just angry."

"I know." Still she stood above him, rigid as the trees, looking down. He wanted to shrivel into the earth.

Suddenly she said, "Did your father ever tell you how First Law was when we had to learn it as children?"

"No. You mean, it wan't the same as now?" He was amazed to think that First Law could ever have been different.

"There was another part to it. It said, 'Male must Live in Shame.' I was one of the ones who insisted we change that."

Male must Live in Shame: it sounded horrible. He had been teased as a child for his difference, and sometimes people still said cruel and thoughtless things to him, but he had never been taught to feel shame. It made First Law as he had learned it seem generous and benign — and Highlands had helped make it so. He looked up at her, grateful, wanting to thank her, but he felt his mouth fill only with one word, a word that was wrong, that was somehow contradiction and denial: *Bluesky*.

He could tell she was waiting for him to say something, but he couldn't speak, simply sat there, staring over her shoulder at a dark surge of rain clouds in the western sky.

Finally she said, her voice cold and irritable, "Just don't think life before the Change was better, for anyone. If you believe that, even for a moment, you've learned nothing. Nothing at all. Don't make me doubt I was right to amend First Law."

"I'm sorry," he said then, making the words come as he looked up at her black, faceless silhouette, Highlands, the one he had always needed to please now suddenly turning her hard judgements against him, too. "I know it wasn't better before the Change. It was just ... Bluesky saying she didn't want me. Because I was male."

He could tell by the way Highlands shifted her feet, the way her arms dropped to her sides that he had regained her sympathy, and he sighed with relief. Slowly she unfolded herself from the sky and sat down again beside him, no longer a dark shape above him, the Leader, but Highlands, familiar, his friend.

"I know it's difficult," she said. "But you mustn't feel yourself diminished. As long as you follow First Law, you're equal to anyone on the farm now that you're an adult."

"Then why did Bluesky say I was unnatural? Why did she choose someone else?"

"She has that right, Daniel. Just as you have the right to choose someone else."

"I know. It's just ... her reason I find so painful."

"Any reason is painful."

He smiled wanly up at her. She was right, he supposed, but, still, she couldn't really understand, couldn't know what it was like.

"Perhaps you should talk to Christoph," Highlands said, as though she knew his thoughts.

"You don't usually recommend my father's advice."

Highlands laughed. "It only seems that way," she said. "You know what your grandmother used to say about us? She said we argued so much because we were interested in each other's opinions. That's true, you know. Your father's a very wise man."

Her comment surprised him. "I always thought you considered him, well, something of a fool."

"Oh, Daniel," she said, shocked. "That's not true, no. Now that piss-head, Montney's father, *he's* a fool."

72

Daniel laughed.

"Come back to the farm with me," she said. "I'll give you one of the chocolate sweet-buns I brought back from Fairview. I ate a whole bag of them after that piss-head left me, and I never lusted for anything better since."

So he got up and walked with her, but although she made light and frivolous conversation he could feel her looking at him with concern. He smiled up at her, eager to reassure — of course he knew the time before the Change was brutal; of course he wouldn't want to go back to that. Even if it meant Bluesky might have admired and wanted him — The forbidden thought clutched at him like a sudden root tangling his feet.

Bluesky: he would have to see her, every day. Every day she would be there to remind him of what he wanted and could never have. A branch Highlands had pulled forward slapped back at him, and although he saw it coming he didn't raise his arm to brush it aside; it thumped into his chest like a fist.

If only he could leave. If only, like the others, he were free to live Outside for a while. He remembered his old dream of University in Leth, how when he was a child and Cayley had gone there he had told his mother proudly that he would go, too. Her hands had stilled on the pair of overalls she was patching, and she looked at him with such sadness that he exclaimed, "What's wrong?"

And, haltingly, she had told him how it was too dangerous for the males to go, how no males could live Outside.

"So I'm trapped here forever?" he cried. "I can never leave?"

"Well, for a day at a time, perhaps. Like your father goes to Fairview sometimes. And Kit from East Farm went to the Farm Conference in Leth last year. But that was only for a week, and others went with him." She looked down at her stitching, pushed the needle through the coarse fabric. "But University?

73

No, Daniel. It would take two, three years. It's just not possible."

Not believing her, he had gone to Highlands, who had told him the same thing.

"But it's not fair! Why should I be denied just because I'm a male?"

"Live is full of denials and disappointments, Daniel. We have to learn to accept them."

He thought of that comment now, coming out of the trees onto the open fields, trying to concentrate on what Highlands was saying about the corn crop. His mother and sister were digging a new compost trench behind one of the sheds, and his mother, seeing them, put down her spade and came over to them. They talked some more about the corn crop, Daniel's mother saying she was more worried about the ergot this year, and then Highlands went on to her house and left Daniel alone with his mother.

She rubbed with apparent thoughtfulness at a smear of dirt on her wrist. Then she put her arm around Daniel's waist and leaned her head against his shoulder. "My dear Daniel," she said. "My sweet child."

He had to smile. His mother was the only one who could still call him "child." Or who could, for that matter, still call him "sweet."

"My sweet mother," he said. He put his arm around her waist and walked with her to the shed.

It was only his second Meeting as an adult, but he was tired and aching from the woodchopping he'd been assigned this afternoon, so he found it difficult to pay attention, especially with Bluesky sitting only three seats to his right. Whenever he glanced her way he saw her looking down determinedly at her hands, which she'd clasped into one tight fist on top of her desk. He tried to keep his thoughts calm and neutral.

They were meeting in the longhouse instead of outside as they'd planned because the rain had blown in from the west. He could hear it rattle in little gusts against the window, and, far away, the light snore of thunder.

They were all there except Huallen, who was minding the youngest children. Sara-Berwyn and Cayley, Bluesky's mothers, sat to his right; then Bluesky and her sister, Shaw-Ellen; Daniel's mother and father and younger sister, Mitchell; Johnson-Dene; Huallen's mate, North, and their daughters, Aden and Fraser-David. Sometimes more of the older children came to the Meetings, but today had been a hard day for them, helping to clear the roads out to the grain fields, so, except for Mitchell, who came to most Meetings even though it would be years before she could participate in Consensus, none of them was interested in coming and listening to more instructions from adults.

There wasn't much to discuss this time, although Johnson-Dene had her usual complaints about last month's supplies and how they were costing too much. Cayley, who was on purchasing shift for the next few months, sighed loudly, but Johnson-Dene ignored her.

"Would you like to change your shift for Cayley's and do the purchasing?" Highlands asked patiently.

And no, of course she wouldn't, but and but and but.

"I know it's more expensive to buy instore, but it takes too much time to get the flour from the mill," Cayley said. "When we did that it meant staying in town a whole extra day."

"Well, I hate paying so much jackup," Johnson-Dene said. She clicked her teeth together sharply several times, as she would when she was annoyed. Daniel imagined her teeth must be nearly

75

ground down to the gums by now.

"If we go to the mill we'd need to take an extra person, and another horse. That costs us, too," Cayley said.

Daniel looked around the loose circle of desks, past Cayley's face to Bluesky's, like a hazed mirror of her mother's, the same sharp nose, the mouth with the lower lip curving out slightly farther than the top one. Only her colouring was different, a reminder of another parent, not Cayley's mate, Sara-Berwyn, but a donor chosen by Doctor, who monitored the farms' kinship bases periodically to avoid inbreeding. Beyond Bluesky he could glimpse the round and small-featured and sunburned face of Shaw-Ellen, with her perpetual anxious smile; although the biological daughter of Cayley and Sara-Berwyn, she looked like neither.

"But we wouldn't save anything," Cayley was saying. She began tapping her forefinger irritably on her desk.

Daniel wished Highlands would just settle it, one way or the other, but he knew that although she could lose her temper when Consensus took too long and could abruptly call a vote or make the decision herself, she resisted doing so. The meeting isn't over, she'd say sharply sometimes, until everyone is satisfied. How can she stand it, Daniel thought, the endless attempts to compromise and placate, when Johnson-Dene was so clearly being obstinate and everyone would have welcomed a ruling against her. But he also knew Second Law: that power-over is never as good as power-with. It would be a lot more efficient, though, he thought wearily.

"Well, no, that's all right," he heard Johnson-Dene say finally, the way she always would, as though all she had really wanted was a chance to complain, to talk.

And then he jerked to sudden sharp attention, because it was Bluesky's soft voice he heard, Bluesky who had never spoken up at Meeting before.

"I was wondering," she fumbled. "I was just wondering if I ..."

If what? He held his breath, waiting.

"... if I could start helping with the teaching a little." She looked shyly at Huallen.

"Of course," Huallen said. "I'd be delighted."

"Good," Highlands said. "Arrange that between yourselves, then."

Help with the teaching, he thought, sinking back into his seat. As though nothing important had happened to her today.

There were only a few things left to discuss — the work loads to fix the east-pasture fence the cows had broken through, the first of the peas to can, who wanted to lead the reading group next or did they want to stop for the summer. Daniel almost volunteered to organize the reading group, to show Bluesky that he, too, could sit here calmly planning his life, but he decided against it; he didn't want to draw any attention to himself. Finally his mother agreed to take the group, and then Highlands said, "Well, I guess Meeting is over," and they all drifted away. Bluesky, he noticed, was the first out the door, casting a quick, nervous glance behind her as though she expected him to pursue her.

His father lingered at the side of the room, adjusting a bookcase shelf that had warped and come loose. Mitchell came over and took Daniel's hand and led him around the room, pointing at all the desks, explaining which of the children used which desk for which lesson. She had, Daniel noticed, cut her bangs this morning, and, unable to get them straight, had kept snipping until she had only a little bristly fringe left, still slanting to the right. She was only trying to cheer him up with her chatter, he knew, but he found it tiring and somehow depressing, and finally he said, his voice sounding more abrupt than he intended, "Leave me alone for a while, will you, Mitchell?"

She looked up at him, her eyes filling immediately with tears. Without a word, she let go of his hand and left. He could hear her footsteps pounding into a run outside. He felt ashamed and angry at himself for his thoughtlessness.

"She's so sensitive," he said miserably, sinking into one of the desk chairs.

"We're all sensitive," his father said. He came over and sat in the desk opposite him. "It's been a difficult day for you."

Daniel smiled wryly, rubbed his hand in a circle on the desktop. "Does *everyone* know about me and Bluesky?"

"Probably," his father said unapologetically. He paused. "It's natural for young liaisons to end, you know. And for others to form."

"Natural. Do you know *why* Bluesky wanted to end it?"

"No."

"Because it was unnatural, she said. Because I was a male."

His father was silent for a long time, the way Highlands had been. At last he said, gently, "We *are* unnatural, Daniel. The world has moved on and left us no place in it. Except here. And even here we have to suffer humiliations from people like Bluesky. Try not to blame her. More and more of the Outside comes in now, and we can't expect our people not to be influenced by it. In the Outside we don't exist. They think of us as monsters who died out long ago. I still don't really know why we didn't, why our people weren't affected as much during the Change. But here we are. We have to make the best of it."

Daniel sighed and picked at a splinter in the desktop. It began to spread, growing thicker and thicker at the root instead of breaking, and finally he stopped trying to make it taper off and snap. He'd have to bring in a knife and sandpaper to fix it now. He felt like a destructive child under his father's eyes, mutilating something carved long ago by someone determined to preserve in them education, literacy, a respect for history.

"When I was talking to Highlands," he said, "I told her I wished I had lived before the Change."

"What?" His father's voice was shocked, as Daniel had expected it to be.

"Because then Bluesky wouldn't have left me."

"Daniel, ah, Daniel ...." His father leaned forward in his desk, stretching his arms as far forward as he could. His hands clutched the edge of Daniel's desk, shook it a little.

"I know," Daniel said. "First Law. I challenged First Law. I didn't intend to. It was stupid of me. I was just angry about Bluesky."

"You're lucky Highlands didn't cut your testicles off."

Daniel stared at his father's serious face. "What?" he gasped.

His father looked at him for several moments before the smile began to twitch at his mouth. Relieved, Daniel laughed.

"Don't laugh," Daniel's father said, starting to laugh, too. "She threatened to do worse things than that to me when we were children. Of course, I usually deserved them."

"Did you ever challenge First Law?"

His father hesitated. "Yes. Someone had said something cruel to me."

"But now, you think it was wrong."

"Yes. Wrong. And dangerous. Pre-Change times were ugly and violent. They're not something to romanticize, even for a moment."

"It wasn't all brutality and exploitation and wars," Daniel protested.

"Daniel — " His father rattled his desk again, a warning. "You can't think that way. If you do, then we've failed you, I've failed you. You've learned nothing. You cannot challenge

79

First Law."

You've learned nothing. Highlands's words. Daniel shifted in his seat, resisted the urge to pick again at the splinter.

"I wish I could leave," he said bitterly.

His father hesitated. Then he said, gently, "You could, I suppose, ask the Leaders for a move to one of the other farms."

"I mean *really* leave. Go Outside. The way the others are able to. To Leth."

He heard his father's intake of breath, saw him pull himself upright in his seat. "To Leth," he said.

"University," Daniel said. His old dream. The word sounded so beautiful he said it again. "University."

"You know that's impossible, Daniel."

"Why should it be? Kit went to Leth for a week."

"It's not the same. You know that."

"First Law doesn't forbid it. It says I must be hidden — but I can be hidden in Leth as well as here. As well as you are when you go into Fairview." He leaned forward, his hands clamping the sides of the desk. "And Huallen says I'm the brightest student she's had. So does Highlands. The best students have the right to go on. I'll learn things the farm needs. Highlands is always complaining that we need more education. And I'd still be here for planting and harvest. We wouldn't have to ask East Farm for a redistribution."

His father stood up, began pacing the room. The floorboards trembled under his heavy steps. "It's just too dangerous, Daniel. You'd have to be constantly on guard. You'd be able to make only the most superficial friends. If you got sick there'd be no doctor you could trust. Even Kit said he wouldn't want to go again, that he was too afraid."

"I'd prepare myself well. I could do it."

"And if you were found out — "

"I wouldn't be found out."

"The farm won't allow it, Daniel. It's pointless for us even to discuss it."

"I'm going to bring it up at next Meeting anyway. I'm going to try to convince them. If I could get Highlands to support me — "

His father smiled. "Highlands. I can just imagine her face."

"Would *you* support me?"

His father stopped his pacing. The room seemed suddenly very still. Then his father sat down, slowly, in the desk closest to him. "You're still upset about Bluesky," he said softly. "You have to want to go for more serious reasons than to run away from Bluesky."

"I'm upset about her, of course I am. But this is not just because of Bluesky. It's something I've always wanted. You know that." He shifted in his seat to face his father.

"It's too dangerous."

"I'd be careful."

His father got up, walked to the door, stood looking out at the rain.

"Would you support me?"

"Yes," his father said. He stepped out the door, walked quickly down the steps.

Daniel sat staring at the grey rectangle through which his father had disappeared. He was astonished at his father's answer. Until he had said that, a simple yes, Daniel had felt their argument was not quite serious, that he was just pressing against a wall he knew would never yield. But his father had said he would support him. A shiver ran over him. Suddenly his going seemed possible, actually possible.

Still, what would his father's support mean? Would he convince the others? Would he convince Highlands? Would he even want to?

And suppose the farm actually *did* let him go — he would be a male in an alien world, at constant risk of exposure, one mistake and his life would be over — if they didn't kill him, they would surely imprison him, quarantine him, use him for experiments, display him as a true and monstrous freak. And they would come to the farms and find the other males.

But still — University: it was fixing itself into his mind, like a stitch mending a tear, and he couldn't undo it. Through the open door he saw the city, room after room of books, the magic of vidspools, teachers whose knowledge went so fabulously beyond what they could teach each other on the farms —

He closed his eyes, leaned his head back until it touched the wall.

He could hear the sounds of the cowbells, their clangs furry and muted in the rain, and he remembered suddenly that he was on milking shift this week. He made himself get up and go to the longhouse door and step outside. He nearly walked into his father, who was standing just beside the steps, under the eaves, watching the rain.

"I'm on milking shift with you for the rest of the week," his father said.

Daniel nodded. He had been scheduled with Bluesky. His father must have asked to change with her.

Little slaps of rain licked at them as they made their way across the yard toward North's house. Daniel kept thinking of things he should say to his father, but he sensed in his quickened pace a desire to be silent, so they walked along together not speaking, a tension between them of two people who had just met, or just quarrelled, or just professed love. Perhaps, Daniel thought, all of those things had happened.

When North came out with the milk pails they accompanied her to the barn. She shook off Daniel's father's guiding hand, even though she was almost completely blind, and stumbled along beside him, one arm out stiff in front of her, flailing from right to left like something mechanical. It was always dangerous to stand in front of North, because one never knew when her arm would leap out in preparation for movement, and everyone had been hit by her at some time or other. But she refused to use a cane, and, since she had never injured herself or anyone else too seriously with her method of navigation, no one urged her to change. Milking was one of the few chores she did better than anyone else, and she was fiercely protective of that distinction, but three cows had freshened lately and they were too much for her to handle, so she had reluctantly agreed to accept extra help this month.

Daniel's father took the cow one of the children had called Moo, and Daniel took the one beside her. When she let down her milk he leaned his head against her hot brown flank. The steady pulsing of the milk into the pail became a trancing rhythm. He didn't let himself think about what had just happened with his father, about what had happened with Bluesky. He made his mind go empty, felt his eyelids droop.

The cow waited until his pail was almost half full before she kicked, knocking the pail loose from between his legs in just the right arch to spill the milk forward. He leaped up, toppling his stool, but of course it was too late.

"Damn," he shouted, "damn!" He wanted to beat at the cow with the empty pail, and, sensing his rage, she danced about the stall, jerking her head up against the rope.

"Start again," he could hear North shout cheerfully from across the barn, her ears better than eyes in seeing what had happened.

He took a deep breath, another, the air trembling into and

out of his lungs. Then he stroked the cow's flank, murmuring, "It's all right, it's all right," speaking as much to himself as to the cow. It was his fault, he knew; he should have been more careful with a cow that had just freshened. He sat down and started again. The two barncats greedily lapped at the puddle of milk that paused at the bottom of the stall before soaking through the cracks in the wooden floor.

When he finished, he milked one of the other cows as well, as a kind of penance, although North said crossly to leave the rest for her, and then he took two of the pails to the milkshed to begin separating. He poured the separator bowl full, set the empty pail under the skim-milk spout and the cream jug under the other, and began to turn the handle. His arm strained with the pressure until the veins in his forearm bulged like thick blue string.

He was starting on the second pailful when his father came in with two more pails. He set them down abruptly when he saw him and exclaimed, "Daniel! Slow down. Look, there's so little cream coming through it's only dripping out."

He looked. His father was right. The cream pitcher was almost empty. Unnerved, he took his hand off the handle, let the machine slow down to a moderate drone. What was wrong with him?

"Well, let me take what you've done out to the calves," his father said, reaching for the skim-milk pail. "We won't have to mix it."

North and one of the children came in then with four more pails, and he continued the separating, watching the cream spout carefully. When he was finished he stored the cream and some of the milk in the icebox, poured the rest into the slop pails for the pigs, and went to his house to wash for supper.

His father came in at the same time, and they washed up

together. Lightning flared at the window above the wash basins, and they were both still, counting the seconds to the thunder.

"Moving away," his father said, when it came, rattling the sky to the south.

They finished washing, then walked together over to Highlands's house, which also contained the farm kitchen. Another crack of lightning split the sky, but when the thunder came it was farther away than the last one. The rain had stopped, and seemed to be rising in a warm mist from the ground.

"Did you mean it?" Daniel said abruptly, unable to stop himself. "Will you really support me?" He had said *will* this time, he realized, not *would*.

"Next Meeting is still a week away."

"So you mean you might change your mind?"

His father hesitated. "I mean *you* might change your mind. Promise me you'll think about it."

Daniel nodded. A week, a week to think about it, to choose.

"I think it might be nice," Daniel's father said as they entered Highlands's house, "if you told your sister you were sorry for speaking to her as you did earlier."

"Yes, of course," Daniel said. He was ashamed to admit that if his father hadn't reminded him, he would have forgotten the incident.

At supper he looked around for Mitchell, but she avoided him and sat beside their mother. He moved quickly across the room and claimed the seat next to her. She didn't look up, only pulled closer to their mother as though she were afraid of him. Her face was brown from the sun, and her freckles, which stood out like pale pink blotches on her cheeks in winter, making her skin seem thin and unhealthy, were almost invisible now.

"Mitchell," he said, putting his hand on her arm, "I'm sorry I sounded rude to you in the longhouse. I didn't mean to be."

She looked up at him with such relief and gratitude in her round child's face that he squirmed in his seat with embarrassment and guilt. "I'm glad you're not mad at me," she whispered, as though she were confiding a secret. She moved closer to him and put her arm around his waist.

How fragile we all are, Daniel thought, putting his arm around her, too, if words can break us or heal us.

Bluesky and Shaw-Ellen came in then, from the kitchen; Bluesky chose a seat close to the door, but her sister came and sat beside Daniel.

"It's all fresh vegetables," she said. "I love the meals this time of year." She smiled at him, revealing the front teeth that overlapped each other, as though they were still pushing for space in her mouth. Daniel had always liked her, and when they were children she had been the most patient and tolerant among them, not caring if she ever won at their games, but today he found her company oppressive and insinuative. He kept thinking she must be laughing at him, enjoying his rejection by Bluesky, who sat across the room from them with her blonde hair curling damply on her forehead from the heat of the kitchen and her perfect mouth biting into a cube of tomato. He clenched his hands in his lap.

Mitchell nudged him impatiently on his right, passing him the potatoes. He took the bowl and stared at the potatoes, nesting like white eggs in the bottom of the bowl.

Across the room Bluesky made a funny face at one of the children who had accidentally dropped a piece of carrot into her water glass, and then they both giggled.

You have to want to go for more serious reasons than to run away from Bluesky.

He was aware he'd been holding the bowl of potatoes too long so he passed it to Shaw-Ellen.

"Aren't you taking any?" she asked, surprised.

He looked at his plate. There were no potatotes on it, only the pale green pile of cucumbers, leaking their sauce slowly across his plate toward the wedges of tomato and carrot and kohlrabi, the pale slice of ling.

"Sorry," he said, reaching for the bowl and spooning out two potatoes. "I wasn't paying attention."

He realized he had made his decision.

CHAPTER FOUR
BOWDEN

I‍T WAS LATE AFTERNOON WHEN WAYNE, one of the patients from Blue Ward, sidled up to Bowden with her sly, eager smile. Bowden turned to face her, attaching a smile to her own face.

"You know what Ellis-Tom said?" Wayne pulled at Bowden's upper arm, forcing Bowden to bend down, as though Wayne wanted to whisper a secret, even though, because of her increasing deafness, she never spoke below a shout. "She said Government is putting extra potassium in our food, and it kills off our brain cells. Isn't that something? Isn't that ridiculous?"

"It certainly is," Bowden declared, mustering her indignation. "That's quite foolish."

It was a game they played: Bowden knew Ellis-Tom probably had said nothing of the kind about potassium, that it was just Wayne's way of trying out her own opinions; and Bowden, freed from her duty to be polite, could openly deride them.

"I thought so," said Wayne, nodding sagely. She wandered off in the direction of Blue Ward.

Marsden, who had been working at the computer to update the hospital address files, looked up as Wayne shuffled past and then glanced at Bowden, rolling her eyes in a complicitous way. Everyone knew Wayne's peculiarities, but then none of the patients, and probably none of the staff, were free of their own. Bowden returned her smile in what she hoped was a relatively neutral way and went over and exclaimed in surprise at how far Marsden had gotten in the files.

"If these merdy hands would work properly I'd be on the pissing *m*'s by now instead of the pissing *g*'s," she said, flexing her gnarled fingers.

"Quit complaining," said one of the four people working on the tapestry commissioned by a clothing store in Commercial. "If you had my legs you'd have something to complain about."

One of the twins helping to shell the peas for supper for the ward snorted. "You should be one of the paras, then you'd have reason to grumble."

The paras were the four paraplegics on the ward, whom Bowden had just finished bathing and who were down in physiocare now. Chastened, everyone went back to work. They were all aware that their own infirmities were less severe than those of others, and that they were in this ward precisely because they were still able to help with the care of others. It was one of the basic principles of Hospital, and not just for old people, that helping others contributed to health, and Hospital was organized so that people of varying degrees of illness and ability were assigned together.

Bowden glanced at the clock. Her shift was almost over. She sat down with the twins and began to help shell the peas. She had barely started when someone touched her shoulder.

"Delacour!" she exclaimed.

Delacour didn't like coming to Hospital. Yet here she stood behind Bowden's chair, smiling down at her. Only her eyes darting nervously around the room betrayed her unease.

"Hi," she said. "I just had to go to Medical Archive so I thought I'd stop by. Look what I got today." She waved an envelope at Bowden.

Bowden stood up, reached for the envelope. "What's in it?"

"Our train tickets. I went down to the station to pick them up."

"We're not leaving for a whole week!" Bowden handed the envelope back.

"I'm impatient. I want to go now."

Bowden laughed. "You're a child. An impatient child."

"Of course I am. I hate waiting for things."

"Well, I hope this will be worth the wait." Acutally, the closer the time came for them to leave the more Bowden's misgivings grew. The long train trip to Peace River Station, renting the horses, camping — it sounded as though it could be more gruelling than fun. But she made herself smile cheerfully at Delacour, say, "It'll be nice to get away together."

"If you can stand me for all that time." Delacour tucked the envelope into her shirt pocket.

"I'll manage," Bowden said, laughing a little uncomfortably, aware of the curious ears around them.

"Aren't you free yet?" Delacour said. "Come on, walk home with me."

Bowden checked the clock. It was after six. She took Delacour's arm, pulled her over to one of the unused work tables. "I thought I'd stop by to see Jesse-Lee on the way out," she said casually. "Why don't you come along?"

Delacour flinched as she heard the name. Her whole posture changed, drooped; her eyes fell from Bowden's face and rested dully on the corner of the work table. She lifted her hand and ran a finger back and forth along the table edge.

"No." Her voice was so low Bowden could barely hear her.

"You haven't been in for more than two weeks. Later you'll blame yourself."

"I know."

"She's *dying*."

Delacour's finger pressed down harder on the table. "She doesn't care if I come."

"Of course she cares."

"I don't know what to say to her. Even when she was well we couldn't talk to each other."

"Well, *find* something to say." She hated this bullying, this dogged insistence, but she knew she should keep pressing, because sometimes Delacour could be persuaded.

But today Delacour wouldn't give in. "I can't," she said, turning her face away.

Bowden sighed, didn't answer.

"I'll see you at home then." Delacour hesitated, fidgeting, as though she wanted to say something more, and then she turned abruptly and walked away, her teacher's-robe flapping behind her, catching on the work table, flying up almost into the face of a startled doctor coming through the door.

Frustrated, disappointed, Bowden watched her go. Of course Jesse-Lee could be difficult, and Delacour had never gotten along with her as well as she had with her birth-mother; but, still, Jesse-Lee was her parent, and she was dying. Bowden's parents had died young, in a lightning fire on their farm, and she would have given anything to have had the opportunity to say goodbye to them. She didn't understand how Delacour could be so stubborn. Jesse-Lee was all the family she had left; how could she not want to take advantage of the little time left to them?

She told the others she was leaving. As she walked past Marsden, who was shaking her fist at the compuscreen, Bowden smiled and squeezed her shoulder. "Courage," she said.

Marsden reached up and tapped her fist on Bowden's hand. "Thank you," she said grimly. "I need it."

Bowden walked on, out of the ward, into the large corridor

leading to Residential. She hadn't actually planned to stop by Jesse-Lee's today, but since she'd told Delacour she intended to, she decided she had better go. It wasn't far — just down the south corridor and through the arboretum, where LaGlace, the mother of one of the nurses, sat in her wheelchair snoring so loudly it must be bruising the plants. Bowden was relieved LaGlace was asleep — awake she spent all her time recounting her dreams; everyone on Blue Ward was familiar with her voice chasing people down corridors, saying, "Wait! I haven't told you what happened *then*!"

Bowden picked up the book LaGlace had dropped and put it on the shelf beside her, setting on top of it the green marker labelled "Arboretum," so that when she woke up, disoriented as she always was, it would remind her where she was.

Jesse-Lee's apartment was probably among the nicest in Hospital in terms of the care and expense that had gone into its design. But it was no secret to any of the patients that these apartments tended to be reserved for Palliatives. Death row, Jesse-Lee called it, when they'd asked her if she wanted one of them. But she'd said if a place was available it might as well go to her as to someone who was really sick. Every apartment had a view across the smooth curve of the coulees, and everything was arranged to allow for convenience and independence. The surveillance camera could be turned on or off by the occupant, so for someone like Jesse-Lee who valued her privacy the camera was off most of the time. The microphone, activated by the word "help," was all the security she needed, she insisted.

"Yes," Jesse-Lee's voice said in answer to Bowden's knock.

She was sitting reading on the sofa by the large sloping window. Outside Bowden could see the grasses in the coulees stirring, brushing against the invisible belly of the wind. Jesse-Lee was naked, as she liked to be in the summer, although it was something with which Bowden was still not comfortable. But she made herself look calmly at Jesse-Lee's old and gravity-worn body, the large red scar on her abdomen from the last surgery which the doctor had thought she wouldn't recover from, the wrinkled face which made no effort to hide its disappointment that Bowden was alone.

"Bowden," she said.

"I'm sorry Delacour couldn't come today." She might as well get it said right away.

"Well," Jesse-Lee said. "Serve her right if I die tonight."

"You won't," Bowden said. "In fact, you're getting better." It was true. If the doctor's original predictions had been right she would have been dead by now. But the illness gnawing at her would claim her eventually, and she had signed the nonintervention document several weeks ago.

Jesse-Lee sighed, and reached for the glass of juice on the end table beside her. Bowden could see her grimace from the spurt of pain it caused, but she knew better than to offer help.

"We'll be going away on our holiday soon," Bowden said. "Delacour got the tickets today."

Jesse-Lee shrugged. "I don't care. Go. I'll try to die while she's gone."

"It's not that she doesn't care, Jesse-Lee. It's because she can't face it."

"Can't face it." Jesse-Lee snorted. "She's selfish, that's all. Like me. When something gets in her way, if she can't sidle around it somehow she'll step on it."

"That's not fair." It was the harshest thing Bowden had ever heard Jesse-Lee say about her daughter. She sank down into a chair by the door, even though she knew she shouldn't do so unless invited.

"Well, you just be careful she doesn't step on *you*, Bowden."

Jesse-Lee set the juice down; a few red drops leaped over the rim of the glass as she bumped it on the edge of the table. She grunted, scratched at her left breast, which swung lightly, describing an arc along the scar on her stomach. "I had a birth-child, you know," she said suddenly, as though she'd only just remembered. "A lovely little thing. She lived for only a week. It broke my pissing heart."

"Oh. I'm sorry. Delacour never told me."

"Delacour doesn't know."

"Why didn't you tell her?"

Jesse-Lee shrugged. "It was a long time before we had her. There just didn't seem to be any reason."

"I think she'd like to know."

"Would she?" Jesse-Lee poked her finger absently into her right cheek, which was indented as though it had grown that way from years of prodding. "Well, if she ever comes to see me before my brain has jellied over I can tell her."

"I'll try to bring her," Bowden said. "Before we leave."

"Don't make her come just to do you a favour. She can come on her own if she wants to."

"She wants to. She's just ... afraid."

"Afraid." She drew out the word derisively. "Don't be naïve, Bowden. Delacour's not afraid of anything."

Bowden bit back a defensive reply. When she spoke, she could hear the phony cheeriness in her voice that others might consider professional but that she knew, and Jesse-Lee probably knew, was the opposite. "Well, I'm sure she'll come of her own accord."

Jesse-Lee smiled. It didn't look entirely sincere. "Don't worry about it, Bowden. I know you're only trying to help, but — "

"Central, cue," said a voice sudddenly in the middle of the room. "Jesse-Lee, please answer."

Bowden jumped to her feet and whirled to see who had

spoken. And then of course she realized what it was, the communicator activated by the word "help."

"Oh, shut up!" Jesse-Lee shouted at it.

There was silence for a moment, and then the voice said, "I assume this means you're all right."

"I'm with her, Central. Bowden. We were just talking. Sorry."

"Okay. Clearing."

They looked at each other and began to laugh, like naughty children caught in a prank, Jesse-Lee's thin shoulders bowing forward like an old wire clothes hanger as she wheezed and snorted. Finally she sank back and sighed. "Ah, merde. I suppose that added another year to my life."

She thought of Jesse-Lee when out the train window at Calgry Station she saw an old person in a wheelchair holding her arms out suddenly to someone, her daughter perhaps, who was getting off the train. She almost pointed the scene out to Delacour but stopped herself in time.

"When we come back, I'll go see her. I promise," Delacour had said, and Bowden knew that was the best she could do, that it would be useless to say, *if she's still alive then*. Besides, Jesse-Lee's condition seemed stable for now, and Bowden was reassured to hear from Central that Delacour had phoned in for a formal check the day before they left, although it had annoyed her, too, that Delacour had gone through Central, as though she didn't trust Bowden's reports or didn't want Bowden to know she'd called.

Bowden looked out at what she could see of Calgry Station. It was hard to believe that once this had been the largest city in the state. Now its population was less than a thousand, and that included mostly the farmers around its edges. Parts of the abandoned inner city were still radioactive, primarily from the old Reddeer accident, which had blown much of its deadly cloud into the bowl the city held out to it. The rest of America had suffered, too, of course, but Calgry was the only city made uninhabitable almost overnight. In the distance she could see the remains of some of the concrete buildings, still stabbing up centuries later into the shimmery sky.

It was very hot. The breeze rummaging through the train did little to cool anyone. Delacour sat back on her seat with her eyes closed, her face pebbled with sweat. Her hair clung to her head like wet leaves sticking to the surface of a road. Bowden wondered if Delacour shared her uncertainties about the trip.

Two young people with a lot of luggage took the seat opposite them, and their careless good looks made her think of Hythe. Bowden had seen her again after that dreadful class, only three days ago, coming out of Bowden's own apartment. Bowden had stopped still on the path, causing someone to bump into her, but she barely noticed — she kept watching Hythe's long, pale body walk away from her. When she entered the apartment she waited for Delacour to mention it, but when she didn't Bowden finally said, casually, "Was that your student I saw leaving?" and, "Oh, yes," Delacour answered, just as casually. "She wanted to borrow one of my vidspools."

The train began to move, and soon they were out in the country again. The breeze pushing strongly in her face cooled her off a bit, and she felt more comfortable, eager to see what was ahead. The farthest north she had ever been was Edmonton Station, and that was years ago, before they had extended the line to the Peace. Delacour revived slightly, too, and they stared out the window together at the thick green forests, the mountains leaping into view occasionally in the distance.

"I was named for an oldtown around here somewhere, I think," Bowden said.

"Oh?" Delacour slapped at a mosquito on her arm. She missed.

"Were you named for one?"

"I don't think so. Rhea didn't tell about it, if I was."

Rhea, Bowden thought. She's thinking about her birth-mother, as though Jesse-Lee didn't exist.

"Is Jesse-Lee named for an oldtown?" Bowden wasn't going to let her get away with it.

"I don't know. She might be."

"You'll have to ask her when you see her."

Delacour sighed, loudly.

Bowden continued as though she hadn't heard. "My mothers were both named for oldtowns. Medley-Barons and Codesa. Aren't those nice names?" The mosquito Delacour had been swatting at was circling around Bowden. She waited until it had settled on her leg, then slapped it. She flicked it away with her fingernail.

"Yes. Very nice names." Delacour yawned.

"I almost took Codesa's name when I became an adult. I wish I had now. Bowden-Codesa. It would sound nice."

"I like it better as it is. It's simpler." Delacour tipped back her head, and her eyelids slid down.

Bowden continued to stare out the window at the green rush of trees. But by the time they reached Edmonton Station she had fallen into a light sleep, the motion of the train swinging in her head; and she woke with a start, alarming dreams scattering around her, only when they were pulling out.

The two young people in the seat opposite them were gone, and in fact the whole train seemed nearly empty. Bowden felt a nudge of panic, travelling now where she had never been, everything strange and wild and uninhabited. But the new rail line was faster and smoother than what they had been on, and it reassured her to feel that confident, civilized beat of metal wheels beneath her.

They were veering west now, she could see on the progess map over her head, but even as she watched, the direction swung more and more to the north, and soon they were up into the SwanHills. The forest outside had changed from deciduous to coniferous, old trees, an old forest, perhaps never cut. It awed her, the total emptiness, no one around them in any direction for several hundred kilometres, the train a small, determined capsule heading into the evening.

Delacour was poring over a temporary-book titled *Current Excavations*, and she learned over to Bowden and pointed to a page labelled "The Peace." "They have a dig there," Delacour said. "I remember they were quite excited at first because they found male remains that seemed to exceed by more than fifty years the latest known ones in Scandinavia. But then they did the artifact-scan and found it was only fifteen years or so later. Still — that's significant enough, fifteen years. I had to change my lessons."

Bowden nodded, trying to look interested. "It's hard to imagine anyone living up here, so far in the wilderness."

"It wasn't wilderness then. There were several hundred thousand people here at one time."

"And now?"

Delacour shrugged. "I don't know. A few hundred at the Peace. A few hundred at Fairview — maybe more because of the hospital. A few hundred on the farms." She turned back to her book on excavations. "How about if we stop at the dig tomorrow before we head out?" she asked. "It's only a few kilometres out of the way."

Bowden looked at her suspiciously. "This is our *holiday*. The dig has to do with your work."

"I'd just like to see it. It might be interesting."

"You knew about it all along, didn't you? Is our holiday just an excuse for you to visit it?" It would explain, she thought, why Delacour, who had never particularly liked travelling, had wanted to come in the first place.

"Of course not!" Delacour's voice rose angrily. "All right, we won't go." She slammed the book shut.

"I'm sorry. I just wanted this to be a holiday for *us*. With no work. Just for us."

"It's okay. I said we won't go." Delacour turned to look out the window at the westerly sun blistering the lake, and all Bowden could do was stare helplessly at the back of her head, her rumpled hair bristling at the edges.

By the time they reached the Peace they had both dozed off again, and one of the crew had to wake them and tell them to detrain. They stumbled sleepily down the steps, Bowden turning and looking back at the train with a kind of frightened longing. They were on their own now, a thousand kilometres from home. If Delacour hadn't strode purposefully ahead Bowden might have run back to the train, wanting only to return to the comfort of her own apartment, her own predictable city. She felt like crying, the fatigue of the last fourteen hours tangling her feet on the rutted, unpaved streets.

They found the Trail Company easily enough only a block from the station, and after they checked in, the manager, a small, dark person with feathers woven into her hair, escorted them to the hotel, where they discovered the electricity had been turned off for the day, so they sat in their room in the dusty twilight eating the sandwiches the Trail Company had provided.

"Well," Delacour said. "Tomorrow will be better."

Bowden nodded, too tired and disappointed to speak.

But the next day *was* better. Once they got their horses and supplies and had climbed out of the Peace valley along the winding Shaftsbury Trail, Bowden felt a rush of exhilaration at seeing the huge river pumping along below them, the air brimming with morning bird song, the suede greenness extending as far as she could see. She liked the feel of the horse clamped between her legs, the way it responded like the horses of her childhood to the pressure of knees, the twist of the reins, as though they were both remembering skills learned long ago. She was pleased to see she was a better rider than Delacour, and she gave excessive instructions until Delacour said she would scream if Bowden said any more. But they were happy with each other, pointing out things in the river valley to each other, saying, look, look, feeling wonder again like children. Bowden couldn't believe that yesterday she had wanted only to go home.

They stopped for lunch at the spot recommended on their Trail Company map, and it made them feel reassured and competent, knowing that if they could keep to the schedule they could also choose not to. They sat on the riverbank watching several deer grazing far below, and Delacour brought out her binoculars and pulled them into a closer view. It was the first time either of them had ever seen wild deer. A breeze from the west rattled the leaves of the poplars behind them, and a large grey bird flew up from the underbrush, the clap of its wings like applause. Their lunch consisted of rich, creamy salads they had never tasted before, and were so good they had to restrain themselves from breaking the safe-seals on their supper rations to sample them as well.

Bowden went to check on the horses, which they'd tethered close by. Large and stolid animals, more Clydesdale than Arabian in their ancestry, they were good-tempered and responsive.

She watched their huge teeth tearing at the plentiful grass. She inflated one of the drink-bowls, filled it with water, and took it over to them. Her horse emptied it in almost one swallow, and Delacour's horse would probably have inhaled the bowl if Bowden hadn't snatched it away. She filled it again. As she walked back to them, she noticed for the first time her horse's penis swinging between his legs. She stopped still and stared as it pushed rawly through its outer skin and protruded like a thick red forearm from its sleeve. It was a long time since she'd seen a male animal with its penis extended.

"Delacour, look," she whispered.

"Oh, my," Delacour said. She came up and stood beside Bowden, watching.

"It's hard to believe he can keep it all tucked away up there when it's not in use," Bowden said.

"You know," Delacour said, "I've never actually seen one out like that before. Except in pictures."

Delacour's horse was straining forward for its water, snorting and shaking its head impatiently. It was also a male, but its penis wasn't extended. Bowden set the water down in front of it, and it guzzled greedily.

"Is it safe it ride him when he's like that?" Delacour asked, still watching the other horse.

Bowden laughed. "It doesn't last forever, you know." And even as she said it, the erection started to subside, and soon it had all pulled back inside.

"Very interesting," Delacour said. "I hope it happens again."

"Poor thing," Bowden said. "It probably misses its mate."

They went back to the bank and just stood for a while looking down at the river curling away into the distance like a thick blue string, at the deer, at the great, unpeopled emptiness around them. The sun lay itself across their shoulders like a friendly arm, and two white butterflies flickered in the grass at their feet.

Suddenly Delacour said, "Ah, lord, isn't it almost too much? A surfeit of beauty!"

And then, her voice so impassioned that Bowden could only stare at her in amazement, she cried, "Oh, Bowden, I feel such a — such a restlessness in my life! I'm so hungry for everything, but all I consume leaves me wanting more. My life seems like just a series of things I have to rush and finish and then move on, when what I *want*, what I truly want, is to stop, to be satisfied, to be still."

The air seemed quieter than before. Bowden waited a long time before she answered. "And am I just something to finish? Before you move on?"

Delacour turned, her face strained, the muscles at the corners of her mouth compressing the skin into bloodlessness. She lifted her arms, put them around Bowden's neck.

"Of course not," she said.

Bowden reached up, took hold of Delacour's wrists and pulled her arms down. Her hands dangled from the cuffs of Bowden's fingers as though Bowden had severed their nerves.

"You've been with that student, haven't you? Why won't you admit it?" Bowden said, trying to keep her voice calm, not allowing it to tremble.

"She doesn't matter — "

"She matters to me." Bowden let go of Delacour's hands. She turned and walked back to the horses.

Delacour's voice followed her, a rope, a lasso she was throwing to try to pull her back. "Bowden, listen to me. The others are just ... transcience, empty experience. But you, you're — please, turn around, look at me."

Bowden stopped, turned. She concentrated on her heart, beating slowly in her chest, as though if she didn't will it to continue it would falter, stop.

"You're at my centre, you're my still centre."

The horses, alarmed at the tense voices, the jerky movements, had been trying to back off from them, raising their heads and pulling at the reins tied loosely around the poplar trunks. Delacour's horse had almost pulled open the knot, and Bowden, relieved at the excuse, hurried over and grabbed its halter. Delacour came and stood beside her, and they stroked the horse's damp, satiny neck.

"Whenever you go with others I feel you've left me," Bowden said.

She thought, with sudden sadness and yearning, as though of a long-absent friend, of the person she had been eight years ago, laughing at the foolish restrictions of a monogamy-bond. *(Why would we need a monogamy-bond? We are everything to each other.)* Monogamy-bonds had been, she knew, one of the things about which people argued all the time before the Change. We have elimated so many larger problems since then, she thought — why did this one seem to defeat us?

Delacour was combing her fingers stiffly through the horses's coarse mane. "How could I ever leave you?" she said. "Without you I'd be even more stupid and confused than I am now." She fisted her hand in the horse's mane, released it.

"You, stupid?" Bowden said. But she felt herself giving in.

"Yes, I am," said Delacour. "In the ways that matter. You're the wise one — "

"Wise!" Bowden snorted, but she was pleased at the word, even as she could see how it was manipulating her, because she knew in some way it was true, that she had a sense of her place in the world, which Delacour didn't. Perhaps it came from holding in her arms every day the dying people of the world, giving them calm and comfort, and to do that she needed a calm and comfort inside herself, which Delacour, with her rummaging through history and sensual pleasure, could never have. A still centre: yes, she thought, I suppose that is what I do have, what I must have. But if that is true, then why do I fear so much losing Delacour, fear her choosing someone else?

"I don't want us to quarrel, Delacour," she said.

Delacour stroked the horse's neck. Then she nodded and said, "All right," as though something had been agreed, settled between them.

But we haven't settled anything, Bowden thought unhappily.

They picked up their lunch packs, mounted the horses, and continued on, quickening their pace without really intending to. There was still an unease between them, but as the rhythm of the horses worked its way through them they began to relax, and by the time they reached the Trail Company's midway cabin, where it was recommended they spend the night, Bowden felt comfortable with Delacour again. Comfortable, she thought — what did that mean? Did it mean she would be able to see Hythe leave her apartment again and say to herself, well, it doesn't matter; Delacour will come back to me? She watched Delacour's lean back rise and fall in the saddle in front of her. Comfortable: if that were only what Delacour wanted, too, everything would be all right.

"We don't have to stay here tonight," Delacour said, turning in her saddle. "It's early enough; we can go on and camp somewhere."

"I'd just as soon stay here," Bowden said. "I'm rather tired." It was a better reason to give Delacour than saying it would be safer at the cabin.

"All right. My buttocks are worn raw, anyway."

They unsaddled and rubbed down the horses, and then they set up in the cabin, which seemed to have been prepared for them fairly recently, with new sheets and a full coal-oil lamp, an emergency beacon and radio, plasti-sealed pails of fresh water, and even, above the bed, a shelf full of books, including duplicates of their maps and instructions. They giggled and shrieked like children as they saw a mouse scuttling across the floor, and finally they managed to get it shooed out the door. They built a fire in the large cleared and charred area outside and ate their supper there, watching the flames send sparks into the darkening sky, and they talked of inconsequential things, careful not to be too serious.

Delacour had brought along some of the books from the cabin, and she flicked through them without interest until she came to a poetry collection, which made her exclaim, "Imagine finding this here! I remember reading some of her work when it was first discovered years ago. A pre-Change poet, early twenty-first century — not much work by our people survived from then."

"Read me some," Bowden said, lying back and propping her head on her bent arm.

Delacour leaned closer to the fire so she could see better and flipped through the pages, pausing to skim and then moving on. "It's rather difficult," she said. "Look at this one, for instance." She tapped a page. "The explanatories take up more space than the poem itself." She turned another few pages, hesitated. "Interesting passage here. Listen:

> The squirrel my brother shot down with the .22
>   so the dog could play.
> The dog just sniffed the dead fur
> & looked up the tree again, eye
> cocked for the squirrel.
> It is always in our damn heads."

"The .22," Bowden said, "is that a gun? So he shot the squirrel? Just for fun? How horrible!"

"Yes," Delacour said. "But the rest of it — what a clever observation. The dog, you see, is only interested in what's elusive, up in the tree, the idea of the thing."

"Killing," Bowden said, in her mind the squirrel still falling from the tree. "It's what they knew best how to do."

"I'll find something less depressing," Delacour said. She leafed through the book for some time before she chose one. "Here," she said. "This one has love in it. It's called 'Gorgeous.'" She lay down and put her head in Bowden's lap, holding the book expertly entwined in the fingers of one hand above her head. "It ends like this:

> What are our chances.
> What are our chances.
> If our cancer can be removed without fear, under
>   local conditions.
> The chromosomes unrolled and kissed,
> until they are better.
> & the woman gets out of the bed.
> The blood on her legs, overflowing the small
>   stopper.
> The bird risen in the branches.
> In what book, concealed, is its name.
> I river, I river, I river.
> Trust the verb.
> Motion
> In the line, too, motion.
> I love you. The book is ended.
> the blood gorges gorges gorges the bed."

Bowden looked at the page Delacour had read, the small print fluttering in the firelight. "I don't understand it," she said.

"Well, it's how they used to write then. More symbolically." Delacour closed the book and set it on her chest.

"All that about blood. What's it mean?"

"It's about menses. A celebration of it."

"But why celebrate that? They didn't have extractors then, so it must have been an inconvenience. I don't understand."

"I suppose the poem is asserting pride in non-maleness. It tells us to have courage, to trust ourselves. It's about surviving, about curing what was wrong with that world."

Bowden sighed. It was just something else of Delacour's world she couldn't understand, that made her feel inadequate, excluded. A still centre: yes, she remembered bitterly, I have a still centre — in a still centre nothing moves; poetry is nonsense, a nuisance of words.

She thought suddenly of how when they would go walking in Commercial people would smile at her, and how it pleased her, that they felt such a commonality with her. But she thought now that their smiles meant something else, too, that they claimed her as predictable and ordinary, boring. Strangers never smiled at Delacour.

Delacour turned her head, looked up at Bowden. "You're more beautiful than any poem," she said.

Bowden laughed, let the easy words reassure her. She pulled her hands gently through Delacour's hair, snagging on a knot and working it slowly loose. She massaged her scalp, the back of her neck.

"Ah," Delacour said.

The delicate colours in the sky drained slowly away, and it grew dark. They looked up at the spectacular stars, trying to find the old constellations. The moon had become entangled in clouds, looking like a great bulge of brightness in the sky. In the west Bowden saw a meteorite, such a brief streak of light it was hard to believe she'd seen it at all. They used to call it a falling star, she remembered. She looked into the dark forest, as though she expected to see it there, fallen, setting the trees ablaze.

"Oh, god, " she whispered, her hands freezing on Delacour's shoulders.

"What?" Delacour leaped to her feet.

"There." She pointed, but the two bright feral eyes she'd seen on the edge of the forest were gone.

"It's okay," Delacour said. "Just something afraid of us."

But Bowden, chilled, insisted they go inside, so they poured water and dirt on the fire, Bowden shining the flashlight on the remaining coals even as she realized how absurd it was to illuminate what was already bright, until they were sure it was completely out, and then they moved their things inside. Bowden wanted to push the table up against the door, but Delacour laughed and said surely it wasn't necessary.

They made love in the narrow bed, more hungrily than they had in a long time, stopping just before orgasm so they could begin again, their bodies like sweetness held in the mouth, brimming with juices saying swallow, saying now, saying yes and yes.

Delacour fell asleep almost immediately after, her hand still cupped on Bowden's shoulder, but Bowden lay awake for a long time, thinking about what had happened during the day. She looked nervously through the windows, expecting a sudden wild face to appear. What she did see, finally, was a flare of sheet lightning on the horizon, and it made her get out of bed and stare anxiously out into the night. She hated lightning, could never forget it had killed her parents, her house ablaze when she came running down the thundering road from school.

A white bolt shot down the south sky. She trembled, clutched her arms tightly to herself. The cabin was in a clearing, close to the river — it was a bad location, she knew. And tomorrow, if they had to travel in a storm — She glanced at Delacour, soundly asleep, little snores puttering from her mouth, and she almost went to wake her, but of course it would have been foolish; what could Delacour do?

She watched the horizon tensely, her eyes circling the spot where the flash had been, but there wasn't another. She stood there for about half an hour, shivering, afraid to go back to bed, as though it were her watching keeping the storm away. At last, the sky quiet and cloudless above her, she took a sleep-pill and went to bed, and the pill closed her eyes against the fear and let her fall into a thick, dreamless sleep.

It was the next day they encountered the bear. They were about halfway between the cabin and Fairview, still early in the day, away from the river now, rounding a curve in the trail, and there it was, right in front of them, a large brown bear snuffling at something in the bushes.

The horses went wild when they saw it. Delacour's reared, and she toppled to the side before she even knew what was happening. Bowden saw her fall and land with a rattly thud in the underbrush. She had no time to think of anything, then, except keeping her own horse under control, as it shied back and fought against the reins that kept it from turning and plunging after its companion down the trail. She couldn't see Delacour at all.

And then the bear stood up. She saw it from the corner of

her eye as her horse danced sideways — suddenly twice the size it had been four-footed, as tall as she was in the saddle, its huge head and predator's eyes fixed on her.

The stunner, she thought, her mind lunging as desperately as her horse for safety. Keeping her left hand taut on the reins, she fumbled in her pack. She didn't dare look down, and her fingers had to identify what they found — food pouches, papers, clothes —

The bear fell to all fours, and, keeping its head high, began to pad forward slowly, not toward Bowden and her frantic horse, but toward where Delacour had fallen.

"No," Bowden shrieked. "No!"

Her fingers were almost at the bottom of the pack when they closed around something metal. It could be something else; it could be the flashlight, the radio band, the soap cylinders — but she had to take a chance and pull it out, spilling what was above it from the pack.

It was the stunner. She glanced at it, cold and alien in her hand. She had never held one before, let alone used one. It had a large round hole in one end, so she knew that must point at the bear, which had stood up on its hind legs again, directly across the trail from where Delacour had fallen. She settled the stunner into her hand, found a trigger that must activate it, and aimed. She was a long way back now, and she knew it was useless to try to urge her horse forward, so she just had to hope she was still within range. She pulled the trigger. She felt a slight vibration in her hand, but there was no spurt of flame, no sharp crack of sound, and the bear did not change position. The batteries must be dead, she thought in horror, as she pulled the trigger again and again.

The bear sank down to all fours, and then, slowly, tidily, its legs folded themselves under, and it settled to the ground.

Its neck and head reached forward as though they had no intention of following the direction of the rest of the body, but then slowly they, too, collapsed, extending rigidly along the ground. Relief flooded through Bowden, but she forced herself to remain where she was, waiting for movement in the bear. Only when she was sure did she slide down from her horse, lash its reins tightly around a tree, and run forward. The bear's glazed open eyes watched her approach. When she was a few yards away she stopped and looked for the first time from the animal to the underbrush.

"Delacour!" she shouted. "Delacour!"

There was a small movement in the bush, and she ran toward it. "Are you okay?" she cried. "You can come out — it's safe. Are you okay?"

Delacour stood up, covered in leaves and twigs, her face white. "The bear," she said.

Bowden ran up to her, grasped her arms, the stunner still in her hand. "It's all right," she said. She led her slowly out of the brush, checking her for broken bones, but the worst she could find was a bruise along her right thigh. Bowden sat her down on the trail facing away from the bear, but Delacour turned and stared at the downed animal.

"You did that," she said. "You knew what to do."

"I have to go after your horse," Bowden said, turning Delacour's face to hers to make sure she understood. She might still be in shock. "Will you be okay here alone? I'll leave you my stunner."

Delacour nodded, rather unconvincingly, but she began vaguely brushing herself off, and Bowden, watching her co-ordination carefully, decided she was regaining her control. She fitted the weapon into Delacour's hand. "I'm sure you won't have to use it," she said. "But just in case."

Delacour nodded dully again. "I wouldn't even have thought of the stunner," she said.

"It was on the pack-list. I remembered seeing them put it in. Now I have to go after your horse. Wait right here. Okay?"

"Yes. I'll wait right here."

Bowden ran back to her horse and pulled herself on. The animal needed no urging to leap into a wild gallop. Feeling the great chest pumping under her, the wind and mane cutting at her face, Bowden felt for the first time the exhilaration of success: she hadn't given in to fear and panic; Delacour was the one lying helpless in the underbrush, and she was the one who had known what to do. Finally she pulled back on the reins, slowed her horse to a canter, and began to shout the word the person at the Peace had told her.

"Come," she yelled, but it was as much a shout of triumph as it was a call for Delacour's horse. "Come!" Her heart beat in strong, exultant thumps at her chest. It frightened her a little, this raw excitement — what had she done, after all, except point a stunner at an animal and pull the trigger? Was this how the males had felt, long ago, the hunters, the ones who killed, finally, just for sport?

The horse did not come, but when she found it grazing at the side of the trail it made no move to resist capture. She picked up its reins and tied them to her saddle horn, and it trotted obligingly along behind her down the trail.

But when they neared the place where they'd met the bear the horses caught its scent again, and it was all Bowden could do to keep them under control. Delacour's horse reared, and then, realizing it couldn't break free, planted its legs and refused to move. Bowden dragged it ahead one stiff step at a time, her own horse shaking its head in frantic disagreement, bouncing forward only with the greatest urging.

What Bowden saw when they rounded the corner almost made her drop the reins. The bear was still where she'd left it, but there was something else on the trail — a supply truck. She'd known they would probably encounter one en route, but she'd expected to hear its noise well in advance; this one had the motor turned off as its driver and Delacour stood looking at the bear blocking its path.

The horses continued to plunge and toss their heads, struggling for escape, so Bowden dismounted and tied them to a tree well back from the road, and then she walked over to join Delacour.

"You did this, eh?" said the driver, an old, small-eyed person smelling of garlic, with a loud, annihilating voice. Her expression gave no hint of whether she approved or not.

"Yes," Bowden said nervously. "I was afraid it was going to attack."

The driver grunted, prodded at the bear with her boot. The lines above her mouth pulled tighter. "I don't like bears," she said.

"Do you think I did any permanent damage? I hit it three times with the stunner."

"It was coming toward me," Delacour added. "I'm sure I was in danger."

"You should close its eyes. So they don't get dried out." When Bowden and Delacour only looked at her uneasily, she sighed loudly, bent over, and pushed down the animal's thick eyelids. The bear looked better that way, calm, asleep.

"Can you get past?" Bowden asked, looking at the supply truck and the way the bear was blocking half the road.

"I got by worse things on this road. One of these days they'll bring the train up here and I won't have to make this pissing trip any more."

"But it must be interesting," Delacour said, "being the one

114

who can have a truck. Who can drive."

"*Interesting*? Merde. It's the worst job there is." She nudged the bear again. "Your horses won't want to go by this thing, you know. You better take a big detour."

"I suppose so," Bowden said.

"Look — you want to see nice scenery there's a better way to Fairview than this road — it's all away from the river now. But you go back up a quarter kilometre and there's a trail that goes south, along the river. It takes a few more hours, but if you want to see pretty country that's where it is. Just watch out for the Isolists."

"Who?" Bowden asked.

"The Isolists. They're some religious group. Harmless enough — I've met some of them. But they want to be left alone. So we respect that. Rumour has it they've been inbred so long some of them aren't, you know, quite right."

Bowden could feel Delacour's interest quicken. No, she thought wearily.

"Quite right?" Delacour asked.

"Well — birth defects. You know."

"The doctors are supposed to prevent that."

The driver shrugged. "Maybe they don't want it prevented. I don't know. It's none of my business. It's just rumours. Well — " She clapped her hands onto her thighs so loudly it made Bowden jump. "I better go. I got frozen stuff in there." And she began to walk back to her truck.

"Thanks," Delacour called after her.

The driver raised her hand and then swung herself up into her truck without using the toe-holds. They watched as she started it up, a loud and ugly roar worse than any animal's. Its four huge tires ground slowly forward, veered off the road and into the brush at the side as it passed the bear, then climbed back

into its usual track. As it passed the horses they reared and whin-
nied in terror, as afraid of the machine as of the bear, and Bowden ran toward them to make sure they wouldn't tear themselves
loose.

"Easy," she said, "easy," patting their sweaty necks. When
the truck was past, its snuffling noise diminishing in the distance, they calmed a little, but their heads kept jerking up when
she reached for their bridles, and their eyes rolled nervously
at any movement. Delacour came up beside her.

"Well," she said. "That was quite an adventure." She reached
out her arms and folded them around Bowden. "You were wonderful," she said. "I'm so proud of you."

It wasn't quite the right word, *proud*, like a parent pleased
with a child doing better than expected, but it would have to
do. Yes, Bowden thought, it would do.

Delacour drew back and held out her hand to Bowden. Bowden was surprised to see it still held the stunner. "Take it,"
Delacour said, "before I shoot one of the horses with it or
something."

"You've one, too, you know." Bowden took the stunner and
tucked it into her pack.

"I'd never have thought to look for it, though."

"Are you feeling all right now? Do you hurt anywhere besides your leg?"

Delacour shook her head. "I'm okay. Don't worry."

"We should probably go, then. I don't know how long the
bear will be out."

"About what that driver said. About the alternate route. What
do you think?"

"We're talking about *kilometres* out of the way, Delacour!"

"But it was so lovely along the river — we can't get lost if
we just follow it. And we've our maps; they show all the trails.

We'll always know the road is straight to the north of us some-where. We can cut back when we're close to Fairview. Come on — we're ahead of schedule, anyway."

Why was it so easy for Delacour? She could have been killed, yet here she was eager to take more chances. Well, all right, Bowden thought resolutely — I can be that way, too; I was the one who stopped the bear.

"Okay. Let's do it, then."

Delacour grinned. "Great," she said. "Wonderful." She un-tied her reins quickly and swung herself into the saddle, winc-ing as her bruised leg slapped into place, and turned her horse back the way they had come.

Bowden had little choice but to follow. The horses skittered nervously at first, as though they were walking on ice, but as the bear's scent decreased they lowered their heads and resumed the light trot they preferred.

It was easy to find the trail the driver had spoken of, and, without comment, Bowden followed Delacour in. Immediately she had misgivings. The trail was overgrown and narrow, not wide enough for them to ride two abreast, and the branches Delacour and her horse dragged forward came slapping back at her. She began to lag behind and then, worried, would urge her horse ahead until Delacour was in sight again. The dense-ness of the forest made her uneasy; she kept peering to the side expecting a bear to lunge at them any moment, and several times she reached into her pack for the reassuring feel of the stunner. Her horse picked up her nervousness and shied at any move-ment around them; when a partridge flew up from the under-brush to her right like a ragged piece of the forest breaking free, it frightened them both so much she almost fell.

She was just about to shout at Delacour that this was ridiculous, that she wouldn't go on, when they broke free of the forest onto the riverbank and were looking down the smooth parabolas of hills to the river flickering in the sun.

"I'm glad we're through that," Bowden said. "I was getting welts from the branches."

Delacour dismounted stiffly, rubbing at her thigh and her buttocks. "I'm getting welts on my ass," she said.

Bowden swung herself down, too. The horses began rummaging through the grass. She wished she felt confident enough to take their bridles off and let them eat properly without the bits chafing their mouths, but she had had such trouble getting the bits in this morning that she decided it wasn't worth the struggle. But she looked at them guiltily, imagining what it would be like to eat with a rod of metal clamped between her teeth.

Delacour wandered to the edge of the bank, startling into flight a flock of small red-winged birds that erupted from behind a stand of white birch trees like a shower of sparks. She pointed at two thick grey stumps in the water, close to the south shore. "Those could be what's left of bridge pylons," she said. "According to the map there was an oldroad here once."

Bowden came over, shaded her eyes with her hand, and squinted to look. "It's hard to imagine. A bridge. So far north."

"There'll probably be a bridge there again someday. Fifty years ago the idea of a train to the Peace would have sounded absurd, too."

"I hope it never happens," Bowden said, "I hope it never changes."

"Never changes? Of course it will change. It has to."

A sudden dense cloud of small flies swept up from the river like a piece of polka-dotted gauze and engulfed them, slamming into their eyes and ears, tangling in their hair. The horses snorted, jerking up and tossing their heads. Then just as suddenly the insects were gone.

"Aagh," Delacour said, spitting. "One in my *mouth*."

Bowden combed her fingers several times through her hair, but even so she continued to feel little tingles on her scalp that made her reach up and scratch.

"That's nature," Delacour said. "Bears and flies."

Thinking of the bear made Bowden uneasy again, and she looked into the bush from which they'd come. "We better get going," she said.

They rode on. Delacour kept pointing at things for Bowden to see, then began some long explanation about the meanders in rivers. "Oh, yes," Bowden would say, but her mind wandered off into anxious little whirlpools of her own as she watched the sun starting to lean into the west.

About an hour later they reached a stream, which, although small, cut a sharp gully in front of them, and they had to head inland for half a kilometre before they found a place to cross. The horses strode into the water without hesitation, although in the deepest part it reached almost to their stomachs. Bowden cried out as she saw Delacour's horse in front of her stumble and almost fall. All she could do was hang on to her reins and saddle horn and wait until it was over. As the horses bent to drink on the other shore, Delacour took out her map and located the stream.

"Look here," she said, holding out the map to Bowden, who was too far away to see anything but a scribble of lines, "just across the stream there's a trail that will bring us out about five kilometres before Fairview — let's take it."

Bowden nodded. Delacour trusted the map; Bowden trusted Delacour. The horses, who trusted no one, beat their wet tails on their riders' legs and drank more water than they needed, just in case.

The trail was just where Delacour expected to find it, and

it was less overgrown and narrow than the one they had first taken away from the road, although they still had to go single file in spots. Sometimes they would break into a clearing that was rich with strawberries or saskatoon bushes, but although Delacour pleaded to stop Bowden kept eyeing the sun and insisted they go on.

"Now what?" Delacour said suddenly, reining to a stop as they were halfway across one of the clearings.

On the other side were two trails, one angling slightly west, the other north.

"Oh, no," Bowden moaned.

Delacour was digging out her map, which was so crumpled by now she no longer tried to fold it along its original creases. "We may be here," she said dubiously, pointing at a wrinkle. "Or here."

Bowden took a deep breath. "Which path should we take, then, do you think?"

"I don't suppose it matters," Delacour said cheerfully, wadding up the map. "They both probably come out at the main road eventually." She urged her horse forward. "Let's take the westerly one. Okay?" She looked over her shoulder at Bowden, who only nodded and nudged her horse to follow.

This trail seemed wider than the one they had just left, and that reassured Bowden at first, but after a few miles she noticed it seemed to veer farther westward, perhaps even southerly, and she confirmed it on her compass.

"Well, do you want to go back?" Delacour asked, "take the other one?"

"I don't know," she said miserably.

They decided to try a few more kilometres to see if the southerly direction persisted, but when they stopped again, on a lightly wooded knoll, to confer, they were still indecisive — the trail was no longer going south, but neither was it going north. Delacour brought out her map again, but it was no help; they could have been anywhere.

"Look," Bowden said suddenly, pointing. "Smoke."

And there it was, a languid, grey curl of it sauntering skyward, a breeze tugging at it slightly near the top. It seemed to be ahead of them on the trail and somewhat to the south.

"Is it Fairview, do you think?" Bowden asked. She felt greatly relieved.

"I don't think so. Fairview should be off to our right somewhere. It's probably one of the Isolist farms."

"Who?"

"You know. The driver told us about them."

"Oh. Yes. She said they were odd. That they didn't like strangers."

"Well, we can head that way, anyway. They could give us directions. It might be interesting to meet them."

"They don't like *strangers*. We've no right to bother them."

"They can give us directions, for heaven's sake," Delacour said.

She kneed her horse forward, not waiting for Bowden's reply, and Bowden's horse, used to the pattern by now, followed obediently behind without waiting for the nudge from Bowden's heels.

When they descended from the knoll, they lost sight of the smoke, but the trail continued its westerly direction, so they knew the smoke was still somewhere ahead and off to the south. They found themselves looking more and more to their left for signs of habitation, the alterations in the landscape that only humans could make. But there was nothing, only the impervious forest, the trees holding out their greedy leaves to the sun to be filled. Once a small path angled off to the north and they considered taking it but decided not to.

Eventually, discouraged, they stopped on a small rise and looked around, but the paring of smoke, which should have been almost straight to the south of them by now, seemed to have disappeared. Delacour dismounted, moaning and holding her bruised thigh. Bowden, after a minute, slid off her horse, too, and they stood there in silence, stretching and rubbing their tense muscles. Delacour took down her pack and pulled out a long-sleeved shirt, which she slipped on over her sleeveless one, and Bowden thought vaguely that she should do the same, that it would protect her from the sun and slap of branches, but it seemed too much trouble and too late in the day. She took a drink from her water pouch, flipped her horse's reins around a branch, climbed up on a mound of rocks, and sat down, closing her eyes and letting the slight breeze paddling through the leaves above dip her face into light, shade, light, shade.

And then she heard them.

Not voices, not quite, but human sounds; she knew that instantly. She whirled to her right and there they were, in a meadow beneath her, where the rocks she was on formed a slight ravine. They were partly obsured by a patch of willows, but she could see them clearly enough to tell they were naked, and making love. One was on top of the other, and was broad-backed and blonde; of the other Bowden could only see a corona of black hair and her widely spread legs and chubby arms, which were wrapped across the back of the first. The one on top was making deep pushing movements with her pelvis onto the pelvis of the other, and Bowden watched, fascinated, wondering how this could be satisfying for either of them. They must be Isolists, she thought; obviously their mating rituals were different from hers. She knew she should stop watching, but she couldn't pull her eyes away.

"What's wrong?" Delacour's loud voice made her start, and

she unfastened her gaze from the couple, who were too engrossed to have heard. As though she had to protect them, she simply shook her head and began cautiously to climb down. But Delacour, curious, was coming up to meet her, and before Bowden could draw her away she had reached the top and looked down. Bowden could hear her quick intake of breath.

"We shouldn't watch," Bowden whispered, but even as she said it her eyes were drawn to them again, to their odd posture, their sounds of pleasure that drifted up through the hot green air.

At last the one on top stopped her plunging movements and lay limply on the other, who slowly loosened her arms and let them drop to her sides. After a moment the other one rolled over onto her back.

Delacour gasped, and Bowden felt her go rigid beside her. For an instant she didn't understand what had alarmed her, and she flicked her eyes, frightened, at Delacour, whose mouth was open in a slight ellipsis of surprise. Bowden looked back at the people on the ground. Then she saw.

There was something physically wrong with the blonde person. Her breasts were covered with a woolly coat of hair, like an animal's, and something thick and white seemed to be protruding or oozing from her vagina. Bowden stared at it, horrified.

She felt Delacour move beside her, but she didn't look over. "I'm going to get the binoculars," Delacour whispered. Bowden heard the slither of her body as she pushed herself back.

And suddenly there was a clatter of stones falling, Delacour saying, "Merde," under her breath as she grabbed for a hold on the smooth surface, found none, and went thudding onto the ground at the base of the rocks. Bowden spared her only a glance and turned back to the couple, who had leaped up in alarm, looking toward her. She pulled her head down as far as she could, hardly breathing, but she was sure she was still visible, her white pants splayed against the grey stone. When she raised her head again she could see them running, clutching their clothes to them, the blonde one frantically trying to tie her shirt around her waist as she ran. The sight of their panic made Bowden feel guilty and ashamed.

Delacour had clambered up beside her again, cursing, but by the time she reached the top of the rocks the couple had disappeared into the trees.

"My god," she gasped, "did you see that?"

"That poor person. The driver said some of them might have defects but I've never seen anything like that."

"You know what it made *me* think? It made *me* think she looked like a male."

"A *male?*"

"Well, of course it couldn't really have been one, but still — "

"Maybe it was just part of their customs, that some of them try to, I don't know, add on things to their bodies to make themselves look male."

"Mm," said Delacour. "That's a reasonable explanation."

"I mean, she didn't really look *disabled* or anything."

"No," Delacour said. "But I'd sure like to get another look."

"Well, we can't. We've frightened them away."

"I think we should follow them. That path obviously leads to their farm."

"No. They must be Isolists, and we've probably already violated some taboo just by watching them."

"Out in the open like that, what could they expect?"

"They could expect nobody to be here."

"Well, I still think we should follow them."

"It's the wrong way. We should be heading north, not south — "

"They can give us directions, Bowden. We're lost."

And there was no argument she could make to that. *We're lost* — hearing Delacour admit it made her feel even more helpless. "All right," she sighed. "But you have to promise we'll just ask directions and then leave."

"Yes, yes." Delacour had already slid down from the rocks and was untying her horse.

"We can't bother them," Bowden persisted.

"All *right*. I'm not going to say, 'Excuse me, would you mind if I looked at you all naked?' " She swung up on her horse, urging it forward even before her right foot found the stirrup. "Hurry up," she said.

They wound their way down to the bottom of the ravine, the horses' hooves scattering pebbles and earth, and then they headed across the meadow to where the path began through the trees. Bowden kept looking behind her, trying to memorize the route so they could find their way back, but Delacour looked only ahead, pressing her horse into a canter across the brief meadow.

When they reached the path they found it almost impossible to ride on. It was clearly a footpath and not meant for horses, but by going slowly and fending off the thick branches with their arms or flattening themselves on their horses' backs they were able to proceed without dismounting. The path branched into two at one point, but Delacour barely hesitated before she chose one, as though she had the scent of something she was chasing. Bowden felt more and more apprehensive as they continued, but her protests only simmered, futile, in her throat: *We're getting more lost. We've no right to intrude.*

What if there really are males?

In the poem, the squirrel, shot, for amusement, falling from the tree.

She felt a sudden terror. Her eyes flickered to her pack, where her stunner was. She remembered how easy it had been to use it. Quickly she looked away, repelled by what had entered her mind, a breaking of law, using the weapon against another person. Not another person, she assured herself: a male. *The male will get you.*

She took a deep breath. Stop being absurd, she told herself angrily; I'm no longer a child, to be frightening myself with ghost stories. There are no males. She forced herself to laugh, but not loud enough for Delacour to hear. A thin branch wiped its leaves along her teeth.

The forest, which was mostly spruce and pine now, lightened up ahead, and they could see the flicker of unobstructed sun through the final rows of trees. Then suddenly, amazingly, they were in the open, a wheat field with the grain turning a thick gold, and beyond that a fenced pasture with cows and horses, then another hectare or two of what looked like a vegetable garden. Windbreaks separated the fields like dark green seams, and at the south end of the wheat field was the farm itself, about a dozen buildings sewn so smoothly into the folds of the landscape they looked as though they had been there forever. Only two or three of the buildings were painted, but in dull browns or greens to blend them even more into the surrounding forests and hills, like embroidery whose purpose is not to ornament but to complement. A windmill turned lazily in the wind beside the sunsavers and the generator at the east corner of the farm.

To Bowden, the scene, unrolling abruptly after the day of seeing nothing but wilderness, recalled to her with striking vividness the farm of her childhood. Whoever these people are, she thought, they cannot be that much unlike us. Delacour simply sat and looked around her, too, her eager rush through the forest calmed by the sight of the farm, so ordinary and still in the afternoon sunlight.

A bell rang suddenly somewhere at one of the buildings, and it startled them out of their reverie.

"Well," Delacour said, pressing her horse lightly forward. "I suppose we should go find someone."

They moved slowly along the edge of the field, trying not to let the horses trample the wheat or snatch a mouthful as they passed. As they neared the main buildings, of which Bowden could now count about eight that looked like dwellings and another ten or so that were storage sheds or barns, she expected a dog to come rushing out at them, and she tightened her hold on the reins, but there was no sign of any animals around the houses. Their narrow path suddenly joined a larger trail, perhaps the main one into the farm, although even it would hardly be wide enough to accommodate the harvesters bringing in their machines. It was possible, she supposed, that they did the harvesting themselves, using only horses; it was hard to know how much self-sufficiency they had, how much they needed the outside world.

The horses, picking up the familiar smells of other horses, tipped their ears forward and nickered, quickening their pace. They were only a few yards from the first buildings now. At the side of one of the outbuildings, a barn perhaps, Bowden noticed something hanging, long and pale, and as she looked more closely she realized with shock it was a slaughtered animal, a pig probably, the blood dripping into a pail from the huge red slit that ran the length of its body.

"Meat eaters!" she whispered to Delacour. It shouldn't repulse her; she knew there were people in the city, too, who would eat meat, but, still, the sight of the bloody carcass sent a chill of foreboding through her.

And then there were the people, four of them, coming out

of their houses with a deliberate casualness. Bowden was sure they'd known someone was coming.

"Hello," Delacour said, in her hearty, confident voice. "We're sure glad to see you. We seem to have gotten rather hopelessly lost."

The tallest person of the four, her grey-streaked hair pulled straight back off her broad forehead with a piece of twine, stepped forward and put her hand on the bridle of Delacour's horse. Her other hand reached up and picked a dead leaf from the corner of its eye. "Nice horse," she said. A scar stood out palely on her sun-browned cheek, making her look even more unwelcoming.

Delacour responded as though she thought the reach for the bridle was an invitation to dismount. She swung her leg over the saddle and slid to the ground. "They are, aren't they?" she said, patting her horse's neck cheerfully. "They're from the Trail Company. In the Peace. We've just rented them for a few days."

"Where are you from?" The tall person flicked her eyes to Bowden, who, afraid to seem unfriendly, swung herself down reluctantly from her horse and moved over beside Delacour. On the ground, she felt the farm suddenly loom over her, giant and threatening. The person who had spoken was even taller than Delacour, who towered over most people.

"We're from Leth," Delacour said. "We're just on holiday. This is Bowden. And my name's Delacour." She widened her smile and held out her hand.

The person ignored her gesture but moved a step toward her; Bowden tensed, forced herself not to step back. The person reached up her hands, placed them on Delacour's shoulders, and dipped her head sideways, all the time not smiling, looking Delacour straight in the eye. Then she did the same with Bowden, who tried not to wince as the large hands, perhaps the same ones that had gutted the pig, descended on her shoulders. The three other people moved forward, too, and methodically, formally, without speaking, repeated the action. Bowden had to stop herself from laughing nervously, and she only stood there, wishing she knew what response was expected of her. She tried to unhook the inane smile that seemed to be caught on her teeth.

When they were finished, the tall person said, "I am Highlands. I speak for my people." The other three moved several steps back and lowered their eyes.

"I'm happy to meet you, Highlands," Delacour said, determinedly conversational, but Bowden could tell the greeting ritual had nonplussed her. She was turning the button on her shirt as though it were the lid of a bottle she was trying to unscrew.

"If you follow this main trail," Highlands said, pointing to where it entered the forest behind them, "it will take you to Fairview. You can make it in daylight if you leave now."

It was clearly a dismissal, and Bowden moved eagerly to her horse, "Thank you" ready on her lips, but Delacour, not moving, spoke first, cutting her off. "That's a relief," she said. "I'm sure we'll have no trouble now."

"This main trail," Highlands said, pointing again. "It branches off twice to the west and once to the east, but if you head mostly north you'll meet the main road from the Peace." She lowered her arm and then stood with her hands clasped in front of her and her legs slightly apart, a posture that seemed consciously symmetrical.

"Good," Delacour said. She patted her horse's neck again, fiddled with the reins.

Hurry *up*, Bowden thought.

"When we were coming in," Delacour said, scratching casually at her cheek, " we saw two of your people in the forest. I think we frightened them, and we're very sorry. Could we talk to them, do you think, and apologize?"

Bowden felt like punching Delacour in the side.

Highlands looked at them both, steadily, without speaking. One of the people behind her took off her shoe and emptied out a pebble; in the stillness it sounded as loud as a boulder when it hit the ground. A horse neighed in the distance, and Bowden's horse jerked up its head, pointing its ears at the sound and grunting back a message of its own.

"None of my people said anything." Highlands glanced at the horse, as though she were responding to it.

"We just wanted to say we're sorry," Delacour persisted. "One of the people, I know, was blonde."

Highlands was silent again. Even Delacour was nervous now, her gaze faltering. She rubbed her right foot on the ground as though the sole were itchy.

"Bluesky is blonde," Highlands said finally. "It might have been her." She turned to the house to her right and said, not raising her voice, "Bluesky. Come here for a moment."

A young person stepped to the door of the house, so quickly it was obvious she had been standing there listening. It was possible she was the one they had seen in the woods, Bowden thought, but she seemed more slender, taller perhaps. Bowden tried not to stare at her chest and groin, both covered with a loose denim overall.

"Were you just in the woods, Bluesky?" Highlands asked.

The person called Bluesky glanced nervously up at them. Then she nodded and looked down as though she might be ashamed, her hair falling over her face like a hood.

"These people think they saw you," Highlands said. "They want to apologize if they frightened you."

Bluesky nodded again, not looking up. Her fingers picked at the door frame. Bowden wondered for a moment if perhaps only the leader was permitted to speak. But they might think the same about her, she thought wryly.

"She accepts your apology," Highlands said. She ran her hand down the neck of Delacour's horse.

"Well," Delacour said, lamely. "Good."

"You'd better leave now if you want to make it back in light," Highlands said.

Even Delacour couldn't pretend not to understand this time, so she produced a hearty smile of agreement and said, "Well. We'll be going, then."

"Yes," Bowden said, determined to say something at last, so they wouldn't think her mute or forbidden to speak. "We won't bother you any longer." She swung herself into the saddle and pulled her horse into a half turn before Delacour had even mounted. "Thank you for your help." From this height Highlands looked much less formidable.

Highlands took several steps back, gave a formal bow, which was matched by the others behind her, then turned and walked away across the yard. The others vanished into their houses as though they had only been pictures painted onto doors, which now swung shut, and then Highlands, too, was gone, behind the building from which the slaughtered pig hung.

"Well," Delacour sighed, planting her foot in the stirrup, "I guess we're going."

"About time." Bowden pulled her horse around and led the way along the trail, into the forest. She resisted the urge to look behind her, to see if Delacour was really following, to see if the people had come back out of the houses to watch them go. She felt their eyes on her back, tangible as a hand. Only when she was well into the forest did she relax, rub her sweaty hands on her thighs, and pull back slightly on the reins to allow Delacour to catch up.

They rode abreast for a while, not speaking.

"That Highlands, the leader," Bowden said at last, "she was rather impressive, wasn't she?"

Delacour gave a little laugh. "She was, yes. I'd hate to make *her* angry."

"I think we probably did."

"No," Delacour said thoughtfully, "not angry. She was too careful for that." She began combing her fingers through her horse's mane. "The person who came to the doorway, Bluesky, do you think she was the one we saw in the woods?"

"She might have been. I don't think so."

"I don't, either."

"Well, it's just something we'll never know. A mystery."

"I hate mysteries."

"I'm glad we're away. They obviously didn't want us there."

"I wonder why."

"It's none of our business."

"Ah, yes," Delacour said, smiling. "That's what makes it so interesting."

And so they rode on, keeping to the directions Highlands had given them. Just as the sun was lingering on the horizon, turning the leaves and trees golden, as though they were lit from within, and they decided they would have to camp, they came around a bend and there was Fairview, so they stayed at the house the Trail Company had arranged.

And the next day, and the next, they rode back to the Peace, a sadness on them now because the trip was ending and it had, after all, been enjoyable.

In the Peace Bowden phoned Hospital in Leth and found that Jesse-Lee had died the day before.

At the funeral four days later, when they did the remembering, Delacour only shook her head when it came her turn, and

Bowden had to do it for her, telling about the time Jesse-Lee broke her arm and splinted it herself, something that was really only Delacour's memory. At the cemetery Delacour hung back, her eyes averted, when the others went up to the grave to say their last goodbyes. For the next two weeks she brought home twice as much work as usual, mortaring the books and vidspools into an impervious wall around her desk. If she cried, she was careful not to let Bowden see.

CHAPTER FIVE

DANIEL

IT WAS THE DREAM AGAIN ABOUT BEING FOUND OUT: in this one he was walking toward his apartment and suddenly a wind caught his clothes and somehow pulled them off and he was standing, naked, while the students around him pointed and screamed, and his legs strained and strained to run but could barely move —

He sat up, flailing at the bedclothes, covered in sweat. Slowly he willed his heart back to its normal beat, and then he got up and went to the bathroom and rubbed himself dry with a towel. He didn't turn on the light, but the illumination from outside trickled through the curtains, filling his apartment with a grainy grey. It was one of the hardest things he'd had to get used to, a room that was never dark, even now, at night in the middle of September.

Five-thirty, said the time-chip imbedded in the wall. He lay back down on the bed, thinking he should probably just stay up and study, but within a few minutes he was soundly asleep.

At eight o'clock the timer beside his bed began to chirp, and he struggled awake, turned it off. Mechanically, he got up, turned on the lights, and went into the bathroom. He set his shower selector for warm, knowing that would double its duration from what he could get at hot, and when it came on he stepped quickly out of his pyjamas into it. The water needled at his face. He leaned back against the warming tile, let his mouth slide open, the water prickle his tongue. Without letting himself think about it, he began to comb his fingers lightly through his pubic hair, cupping his genitals gently in one palm. When his penis thickened under his touch, he stroked himself easily to climax, almost choking on the mouthful of water he gargled into a moan of pleasure and release.

The timer above his head beeped, reminding him he had only a minute left, and quickly he rubbed his underarms and genitals with soap, barely in time to let the last of the shower carry it, frothing, away. He was getting too slow, too self-indulgent, he told himself as the water clicked off.

He dried himself and began his other morning rituals. The last thing he did, and the most careful, was to shave, with the razor he kept hidden behind his allotment of soap and shampoo. Not that having a razor would have been seen as all that bizarre — they were used for other purposes, after all — but still he made sure he never left it out like something used daily. He was lucky, actually, that his beard was so fair. Once, during his first term here, when he was so miserable and homesick that nothing seemed to matter, he went out one day without shaving, and no one noticed. But he vowed never to do that again. If he wanted to quit and go home he could — but it was inexcusable to take chances like that. When he thought of how hard it had been to convince the farm to let him come here — how could he betray them through sheer stupidity? They had argued about it for weeks, even sent him to East Farm to discuss it with the Leader there, but at last Highlands, largely because of the calm and unwavering arguments of his father, had agreed, and the others, reluctantly, finally gave in, too.

"I won't disappoint you," he had said fervently. And he hadn't.

Highlands, who had approved his return for second term only because he had done so well first term, cautioned him, with at least a degree of seriousness, not to be quite so outstanding a scholar this time.

He took out the flesh-coloured cream that Kit had told him about and that he'd bought in Hospital's specialty store, and he began rubbing it on his cheeks and chin. The face in the mirror turned stiff, impassive, as though the skincream were smoothing out all expression, all personality. He thought of his grandmother years ago teaching him the few words she knew of the oldlanguage his people used to speak many generations ago. The word for "lonely," she said, meant "me, I don't even look like myself."

He made himself smile at his mirrored image, the lonely face he would take with him outside. He was ready to "pass." It was a pre-Change word he'd learned, what some black people had tried to do to gain acceptance in the privileged white world. And of course, in the times when universities were open only to males, there were people who, hungry for the forbidden knowledge, tried to pass as males. What would they think now? he wondered. It was certainly a better example of irony than the one in the back of his literature book.

He brushed at a speck on his cheek, and then he went into his somewhat cramped centreroom, furnished with a desk, a sofa, a bookcase, and two chairs and small side tables. He had bumped his knees several times on all these things, seemingly incapable of manoeuvring around them as easily as did the people who had grown up in rooms such as these. He glanced up, as he did every morning, as though in greeting, at the place where the pale blue north wall met the ceiling and where someone, a former student, perhaps, had painted two fluffy cumulus clouds. The painting was rather crudely done, but it cheered him to look at it. He picked up from his desk the book he used for his geology class and went down to his apartment section's common dining-room, which was a flight below his own level. He still felt vaguely guilty eating here when he had done nothing to help with preparing or serving the food, and he was probably one of the few students who didn't mind the several hours of clean-up duty to which they were all assigned once a week.

He sat with the one friend he had made here, Mitchell-Star. Last term someone from East Farm had been here, and sometimes he felt it was all that kept him sane, knowing there was one other person who knew his secret, to whom he could go if he had to. She had been sympathetic at first, clinging to him a little, too, someone else from home, but as she made her own friends and romantic liaisons she became impatient with him, embarrassed to have him around, and eventually they began to avoid each other. Still, he was reassured to know she was there in case of an emergency, someone he could trust. But she didn't come back after harvest leave, and so this term he was alone.

He didn't let himself think about it. He was stronger now than he had been in first term, more able to deal with the isolation, the difficult times, when he would sit in his room with his books and the knowledge in them suddenly seeming like his enemies, aware of himself as an imposter, carrying an explosive secret. Most of the time, he realized, he was quite happy. Sometimes he would look around himself and laugh in sheer joy: he was at University. The dream everyone had told him was impossible had come true. He would write long and grateful letters to his mother and father and to Highlands, wanting them to be proud, wanting to reassure them they had made the right decision, wanting to share with them already the things he was learning.

It helped, too, having a friend like Mitchell-Star. He had been drawn to her because her name reminded him of his sister and also because he felt no physical desire for her. He could only hope she felt none for him, but then, he thought grimly, his body was not exactly an attractive one, which was fortunate under the circumstances. For a moment the image of Bluesky burned in his mind, and quickly he snuffed it out, feeling now not pain as much as guilt at the thought of her, for it was her sister, Shaw-Ellen, with whom he was expected to mate when he returned — and he *would* have to return, he had resigned himself to that, that he could never have a permanent place here, no matter how much he might yearn after the dazzle of University. And when he went back Shaw-Ellen would be waiting for him, Shaw-Ellen, with whom he made love but did not love, whom he would have to learn to love.

"G'morning," Mitchell-Star said, her pudgy cheeks pushed out even farther now with a mouthful of toast. An acne pimple glowed redly on her chin, but she wore it defiantly, refusing to take the Metane tabs that could clear her skin overnight. "You get that report done on *The Montrose People*?"

"Sure," he said. "You?"

She groaned. "Not yet. Merde. That wordstyle is so *tedious*."

"I thought it was okay." He poured himself a glass of milk.

"Everything is okay for you. It must be nice to be so smart."

"I'm not that smart. I just work hard." Which isn't difficult, he thought, if you have no extraclass life. But it was true that he found the work easy. He spooned a large helping of beancurd onto his plate.

"You'll get fat if you keep eating like that," Mitchell-Star observed.

"I'm storing up for winter."

"It's winter now."

"Fall." He took a large mouthful and grinned at her, letting the beancurd ooze slightly from the corner of his mouth. She groaned in delight, stuck out her tongue at him; it was covered with bits of chewed toast. He had to stop himself from making an even more disgusting face back; already the people across the table were watching them. He wiped away the beancurd. "So," he said. "Are you going to Geology today?"

She took a beancurd helping at least as large as his. "I thought I'd try some of the history sections. I heard they're pretty good. Why don't you come?"

"Oh, I don't know," he said vaguely. "I like what we'll be doing in Geology today."

His first term all he had taken were agriculture and mechanics courses — knowledge he would be able to use directly back on the farm — but now he was trying a greater variety — literature, meteorology, geology, anthropology, nutrition, internationalism, algebra, taking advantage of all his exploratories. They were interesting and gratifying; but they were safe courses, ones that dealt mostly with the world today, a world in which he didn't exist. It was still easier than history, than examining the past.

He had gone to one history class last term, and it had completely unnerved him, the way he had to see the story of his own kind as one of progressive brutality and destruction, the way it made him feel guilty and fearful just to be alive. He thought he had prepared himself for such situations, but it was one thing to read the information in books at home and discuss it with his classmates there and quite another to encounter it here, where he dared make no response, among people who thought males were long and safely dead.

After that he began to make a habit, when he encountered references to pre-Change times, of mentally excusing, disputing, what he read or heard. Nine million people were tortured and killed as witches during the Renaissance: but surely that was the result of primitive religion, not the organized malevolence of males. Wars were imposed, not by the aggression of males, but by expectation, precedent. The "domestic violence" that killed millions of people was committed by males themselves brutalized as children, not because of their intrinsic evil. Males owned more than ninety-nine per cent of the world's property although people did most of the world's work: but perhaps people then, like now, simply cared less than the males did about property, ownership, possession. And the mass murders of people during the Change: well, those were terrifying, chaotic times, and the majority of males, after all, were probably not involved.

So when Mitchell-Star urged, "Oh, come on. Let's try a History. Just this once," he gave in. He would be able to handle it, he assured himself. And he supposed he would have to try a class again sooner or later.

"All right," he said. He took a deep swallow of milk.

❖

It was Delacour's class.

He didn't recognize her at first, sitting at the back as he was with the non-registrants, but gradually something about her began to seem familiar, the way she held her head jutting forward a little as she spoke, the way she scratched now at her arm —

And suddenly he was back in the longhouse, dizzy with fear because the people he was watching through the crack had seen him naked, *naked* in the woods with Shaw-Ellen —

And one of those people was in front of him now, in this room. He felt dizzy again, clutching the desk as though a spasm had shot through him. Highlands had told him the two were from Leth, that he must be careful in case he saw them, and when he came here his first term he often looked nervously around for them. But then, eventually, he'd put them out of his mind, telling himself that, in a city of thirty thousand, it was highly unlikely he would run into them, or that they would recognize him or he them even if he did.

But here she was, the one that had been most persistent, incarnated from nightmare, pacing up and down in front of the room, her eyes jumping from student to student. He bent his head forward, let his hair, which he'd let grow long and never braided, fall forward to cover as much of his face as it could. His heart was charging at his chest.

" ... so we can see the male empowerment techniques used to cover feelings of inadequacy," she was saying. "Of course, compensation theory is not incompatible with theories viewing the Change as natural evolutionary process, or even with the more peculiar viral theory, which posits the Y chromosome as a virus — "

Daniel bent farther forward and his pencil fell from his fingers onto the floor. When the student beside him picked it up and handed it to him, he looked at it as though he'd never seen it before. Panic began to rush over him, as it hadn't since the first days of his first term. There was a roaring in his ears, nothing of words, language, sense. Before he could force his panic under control, he felt himself pushing back his chair and stumbling to the door. He caught a glimpse of Mitchell-Star's face, her mouth moving, her eyes alarmed, and then he was at the door, wrenching it open. The roaring in his ears stopped suddenly, and he knew it had been the teacher's voice, pausing now, as she watched him flee, but it was too late, too late to think it might remind her of another time she had seen someone running away —

Then he was in the hallway, running down a corridor, turning right into another, lost, looking for a door out but seeing only more corridors, blurs of faces coming at him. Finally the throbbing in his side dragged him to a stop, and he collapsed against a wall, wheezing, horrified at what he had done. Across from him he saw a bathroom, and he stumbled inside and leaned against the door. He reached behind him and snapped the lock in place. Safe, he thought bitterly, safe.

How could he have let himself panic like that, after all this time, lose the control he had disciplined himself to acquire? It was the combination of shock, the sudden fear, the words she was saying —

On the wall opposite him was a mirror throwing back at him his flushed and miserable face, his hair sticking to his forehead and cheeks in wet streaks. The mirror had a crack across the bottom left-hand corner, and it sliced off a piece of his chin, lifted it several millimetres, then glued it back on so the edges didn't match. He looked at himself for several moments, the breath sliding more and more slowly in and out of him. *The Y chromosome as a virus* — he heard her voice again.

"A disease!" he shouted at his image. "A goddamned disease!" He wanted to throw something at the mirror, smash the ugly face that would never be right, never belong. But he clenched his hands at his sides and let himself sink slowly to the floor. He sat there for a long time, his knees pulled up to his chest, staring at the thin skin of dust on the floorboards.

Twice someone rattled the door trying to get in, and he heard the bubbling of voices in the hall as classes let out, but still he stayed where he was, his mind a muddy churn of feelings.

Finally, when the noise outside abated, he got up and, avoiding looking at himself in the mirror, splashed some cold water on his forehead and cheeks, trying not to wash off the skincream. He rubbed at his eyes, which felt as gritty as if he'd been in a dust storm, and then, taking a deep breath, he opened the door and stepped into the hallway.

The one student walking past had the glazed, preoccupied look of someone composing a late assignment, and Daniel felt reassured by the fact that she didn't scream at the sight of him. He began walking down the corridor, continuing in the same direction as he'd run, although he knew he should try to retrace his steps if he wanted to find his way out. But he was too afraid of meeting someone from the history class. He wandered the corridors for about twenty minutes, leaving the History section entirely and winding up in Archaeology, before he saw the glint of outside light. Relieved, he hurried toward it. It took him another ten minutes to find a door that led outside — he couldn't understand the aversion the city people seemed to have to going outside. He pulled the door open and gratefully sucked in the sharp scrape of cold air. It felt more like January than September.

He wasn't dressed warmly enough to walk outside today, but he was reluctant to return to the labyrinth of corridors, the people, the heavy, heated air, so he turned in the direction of the huge Hospital sector that loomed off to his left and began to walk; he knew his apartment was somewhere in the long connector that ran beside him between here and Hospital.

The sun shone weakly on his face, barely warm enough to be noticeable, but it glinted off the snow with such extravagant sparkle that he felt his spirits lift a little in spite of himself. He let himself think of the farm, home, of his father and mother, of Highlands, of Shaw-Ellen, the people who trusted him and would welcome him back.

He convinced himself that no real damage had been done. He had made a bad mistake, but it wouldn't happen again. He was a non-registrant; he just wouldn't go back. He had no reason ever to go near the History section again. And the teacher — surely she couldn't have recognized him, not after all this time, not from just a glimpse. Even on the farm she had seen him only from a distance.

He began to feel better. But the cold was pulling up through his legs, so he walked faster. Ahead he could see the end of the blue awnings and windowsills and the beginning of the yellow section, which was where he lived. He began to run, a stiff-legged trot, and then he thought of the windows looking down on him, and he forced himself back to a walk. *Don't draw attention*, he told himself through clenched teeth, and he headed for the closest door.

Inside, the cold held him like a sealed envelope, and it was several moments before he could stop shaking and let the warmth penetrate. He sat down and took off his shoes, held his icy feet, one after the other, in his hands. What would his mother say, he thought, his mother who feared frostbite above almost anything else, who had lost two of her own toes in a blizzard on her way home from Fairview five years ago?

Finally he put his shoes back on, got up, and began walking down the long, straight corridor he knew would lead him to his own apartment. He had been in this section once before, last term, at a gathering one of his classmates had invited him to. It had not been fun, he recalled, him sitting huddled in a corner with a moronic smile hooked on his face, cringing whenever anyone tried to talk to him. It had been painful to watch his classmates pairing with each other, the erotic touchings and flirtations from which he knew he would be forever excluded. His own desires had begun to feel strange, abnormal to him, and he had to fight against imagining the horror and repulsion on those cheerful faces around him if they could see him as he truly was.

The corridor branched out to circle a large rotunda, and he took the hallway to his right. His ankle began to hurt, and he wondered if he might have twisted it as he fled from the classroom. But he could see his apartment section ahead, one more corner and he would be at his own door. He felt exhausted now, wanting only to get inside and drop onto his bed.

But in front of his door sat Mitchell-Star. She saw him as soon as he turned the corner, and she leaped to her feet.

"*There* you are!" she said loudly. "I was so worried — what happened to you, anyway? Did you get sick or something? Why did you — "

He reached her then, and grabbed her arm. He felt like clapping his hand over her mouth.

"Stop shouting, will you?" he said.

She pulled back from him, hurt. "Well, I'm *sorry*," she said. "I just came by to give you your books. You left them in the room." She pushed them at this chest and let go; he had to grab at them as they fell. She turned abruptly and started to walk away.

"Don't go," he said, ashamed, to the back of her head with its independent leaps of hair that always made her look as if she had fallen asleep against a bush. "Please."

She stopped, turned around. He could see the relief on her face.

"Come in," he said, not wanting her to but knowing he had to ask.

She came over to him as he unlocked the door, laid her hand on his shoulder. He tried not to pull away from her touch. "Really," she said, "are you okay?"

He attached a smile to his lips and pushed the door open for her. "Yes, I'm fine."

She came in, dropped herself into a chair in the centreroom.

She had been in his apartment twice before, but still her presence made him nervous, made him look furtively around for something that might give him away. He knew he should offer her a glass of juice, a piece of fruit, something, but he hoped his inhospitality might persuade her to leave.

She reached over to pick up a book lying on a side table. As she leaned forward he noticed she hadn't bothered doing up half the small buttons that ran up the side of her shirt. She began flipping through the book. "You read this?"

"Not yet."

She set it down. "If you're feeling sick, you know, you should see a doctor — "

"I'm not sick," he said, exasperated. "Sometimes I just get a little ... claustrophobic." It was true, after all. "Most of us from the farms are like that."

"I *thought* it must be something like that," she said. "That's what I told the teacher."

"What?"

"The teacher. I guess she'd seen us come in together, and after the class she asked me if you were all right."

"And what did you say?" His voice sounded high-pitched and shrill.

"I said you were probably okay. I said you were from one of the north farms and maybe were still not used to things here."

He sank down into a chair. He pressed his hands onto his thighs to keep them from trembling. "And what did she say?"

"I don't know, just that she hoped nothing was wrong. She was concerned about you. I thought it was rather nice." She was watching him curiously.

He felt too numb to answer. If the teacher hadn't been suspicious when she asked about him, then Mitchell-Star's answer could have made her so, jarred loose that memory of two

147

summers ago, a figure fleeing across the meadow from her predatory eyes.

Mitchell-Star had said something else, but he didn't reply, only sat there, staring blindly across the room. When next she spoke, he realized she was at the door, leaving, and he made himself concentrate on what she was saying. He nodded, not caring what he was agreeing to.

She looked at him doubtfully. "You better be okay. You better not be getting depression or anything."

"I'm okay, really. I've just been working too hard. That Sociology study. You know." He gave her his best reassuring smile, behind which his teeth were clenched so tight he thought they might break.

For the next few days he lived in constant fear, unable to concentrate on his studies, barely able to eat or sleep, waiting for the moment he would see her come striding toward him, her black teacher's-robe flying behind her like a net in which to capture him, pointing and saying, "You! I know what you are!" He remembered how Johnson-Dene on the farm insisted he had broken First Law when he had let himself be seen naked with Shaw-Ellen and that his punishment should be denying him his hard-won right to leave. If it hadn't been for Shaw-Ellen saying that going into the forest had been her idea, and Highlands saying he had the right to make love outside, that it wasn't his carelessness that caused the strangers to come, and to such an unlikely spot, perhaps Johnson-Dene would have convinced them to reverse their positon. And perhaps she would have been right to do so — if he hadn't been seen then he wouldn't be in danger now. His head was thick with recrimination and anxiety.

But he forced himself to go, as usual, to his classes, and by the end of the week his fears had subsided; he began to feel foolish for letting himself become so alarmed. The teacher knew enough about him to find him if she was intending to; the fact she hadn't by now must mean that he was safe.

And of course it was then that she came to the door.

He thought it must be Mitchell-Star, coming to walk with him to his literature class, and he didn't even bother to check the scanner-image beside the door before he opened it. And there she was, only a few steps away from him, wearing her teacher's-robe and smiling down at him. He held the door frame so tightly he could feel his nails biting into the wood.

Stay calm, he whispered frantically to himself; stay calm.

"Hello," she said cheerfully. "You might not remember me, but I'm Delacour, the History teacher. I think you came to my class a few weeks ago?"

He couldn't look at her, her calculated smile, her intense eyes that moved up and down his body and then fixed on his face like a hot light that made his cheeks burn. He only nodded, looking down at her long, thin fingers that were rubbing a pleat into the black teacher's-robe.

"I wondered if you might be ill," she said, "the way you had to leave the class so suddenly."

"No, I'm all right." He tried to make himself sound confident, convincing. "I'm sorry I left like that. I just felt a bit claustrophobic."

"Ah, yes. I spoke to your friend. She said you were from one of the northern farms. I can imagine being here is something of an adjustment for you."

He nodded again, watching her fingers move, over and over, pressing a fold into the cloth. Her nails were cut so short no white at all showed.

"I'm getting used to it."

"I'm sure you are. This is your second term here, isn't it?"

So she'd checked his records. "Yes."

"Ah. And are you enjoying it? University?"

He made himself raise his eyes and look at her, because he knew somehow she wouldn't leave until he did so, until she had willed him into it. He looked into her sharp blue eyes, eyes that dominated her other thin features — her nose that narrowed so precariously at the bridge that she must have trouble breathing, her small mouth, her chin that sharpened itself into a curve of bone over which the skin seemed stretched too tightly, like cloth held in sewing hoops.

He smiled. "Oh, yes," she said. "It's very rewarding. I'm learning a lot." He made himself lean his forearm against the door frame, trying to appear casual, but his hand dangling in front of his left cheek looked suddenly ridiculous.

"Good," she murmured. "Good." Her eyes slid away from his face, moved over his shoulder to scan the room behind him, then snapped up to his face again, quickly, as though to catch some unguarded expression there. "Well, then," she said, releasing her robe from her fingers and smoothing her hands firmly over it, "I guess I'll go." And she turned abruptly and began to walk away.

He couldn't believe it was over, that easily. Watching her back, he almost laughed out loud.

Then, as though the idea had just come to her, she turned and said, "Look, why don't you come to my apartment tomorrow for supper? My mate, Bowden, sometimes likes to cook for us, and someone's just given us some fresh vegetables — a pumpkin, I think, she wants to make a pie — so why don't you come? It must be lonely for you here, so far from home — "

"No, really — " He could hear fear in his voice and struggled to control it. "I don't want to make extra work for you — "

"It's no extra work. We'd like to have you."

"I have to finish my reading for Sociology — "

"You have to eat. We wouldn't keep you long. You can spare an hour."

Desperately he thought of other excuses, tried to invent some Isolist custom that might forbid him from accepting, but everything that came to his mind seemed implausible. He only stood there staring at her.

"Well, then," she said, making one hand lightly into a fist and snapping the other over it, like a lid, "you'll come. We're in Hospital unit. Red, South, 240. About seven o'clock."

"All right." It felt as though she'd reached in and pulled the words from his throat.

Tomorrow, he thought numbly. Red, South, 240. About seven o'clock. Between now and then what could he do; how could he escape?

He knew he had no choice but to go, of course; if he didn't she would only be more suspicious. He wished he'd asked if he could bring Mitchell-Star; he was sure she would have liked to come and it would have given him some protection, another layer of normalcy he could wear.

The whole day for him was an agony of waiting. In his classes he didn't hear a word, distractedly drawing geometric designs in his notebook. Back in his apartment he sat staring at the time-chip, watching the minutes flick by. He remembered suddenly, and with a fierce longing, the sundial his mother had built for him behind their house. He picked up the trousers with the torn seam he had been meaning to mend, but his sweaty fingers kept pulling and knotting the thread, so finally he gave up and threw the pants across the side table. He twirled the needle between his fingers, bounced his thumb lightly on the sharp tip until he pricked himself. He sat looking at the tiny bead of blood for several moments before he went to wash it off.

At six o'clock he began to get ready. He'd saved his shower allotment from the morning, so he took it now, and then he shaved with particular care. He changed his mind several times about what to wear and at last chose a dark overshirt that fell to mid-thigh and a loose pair of cotton pants. It was what he felt safest in, what he had worn almost every day when he first came here. He tied a lacy blue ribbon around his upper left arm, a fashion he had learned to mimic, but then he took it off, thinking it looked too deliberate.

He could already smell his own sweat, and he almost moaned with the frustration of it. He thought perhaps he should wash himself quickly again in the sink, but by now it was six-thirty and he would still have to find Delacour's apartment; Red, South was a long way from here. So he clapped his arms to his sides and, with a last look around his apartment, at the two cheerful painted clouds floating on his north wall, he stepped into the hallway.

He stayed inside the building, where at least there were maps periodically to guide him, but even so he got confused, winding up in the big southern sector of Commercial before he would ask someone for help. It was after seven already. He tried to follow the directions he'd been given — left at the weaving shop, left again at the rotunda, past the Kindercare — he wondered how he would ever be able to find his way back to his own apartment.

Finally he found the red section and took the south arrow, although it felt to him like west, and then it was just a matter of following the numbers to 240. It was past seven-thirty by now, he saw by the time-chips in the walls. He could feel scoops of sweat on his shirt, could feel it running down his stomach and thighs — he wanted to stop at a bathroom to clean himself, but it would only make him later, so he pulled at his shirt as he walked to let the air circulate and continued on, following the numbers — 238, 239, 240.

He stood outside the door. He couldn't remember ever dreading anything so much. He took several deep breaths, pushed the damp hair from his eyes, and knocked.

It was the other one who answered, Delacour's mate. He recognized her from the farm, by her thick red hair that fell in loose spirals to her shoulders. She smiled at him warmly, and in her round face and eyes with wrinkles in thin fans at the corners he read none of the greedy curiosity he had seen in Delacour. But perhaps he was misjudging her — perhaps this was all part of a plan to disarm him — he would have to be just as careful of her as of Delacour. Still, he felt oddly relieved to see her, to know he would not have to be alone with Delacour.

"Come in," she said. She stood aside to let him enter. He could see Delacour in the kitchen, stirring something on the stove.

"Hello," she said, waving the spoon at him. Something green dripped from it onto the heatcircle, and a coil of grey smoke leaped up. "We were beginning to wonder if you were coming."

"I got lost," Daniel said. "I'm sorry. I got over into Commercial somehow, and — "

"Commercial!" Delacour exclaimed. "Good heavens, you *were* lost."

"I'm sorry," he said.

"It's all right," Delacour's mate said, touching his arm lightly. He tried not to flinch. "We weren't ready to eat at seven, anyway."

It was a good thing, then, he thought, that he'd come late; it would be one less half hour of discomfort.

"My name is Bowden, by the way, " the red-haired person said. He took the hand she held out to him, remembering too late that perhaps he should have performed the Isolist ritual of greeting. He hoped they would think he was simply adapting to the ways of the city.

Bowden took him to the small table that folded out from the counter and seated him so that he was facing into the centreroom. He was amazed at how luxurious it seemed, even though it was only about twice the size of his own centreroom. There were soft lights inset into and behind the walls, thickly padded blue armchairs placed at intersecting angles to each other, a bookcase reaching to the ceiling on one wall filled with books and files and vidspools and long grey boxlike shapes he couldn't identify that might have been either functional or decorative. Music was coming from two different corners of the room, although he saw nothing there that could be producing it, and the lights appeared to be reflecting on something that was casting dazzling patterns on the walls.

Delacour had said something to him, he realized suddenly, and he jerked his attention back to her. She was looking at him, waiting for an answer.

"I'm sorry," he said. "I was admiring your centreroom. It's more beautiful than any room I've seen before." It sounded too ingenuous, like foolish flattery, but Delacour gave a little deprecating laugh he thought meant he had said the right thing.

"It *is* comfortable," she said.

"Delacour made the water-reflector," Bowden said. "I've never seen one I like as much. I think she should stop teaching and make them to sell."

Delacour poured the contents of the pot she was stirring into a shallow bowl and set it on the table. "Making one was challenging. Making two would be boring."

"It's beautiful," he said. They must be talking about whatever was casting the patterns on the walls.

Delacour and Bowden sat down, one on each side of him, and started passing him the plates of food. The table was small, not really built to seat more than two, and he pressed himself back in his chair, keeping his knees together and his legs tucked under.

Bowden began to explain what the various foods were, but while he recognized the names of the vegetables and grains and cheeses, he was unfamiliar with the dishes themselves, the sauces and spices that made the peas taste tangy, the cheese curds so rich and strangely sweet.

"And the wine!" Delacour exclaimed, reaching for it behind her. "We mustn't forget the wine." As she leaned back, her leg brushed his under the table; he pulled quickly away. It was just an accident, he told himself, but his thigh muscles contracted so much they ached.

"You don't have to have any if you'd rather not," Bowden said.

"I've never had wine before," Daniel said. It wasn't true; he *had* had some, once, when Highlands brought a flask back with her from Fairview, but he decided it might be wiser to play the innocent.

"Never had wine!" Delacour said, filling his glass to the rim. "What deprivation!" She put her fork down and lifted her glass, and since he saw Bowden do the same he realized he was expected to do so now as well. He lifted his glass, almost spilling it, and took a sip. It tasted sweet, not unpleasant.

Delacour emptied her glass in, it seemed, one swallow and poured herself another. Daniel took another sip, larger this time, hoping he wan't expected to drain his glass so readily. Wine was an intoxicant; he would have to be careful.

"So," Delacour said, picking up her fork again and stirring it vigorously through her asparagus dish. "You're from one of the Isolist farms, are you?"

"That's right." Daniel set his wine glass down, willing his hand not to tremble. His other hand clenched in his lap.

"I thought you people liked to keep to yourselves. How come you're here, in the city, at University?"

"We have certain restrictions about visitors and strangers coming to see us, but there aren't any strong ones about us going Outside. I'm not the first from the farms to have come here. Our leaders have always valued education." Did he sound convincing? He quickly looped it through his mind again — it sounded believable, and it was, after all, basically true.

"That sounds very sensible," Bowden said.

"Yes," he said gratefully. "I think it is."

"And if someone doesn't want to return to the farm, if someone wants to stay in the city?" Delacour asked.

"She can do what she chooses," Daniel said. *But I can't*, he thought, with a sudden distracting bitterness. "Almost everyone who leaves comes back, though. They miss that way of life." He didn't tell them about the pressures, the guilt, put on anyone who didn't want to return. The farms did not absolutely forbid one moving permanently away, but they made it as painful as possible; everyone living outside was a loss, and a danger.

"I grew up on a farm, too," Bowden said. "It was a wonderful time."

"We were at one of your farms. Two summers ago." Delacour's voice was casual, but he could tell from the way she leaned forward a little, swallowed, and didn't take another mouthful that her calm was an illusion, that inside she was excited, intent. He forced himself to meet her eyes, briefly, their vivid blue a whirlpool trying to suck him in before he could step back.

"Oh? Which one?"

"I don't know. How many are there?"

"Four."

"Well, I don't know which one." She sounded petulant, annoyed. "One of them."

"We got lost, you see," Bowden said quickly. "We were on holiday and had rented horses in the Peace and were going to Fairview, but we got lost and wandered onto one of the farms. They gave us directions on how to get to Fairview."

"It could have been any one of them, I suppose." He took another sip from his wine, carefully raised a mouthful of the cheese curd to his mouth. Under the table he was aware of Delacour's legs only centimetres from his.

"The person who came to talk to us was tall," Delcour said, "with a scar on her cheek. Does that sound like the leader of your farm?"

He watched his hand move the empty fork back to his plate. He could feel Delacour closing in, narrowing her interrogation down to the point at which he would be trapped, unable to answer, his silence confirming everything. He swallowed the cheese curd without chewing; it felt like a lump of wax in his throat. "I guess it might have been. Or it might have been Seba, from East Farm. That's our lead-farm, the largest one."

"No," Delacour said. "That wasn't her name. What's the name of your leader?"

He had to say it. She might have ways of checking on a lie. "Highlands," he said, feeling as though he were betraying her, that she had been safe until he named her.

"That's it!" Delacour said triumphantly. "Highlands, that was it, wasn't it, Bowden?"

"It could have been," she said.

"You know — " Delacour cut her asparagus with the edge of her fork so vigorously it almost squirted off her plate. "We saw two people there. In the woods. They were making love. We startled them, and then they ran off — "

"Delacour, that's none of our business." Bowden set down the bowl she was holding with a harder thump than necessary.

Delacour ignored her. " — and I wonder if you know who they were. If anyone said anything." She paused. Daniel felt her eyes tearing at him. "One of them was blonde," she said. "Like you."

He concentrated on the pain in his palm from where his nails were cutting into it. He inhaled, let the breath come out slowly, spacing his words carefully in it. "It might have been Bluesky. Or Huallen. Or my mother." *My mother.* He should have said, *One of my mothers.*

Quickly he looked up, at Bowden, and he forced a smile to his face. "That cheese curd is delicious. Could I have more?"

"Of course." She handed him the bowl, smiling, but not as much at him as at Delacour, a smile he couldn't interpret. "I'm glad you like it," she said. "I've never made it with parsley before."

"You're such a good cook," Delacour said, in her voice, too, an inflection he couldn't interpret, something between her and Bowden.

"I'll have to remember to use parsley again next time," Bowden said.

"I liked it when you used it as a sauce," Delacour said, "that last time. With the potatoes."

"Oh really? It was so easy to make — "

Daniel listened, not believing he could have deflected the conversation so easily. He waited for them to finish, for Delacour suddenly to turn to him, the moment she thought he was off-guard, and accuse, "*You* were the one, weren't you? I saw, I know — "

He made himself finish the extra cheese curd he'd asked for. It seemed to grow in his mouth as he chewed. He had no idea what it tasted like; all he cared about was getting it swallowed, his plate clean, as a reason, another test he had passed for the reward of going home.

But they only kept talking about the food, something now about radishes and basil, and slowly he let himself relax, his hand unclench.

Bowden asked him about the kinds of things they ate on the farms, how they cooked, and he answered her willingly, telling her about the gardens, the canning, the milkcows, anything she wanted to know, although not about the meat because he knew it would repulse her. He told her how one day Highlands came back from town with a pineapple and no one knew how to open it. He embellished the story, made it funny, and they laughed, Delacour's laugh a surprisingly high-pitched, breathless sound. He tried not to think of his father, holding the pineapple in his hands like some huge hairy potato and saying, "We shouldn't be bringing in so much from Outside. It will make us dependent. We have to be careful," and how he'd thought impatiently, *Careful! Can't he think of anything besides being careful?*

Delacour poured him more wine, and he sipped at it politely, checking to see if he was feeling any of its effects. But he felt no different — obviously he hadn't had enough to affect him. Bowden brought out a dessert — not, he observed, the pumpkin pie Delacour had promised, but something special with chocolate, which was rare and expensive, and this, at least, he was able to taste and enjoy. He had never eaten anything so delicious. Bowden smiled happily at his compliments.

By the time they finished it was after nine o'clock. Surely, he thought, he could leave now; most people went to bed here around ten.

"You don't need to go *yet,* " Delacour said. "I want to know more about how you live."

"Leave her alone," Bowden said. "It's none of your business."

"I really have to go," Daniel said. "I might get lost again on the way back."

It was the wrong thing to say.

"You won't get lost," Delacour said. "Just take the blue moveway. It goes right by your unit."

"The moveway?"

"The moveway. You know." He only stared at her blankly. "You mean you don't know what the moveways are?" She laughed, incredulous. "You've been here all this time and never used them?"

"A person doesn't need to," Bowden said. "It's healthier to walk."

"You'll be home in five minutes," Delacour said, ignoring her.

"What are they?" He felt foolish, having to ask. But if his ignorance amused them it was to his advantage. Moveways must, he thought, be just a kind of train.

"I'll show you," Delacour said, pushing back her chair and standing up. "Come on."

Daniel stood up, too. He felt her tallness overwhelming him again.

"Now?" Bowden's hand stilled on the large spoon she was pulling from the dessert bowl.

"If you want to go," Delacour said, looking at Daniel. "We'd be happy to have you stay longer."

"No, no," Daniel said. "I should go."

Delacour shrugged. "All right. Then I'll take you home." Bowden's spoon banged three times on the dessert bowl.

"You don't have to come with me. You can just show me

where the moveway is and how to work it."

"It won't take long." Delacour came out from behind the table, dipping her finger into the chocolate dessert as she passed. Bowden hit her on the knuckle, hard, *crack*.

"You don't need to go, Delacour," she said.

"I won't be *long*." But there was no annoyance in her voice, just a cheerful insistence that Daniel found even more worrisome. Her voice was louder than it had been, her gestures more wide and expansive, and he wondered if she might be a little intoxicated — she had drunk considerably more wine than he or Bowden had. "Come on," she said, holding her right arm up and out, like a bar she was placing between him and the rest of the room. He backed toward the door.

"Thank you very much for the meal," he said formally, snapping his eyes from one to the other. "It was delicious."

"You're very welcome," Bowden said.

Delacour reached behind him and opened the door. He stepped back over the sill. The light from the centreroom behind Bowden shone though her hair, turning it into a bright arch of flame around her head and shoulders. He wanted to reach his hand out to her, entreat her to come with them.

Delacour nudged Daniel out and closed the door behind them. "The moveway's over there," she said.

"Just show me how to work it," he said. "You don't need to come." He was alone with her. Bowden had seemed like a protection, and now she was gone.

"This way." Delacour took his arm and pulled him to the left, away from the hallway he knew he'd come down. He shivered. Perhaps she noticed, because she took her hand away and pointed instead down a narrow corridor. *Moveway Access*, said a sign. He'd seen such signs before, he realized, but, since they were nothing he was ever looking for, he'd paid no attention.

Delacour pushed open a door, and he could see what the moveway was — a moving strip of floor. A person was on it in the distance, and as he watched she came rapidly closer, at about the speed of someone running. She was holding onto a guardrail with one hand to keep her balance and holding open a book with the other; as she whisked past them she didn't even look up.

Delacour was watching him, a light smile on her face. "Well," she said. "Here it is. Progress."

"It's very interesting," he said.

"Interesting." He heard the amused mockery in her voice, and fumbled for a less banal opinion.

"It's ... well, is it really necessary? I mean, a person could run as fast as it goes."

"You sound like Bowden," Delacour said. She poked several times, hard, at a button on the wall. The moveway began to slow down. "We can get on now," she said. "You're supposed to wait until it comes to a complete stop, but no one does. Just be careful and hold the guardrail. When you want to stop it, push one of those red buttons on the rail."

She stepped onto the moveway, easily, her hand grasping the rail at the same moment as her foot touched the belt. Daniel hesitated a moment, then did the same. He almost lost his balance, but caught himself before he fell. The moveway, knowing somehow that now it did not need to stop, accelerated again. Delacour stepped back to stand beside him. "Okay?" she asked.

Daniel nodded. The movement was making him feel dizzy, a little nauseous. The rail was moving at a slightly slower speed than the moveway, drawing his hand gradually behind him, so he finally had to let go and shift his hold quickly forward. But he was able to keep his balance easily enough, and it made him feel a bit better. He risked a smile at Delacour, who smiled back. She was standing so close to him her shirt brushed against his arm, a slight back-and-forth motion produced by the moveway.

"There it is," Delacour said suddenly. "Yellow. Your stop." She reached under the guardrail and pushed a red button that protruded from it. The moveway slowed, came to a stop so quickly that Daniel had to take a few steps forward with the momentum. They stepped off, and the belt lunged forward again.

"How will you get back?" Daniel asked.

"There's one over there going the other way." She gestured vaguely off to the right, but she began walking in the opposite direction. Daniel knew where she was going. Desperately, he called to her back, "I can find my own way from here. You don't need to come."

She turned, smiled at him, her mouth a rectangle full of teeth. "Why, of course I do." She widened her smile.

Without waiting for him, she turned and headed off down the corridor. He had no choice but to follow. He concentrated numbly on his walking, the placing of his feet, as though each step required conscious direction. He still felt a little dizzy from the moveway — or perhaps from the wine, he thought with alarm; perhaps it affects you later.

At his door he fumbled with the key, almost dropping it before he could get the door open. When he heard the bolt retract, he put his hand on the doorknob, turned to face Delacour. He *wouldn't* let her in; he would stand here all night with the door closed if he had to.

"Well," he said. "Thank you again for the supper. And for showing me the moveway."

"You're welcome." She made no move to leave.

"Good night, then."

"Actually — I was hoping I could come in and use your bathroom. Wine does that to one, you know." She laughed apologetically.

She knew he couldn't refuse. Not trusting himself to speak, he turned and opened the door, stood back so she could enter.

"This *is* kind of you," she said.

She walked through his apartment, in no hurry, taking it in, and went into the bathroom. He could imagine her there, opening the drawers and cupboard, looking for what would betray him. He tried to imagine what she might see: had he left the razor suspiciously exposed? Would the skincream seem odd to her? Should he have left the menstrual extractor, which of course he never used, in a more prominent place?

He let himself drop into the armchair by the door and sat there staring at the time-chip in the wall across the room, the minutes glazed and unmoving, as though time had stalled. When he finally heard the toilet flush, he got quickly to his feet — he mustn't seem to be inviting her to stay.

Delacour came out, walked casually into the centreroom, sat down.

Daniel stood by the door, his hand on the knob. They looked at each other, for what seemed to Daniel like an hour.

At last he said, his lips feeling numb, "I really would like to get to sleep. I'm not feeling that well."

Immediately he knew he had made a mistake.

Delacour stood up, an eager concern on her face, and came over to him. "Oh, I *am* sorry," she said. "We shouldn't have given you any wine. If you're not used to it — " She stood close to him, put her hand on his arm. A spark of static electricity snapped at them. He swallowed, trying to clear his head, to think of what he should do.

"Come to bed, then," she said. "You just need some sleep."

Perhaps that would solve it, he thought; perhaps if he just collapsed onto his bed she would think he had passed out, and she would have to leave then —

"Yes," he said. "I'd just like to get to sleep."

She kept her hand on his arm, as though she might be concerned that he would fall if she removed it, and walked with him to his sleeproom. He could think of nothing but her hand, burning through his shirt.

And suddenly to his horror he could feel himself getting an erection. He clenched his teeth, tried to will away his uncontrolled desire.

They were at the doorway now. Daniel took a quick step forward, wanting to squeeze through first, but it made him bump the door frame. Delacour tightened her hold on his arm and, as she reached up with her other hand as though to steady him, she passed her hand heavily over his groin.

He turned quickly away, but he knew it was too late — he could still feel her hand, pressing not against the flat, bony slope that should have been there, but touching what was alien, forbidden. *Male must be hidden.* He felt like screaming, beating at her. What had he done? How could he have let this happen?

He pulled free of her, dropped himself face down on the bed. His brain felt empty, a skull full of air, not one thought condensing into a plan, a solution, escape. His chest muscles tightened, his heart thudding into them like a dull axe.

Delacour stood in the doorway. He could sense her there, her hungry eyes on him. Perhaps he was wrong; perhaps she had not guessed —

"It was you, wasn't it?" Her voice was soft, gentle. "The one we saw in the woods."

She knew. There was no escape. Mother, he thought, oh, Mother, forgive me, help me. Father, Highlands, help me.

He said nothing.

Finally Delacour broke the silence, her voice still soft, careful.

"You don't need to be afraid, you know. I'm not going to hurt you." She paused. Daniel said nothing. He thought he heard her move into the room, but he didn't look up. "Do you know what I think, Daniel? I think you're a male."

As she said the word, her hand settled on his waist.

"No!" he shouted, rolling away from her. "No!" But even to his own ears he sounded guilty, his denial a confession.

"My god," she said. Her voice was trembling. "So it's true."

"Leave me alone," Daniel cried. "Just leave me alone!"

He rolled off the bed on the other side, stood facing her across the room.

"Now look," Delacour said, smiling. She was making an effort to sound calm, her voice the kind you use to soothe frightened animals. A vein in her neck was throbbing. "Of course I'm ... surprised. I mean, this is quite incredible, after all this time, who could have thought it possible — a *male* — it's just so unbelievable — " Her voice became louder, as though the room were full of students listening.

He was crying now, the tears running down his cheeks, catching on his lips, uncontrollable sobs breaking up from his throat, sobs that were turning from ones of fear to ones of mourning, like when his grandmother died in the threshing accident, something good and beautiful gone forever, the loss unbearable. He had a sudden vision of the farms burning, the obsessed hunt for others like him; and he was the one who had lit the first torch, begun the destruction.

"You mustn't be so upset," she said, lowering her voice again. But her fingers twisted themselves excitedly around and around each other in front of her. "Please now. Stop crying — "

But he couldn't. He stared at her hands, seeing himself pressed and twisted between them.

"Now, look, Daniel. Don't be afraid. If you're honest with

me I'll keep your secret."

Her words cut through his despair. *I'll keep your secret.* He had to be calm — things were not hopeless. She didn't seem to be horrified by him; she was willing to discuss. He swallowed, took a deep breath.

"Why? Why would you?"

She took a moment before she replied. "Maybe I like secrets, too."

"Don't you think — " He stopped, realizing it was a stupid question, only giving her evidence against him.

"Don't I think what?"

His mind was in too much turmoil to invent a better ending. "Don't you think I'm dangerous?"

She laughed, a little wildly. "You don't seem dangerous to me. *Are* you dangerous?"

"No. Of course not."

"Not part of some plot by murderous bands of males to reclaim their history, their territory? Not a spy sent to hunt out our weaknesses, send secret reports back to headquarters?"

"No," he insisted, frightened at her language, one he had seen only in books, a vocabularly of war. "I'm just here to learn. That's all. I just wanted to learn."

"Yes," she said. "All right. Now. You've got to answer my questions. How many of you are there? Males, I mean."

He looked her straight in the eyes. What made them so compelling, he realized, was not just their vivid blue colour but their clarity, making it seem as if he were seeing the iris as well as the pupil down the tunnel of optic nerve, down a passage of light and neuron and synapse to brain, to pure and absolute intelligence.

"Just my father," he said. "We're all that's left." He had to try to protect the others. To his surprise, her gaze dropped first, slid over to the pillow on his bed, as though she were thinking it over.

"All right," she said. "I suppose that's possible." It wasn't the same as saying she believed him. "But how did you survive? Your kind, I mean. During the Change."

"The Leaders have different explanations." That, at least, was the truth. "We used to live farther north two or three hundred years ago, much more isolated than we are now. I suppose that might have made a difference. The climate, the way we lived, the things we ate."

"So it's possible there could be others, in other parts of the world. My god. What a discovery — "

"I've never heard of any others," he pleaded. "We're no threat. We just want to be left alone, to live out our lives. It's not our fault we're who we are; we didn't choose it."

"No, no, of course you didn't." But she sounded preoccupied; he imagined her mind rushing ahead, making her sinister plans. To what ? To announce him to the world? To have him caged or killed or mutilated?

"You said you wouldn't tell," he said. "Please." His voice sounded thin and pathetic; perhaps it would only provoke her contempt. But contempt might be better than fear or anger. If it helped to beg, he would beg. He waited for her response.

She kept looking at the pillow. It was a long time before she answered. Then she raised her eyes to his face. Her voice was soft again, the way it had been when she first stood in the doorway. "I won't," she said. "But you'll have to do something for me."

"What?"

"I want you to make love with me."

He almost laughed, incredulous. Why would she want that? She had Bowden. Why would she want him, an alien, a mutation, a virus — her words from her class leaped back to him.

"Well," she said. "Will you?"

"You mean — if we make love, you won't tell?" It was incredible, her wanting that.

"Yes."

And suddenly he felt a surge of outrage — how dare she ask that, to buy her silence by making him perform —

"You think I'm a freak," he said bitterly, knowing that he shouldn't risk antagonizing her, that he should agree to anything, his own pride a small price to pay for such a large silence, but he couldn't stop the angry words. "That's why, isn't it? You want me to amuse you? Repulse you?"

"I'm sorry — I suppose it must seem that way. But, really, I think it's just —" she paused, thrusting her thin finger knifelike up and down the bridge of her nose; he almost expected to see blood " — just curiosity. There's nothing disgusting about that, is there? Curiosity? That's why you're here, isn't it? Curiosity? Wanting to experience something new? To learn?"

"I suppose so, but this — "

"Well, then. Unless you find me utterly repugnant, why don't we satisfy our curiosity?" She shifted her position and a shadow fell on her face, darkening her eyes.

He stood there, helpless, unable to find an argument. He didn't dare refuse.

Well, would it be so bad? He remembered his erection at the touch of her hand; even if his mind was frightened and repelled, his body must have wanted her.

"And you promise, if I do this, you won't tell?"

"I won't tell." Her fingers reached up to her throat, began to unbutton her shirt.

He knew he had to do the same, so, avoiding her eyes, he began to undress, his fingers like pieces of wood he had to manipulate around the buttons, the reluctant cloth.

At first all she wanted to do was stare at him, her eyes on him insatiate, exclaiming first at his chest, his sudden humiliation of no breasts, which made him slouch forward and pull his arms in, trying to force a swelling , a softening of muscle into normalcy. And then at his genitals — there was nothing he could do to disguise them, although his penis cringed to the smallest size it was able. He felt horribly ashamed, an exhibit on display.

Delacour came around the bed to him, comfortable in her own nakedness, her body thin but different from the people on the farms, her muscles lacking their tautness. She stood in front of him, her breathing loud in the still room, and reached out her fingers for his genitals. He closed his eyes. What should he think, what should he imagine? When he felt his penis jerk and swell under her touch he wasn't sure whether he was relieved or dismayed. Delacour said something, but her words were meaningless; he simply stood as he was, his eyes closed, his mind a rumple of confusion. He could feel his penis fully extended now, a tightness in his testicles.

"The penis," she said, pronouncing the word as though she were reading it in a textbook. "It's the part that goes inside me." She ran her finger lightly along it. He could feel his whole body tremble. "And these are the testicles." She cupped them in her hands, felt their grainy texture. He winced.

"Don't," he said wretchedly. "It hurts."

She took her hands quickly away. "It *hurts*?" She touched his penis again, lightly. "Does that hurt, too?"

He shook his head.

She sat down on the bed, took his hand and drew him down to her. "Show me what you do," she said.

Blindly, he pulled her under himself and thrust himself into her. She gave a sharp cry, which she cut short. To his horror he found himself thinking, *I've hurt her — and I'm glad*. The strength of his feelings almost made him withdraw, but he blotted out everything but the rising sensation, and it took him only a few strokes to reach orgasm, moaning in that voice that had nothing to do with consciousness, with volition.

He rolled over on his back and lay staring up at the ceiling, waiting for his mind to understand what he had done, and what he should do now. Exhaustion dropped on him like a suffocating blanket, and he struggled to keep himself awake. He knew Delacour must have felt little pleasure, and he knew he should reach over and stroke her to orgasm, but there was nothing he felt less like doing. Still — he was not free to choose, and surely it would be a mistake not to try to please her as much as he could. Reluctantly, he turned on his side, facing her, and ran his hand across her breasts, her tight brown nipples, down the small bowl of her stomach, into her damp pubic hair, and he began the slow rubbing he had first learned from Bluesky. Bluesky, the image of her cutting through him like pain.

But Delacour put her hand on his, pressed his movements to stillness. She sat up, sliding back on the bed, away from his hand.

"It's okay," she said. "You don't have to do that."

He sat up, too, looked at her, confused. "It's ... the way I learned," he said. "I thought you'd like it."

She smiled. "And I do," she said. "But, well, not right now."

And so he understood — she was unwilling to surrender to it, to lose her power over him. They had not made love; he had given a demonstration, that was all, a performance to an audience. The anger against her surged up in him again. But he choked back the bitter words — he mustn't allow himself to give her more knowledge of him than their sordid bargain required.

She rolled off the bed, reached for her shirt, and slid into it. She did up the buttons slowly, looking down at him. "So," she said at last. "This is how it was before the Change. Very interesting."

Interesting. A euphemism. He remembered the mockery in her voice when she had used the word to describe the moveway.

"There was a certain violence to it, that's all," she said.

He didn't know what he should answer, so he only lay there, looking dully at her as she finished buttoning her shirt and reached for her pants. He felt incapable of movement or thought or argument. All he wanted was for her to leave, to let him sleep; perhaps they would come in the night to kill or capture him, he didn't care, all he wanted was the negation of sleep.

"I'm sorry," he made himself say, the only words he could think of, the words he had learned to use as a child to buy forgiveness, to divert punishment. His eyes slid shut, just for a moment, he thought, but when he opened them again she was gone.

When he awoke in the morning the first thing he noticed was the smell: the sour stink of old sweat and semen. His head ached, and his mouth had a rancid taste. He stumbled to the bathroom for a drink and to wash himself. Only when he looked at himself in the mirror did he remember everything. Trembling, he sat down on the toilet, pressing his hands over his ears.

Delacour. She knew his secret. That was what it came down to, no matter how his mind twisted to avoid the knowledge. He had betrayed the farm. He had broken First Law.

He tried to remember everything Delacour had said, clutching eagerly at her promise: *I won't tell. If you make love with me.* He had done what she wanted, but would it guarantee her silence? How could he trust someone like her? Had making love with him only convinced her of the evil of his kind? *There was a certain violence to it* — what would that mean? History taught that violence was what the males had specialized in, carried around like an extra chromosome. So if Delacour saw the violence in him even in the act of making love — His own ugly thoughts returned to him, how he had hurt her and not been sorry.

He pressed his hands harder against the sides of his head. At last, he sat up, took a deep breath, and made himself start thinking about what he would do now.

His first impulse was to go home, simply to run away. He looked quickly around his apartment, his eyes like suitcase locks snapping shut on his few possessions. But he knew leaving would be a mistake. Eventually Delacour would follow him, and he would only bring the danger back to the farm. He had to continue, he decided, as though he trusted her promise; he had to go to his classes and do his assignments and behave like a normal, innocent person.

But if he didn't go home, what he must do, he knew, was to write Highlands and tell her what had happened. Yet the thought of telling her made him leap up and pace his apartment in despair. She would be furious, that he had let it come to this, that from the moment he had first seen Delacour here he had made one stupid mistake after another. And what could she do to help? Involving her might only make things worse. He stopped at the window facing the outside and leaned his feverish face against it.

Finally he decided to wait a few days before he wrote; it was possible, after all, that the worst was over, that Delacour had simply satisfied her curiosity and would leave him alone now.

He set the shower selector for hot and quickly washed himself clean. He was finished before the timer beeped. He shaved, applied the skincream, and dressed, not letting himself think about anything but the movements of his hands, and then he went down to the common dining-room, where he sat as usual beside Mitchell-Star.

"You look like as if you've just been exhumed," she said when she saw him.

"Thank you."

"I mean it. You look awful. You should get more sleep."

"I know."

"You better watch out." She jabbed a piece of buttery toast at his elbow. "Anatomy lab's always looking for more cadavers."

He laughed sadly, thinking already how he would miss her when whatever terrible future Delacour was planning for him arrived. He had a sudden urge to confide in Mitchell-Star, tell her everything, and appeal to her for compassion, for help. But the impulse passed.

"Well, gotta go," Mitchell-Star said. "See you in Geology."

Daniel sat there for longer than he should have. But finally he got up and made himself go to his first class.

As he opened every door he was sure he would see Delacour, turning toward him with her ironic smile. But it was an ordinary day, and an ordinary evening, even though his eyes would rise repeatedly from the pages he was supposed to be reading, waiting for the knock, the door opening, someone stepping through to claim his life.

After a week he was ready to consider that he might be safe, that she would keep her word, and after two weeks he was almost in a delirium of joy, someone recovered from a critical illness. He went everywhere Mitchell-Star asked him to, and people who had ignored him before now greeted him in the hallways, responding to his eager smiles, his sudden extroversion. When he told Mitchell-Star how his Internationalism teacher had singled out his report on desertification for special commendation, he was so uncharacteristically gleeful Mitchell-Star accused him crossly of being a braggart.

But of course it wasn't over. Three weeks later Delacour came to see him again. When he opened the door she stood in his doorway exactly the way he had feared seeing her, with a light smile on her face.

"Hello," she said. She was wearing her black teacher's-robe and, incongruously, a large red ornament in her hair.

"Hello," Daniel said. He was surprised at how even his voice sounded. He felt not panic, not fear, only a kind of dull despair, someone seeing Doctor at the door and knowing she had come to tell him the cancer was back, the cure illusory.

"I've just been wondering how you were," she said. "May I come in?"

He stood aside to let her enter, not bothering to answer. She went over to the sofa in the centreroom and sat down, gesturing for him to join her. He sat on a chair facing her, but he fixed his eyes on a point somewhere behind her left ear.

"So," she said, sitting back. "How have you been?"

"Fine."

"I was afraid you might have panicked and gone back to the farms. I'm glad you didn't."

"I just want to finish my courses and then go home. I'm no threat to you."

"I didn't say you were." Her smile widened. "You mustn't be so defensive."

"I'm sorry," he said. "But you promised to leave me alone."

"Ah, no, not quite. I promised to keep your secret. That's

not the same thing."

He let his eyes snap her back into focus, her features so sharp and distinct in her white face it was as though someone had drawn them on with coloured pencils. "What do you want from me?"

But already he knew. Or his body knew, had known from the moment she appeared at the door. She took his hand, and he followed her blindly into the sleeproom, their clasped hands like a knot she had tied somewhere deep inside of him.

This time she allowed him to bring her to climax as well. After, as they lay beside each other, she reached over and ran her fingers through his hair, clenching it lightly and then releasing, sending small stings of pleasure through his scalp. "Such beautiful hair," she murmured. Daniel lay with his eyes closed, watching the geometric patterns form and reform on his eyelids, not letting himself think.

The next day his head was thick with despair and self-loathing. How could he have gone with her as he had, unprotesting? She was his enemy. Yet even now, remembering it, brought a quickening in his body, a pulse beating through him like an adreno injection from Doctor's needle. But this was no drug to bring him health; it was madness, anarchy. The first time, at least, he could blame her coercion, but this time — He tried to tell himself that he had only done what was most prudent, what might seem to Delacour most normal, but he knew he was just making excuses. He paced the floors of his apartment, picking up books and putting them back down.

He missed his first class, and in the others twice Mitchell-Star asked if he was all right. Finally he accepted the excuse she offered and said he *was* feeling rather ill, and he cancelled the theatre-play tickets he had reserved with her and went home, sat in his apartment without turning the lights on. When he eard voices outside his door, he looked up in what he realized vas eagerness, that it might be Delacour. Appalled at himself, ie went into the bathroom and masturbated, not for pleasure »r even release, but as a kind of punishment.

When at last he fell into a restless sleep it wasn't Bluesky vhose face filled his dreams; it was Delacour's, an erotic and onfused dream of running and capture and harsh desire, and ie awoke in the morning covered in sweat, exhausted as though he dream had been reality, which after all was no more strange.

It was three days before Delacour came again. They made ove on the sofa in the centreroom.

After, she pulled her shirt on and went to the kitchen to get herself a drink of water, rummaging for a glass in his cup->oards as though they were her own. She came back and sat lown beside him, one leg stretched straight out on the sofa and he other on the floor, giving her the look of someone prepared ooth to rest and to leave. He could see the dark scribble of ier pubic hair under the bottom of her shirt.

"Talk to me," she said.

"What about?" He wished she would go — what was the point of pretending they were like other lovers, beginning a com-panionable evening? It was a mockery of the lazy tenderness of afterlove, and he knew that what he must be wary of now was imagining her a friend, a confidante. They were not two equal, free people; he mustn't be deceived into believing they were.

"Yourself." She reached over and picked a thread from Daniel's shoulder.

"You know who I am."

"Do I?" she said, leaning back.

"I'm not very complicated."

She laughed, a loud, confident sound, but one that seemed

to end prematurely, incomplete. "Ah. No simple person ever says she's not very complicated."

"I'm not as complicated as you."

She set the water glass in the palm of her hand, turned it back and forth like a key in the wrong lock. "On the farm," she said suddenly, "when I saw you, who was it you were with? Is it someone you're mated to?"

"Not yet. But we have an agreement. We've planned to be mated when I go back."

"How did she decide to choose you? Or was it her choice? Does the Leader arrange the matings?"

"Of course not. We choose whom we want."

"And there's no ... difficulty for her in choosing a male, when others don't?"

He shifted uncomfortably, thinking of Bluesky. "She sees no difficulty with it," he said stiffly.

"When you go back, will you tell her what happened here, with us?"

"I don't know."

"Would she mind?"

"Perhaps. A little. We have no claims on each other until we're mated."

"And then?"

"It depends on the people. Most of us have monogamy-bonds. It's just too difficult, otherwise. The farms are so small."

"So there's no rule about it. It's just a matter of practicality?"

"I suppose so. What does it matter? Why do you want to know?"

She smiled lazily, closed her palm on the bottom of the water glass. "Just curious. The mating patterns of others interest me."

"What about you and Bowden? What kind of mating pattern do you have?" He knew he had no right to ask, but then neither did she of him.

She took several moments before she replied. "We have no monogamy-bond. Still, it ... troubles her when I go with others," she said finally. There was an edge to her voice, so he only nodded and picked at the edge of the sofa, where a thin curl of stuffing was leaking through a frayed seam.

"Anyway," Delacour said, her voice cheerful again, "your mothers, your male mother —"

"Father."

"Yes, of course — how odd to use that word for humans. Your father. What's he like?"

"He's a very kind man, very patient and gentle." Thinking of him brought such a surge of love and pain that he could hardly speak.

"Gentle and kind? That doesn't sound like what we know of males. Isn't he ... aggressive, dominating?"

He shook his head vehemently, determined to convince her. "He's the least aggressive of any of us. Even less so than my mother. When the animals have to be killed, he refuses to do it. And Kit — " suddenly he remembered: he had told her he and his father were the only two males " — thinks so, too," he finished lamely.

If Delacour noticed anything, she didn't pursue it. "I suppose there always were males like that," she said. "But they were in the minority."

"We're not that different from you."

"Don't you see ways in which you think, feel, behave differently from the rest of us?"

"I don't know. How can I tell if the way I am is the result of my just being an individual or of my being male?"

"But your response to things — do you think you get angry more easily than others, for example?"

179

Daniel shifted uneasily. "Of course I get angry. Highlands says I have a bad temper. But hers is just as bad."

"Do you find yourself wanting to — hit things, people, animals?"

How much should he tell her? Thinking about it frightened him suddenly, too — how much of his temper *was* his maleness? Because Highlands and Cayley and Johnson-Dene seemed to him just as bad might mean nothing; perhaps he was only perceiving them so to justify himself. "Sometimes," he said carefully. "Don't you?"

She laughed. "I've been known to be ... cranky. I suppose it's a question of where you stop. Feeling and acting aren't the same thing."

"Yes," he said, relieved.

"Still — how do you explain the world we've made, so different from the male world? Consensus governments, no wars, no killing — except by very ill people, and there were only two in the whole country last year. Violence against others as it was before the Change is virtually nonexistent."

"But perhaps that's only because this world had an unnatural beginning. It would pick what it liked and discard what it didn't. It seems to me that so much of life around us — " he waved his hand vaguely in the air " — the university, the way we work and think and live together — all that is chosen from the ways of the pre-Change world. This world didn't have to struggle through centuries of trial and error, of primitive science and religion and medicine and survival of the fittest."

She was watching him, listening to him, with what he thought was interest. But it reminded him of the kind of interest Cayley showed in him as a boy in her classroom when he tried to impress her, not the kind of interest that really came from an engagement of intellect, from the excitement of hearing new ideas.

"Ah, yes," she said. "Survival of the fittest. Of course there are those who say that's what happened during the Change. When creatures continue to use responses no longer appropriate to survival, nature eliminates them."

"Except now there's me to account for. An error made by nature."

"Or nature giving males another chance."

Daniel laughed. But her comment made him vaguely uncomfortable. "I wish you didn't see me as so different from you," he said. "I have one very small chromosome unlike yours. That's all. Otherwise we're the same."

"Yes — but what a chromosome! It's the one that wanted to destroy the world."

He thought from her tone that she might be mocking him, but he wasn't sure. She was only repeating, after all, the judgement of history. "I don't think it was that simple," he said.

"No?"

"The males might have been victims, too, just doing what they were taught, what they thought was expected. The males who were like my father never sought power-over, so they were discounted, unvalued."

"I see." She gave him a teacherly smile. "It's a clever student who perceives the opposite of a truth might not have to be a lie. It might simply be another truth."

"I'm not your student."

"You came to one of my classes."

"Only one. The day you talked about the male as virus."

She laughed. "An absurd theory, that's all. You mustn't take it personally."

"I suppose I can't. I'm not a person. I'm a male."

She looked at him for the first time with something like sympathy in her face, and she leaned over and stroked his arm. He tensed, but didn't pull away. He stared at her nose, so small, the skin stretching over it as smoothly and tightly as bark over a knot in a tree.

She took her hand away. "Perhaps I should go," she said.

He nodded. She stood up, put on her clothes. At the door she paused, turned. "Do you want me to come again?" she asked softly.

He looked up at her miserably. "No," he said. She put her hand on the doorknob. "Yes," he said.

The next day he pulled himself dully through his classes, trying not to think of anything but his work. He sat in a library centre for hours, his brain beginning to feel like a pencil worn down to a stub by all it was expected to understand. He finished his report on the new weather study, but when he read his paper over it seemed confused and chaotic, endorsing the report at the same time as saying it was too conjectural. No. Yes. He took a drink from the glass of water he'd brought with him to his table, and when he set it down on the corner of one of the pages he noticed how it magnified the words and letters underneath. ISOBARS AT HIGH level. SUCH A CONCLUsion. He moved the glass across the page, pausing to read the magnified portions, as though it were a code, a hidden message telling him what to do. TEMPERATURE RIses. aneMOMETER READings. Finally he drank what was left of the water, set the glass aside, and put his head down on the desk, willing himself to sleep, the only escape possible. He fell into a light doze, and when he awoke he found he had drooled on his paper. He had to stop himself from laughing hysterically.

He walked wearily to his apartment. It was late; the night-lighting had already come on, and the corridors, empty of all but the occasional cleaner, seemed wider than they did in the daytime. He became aware of a low hum, perhaps from the lights, or from the invisible machines that ran the building.

And then, his hand reaching for his doorknob, he remembered something Delacour had said to him last night, when she'd asked about Shaw-Ellen: *When you go back, will you tell her what happened here, with us?*

The implication of her question was suddenly clear to him — she was giving him choices; she was giving him the freedom to go back.

And if that was true, then he wasn't just a tethered animal growing fond of its jailer.

So when she came to him two days later he greeted her at the door with a smile.

"Well," she said, "you're looking cheerful."

"Would you rather I weren't?"

She looked at him oddly. "Of course not."

She pulled a bottle from her coat pocket and set it down on the counter. "I've brought us some wine. We can celebrate your being cheerful." She came up beside him, slid her hand inside the collar of his shirt, along the ridge of his neck, settling on his chest, her thumb circling in the small depression in his throat. With her other hand she took the bottle from him and set it back on the counter. "For later," she said softly.

They made love, as they had the last time, on the sofa in the centreroom, but taking longer this time, trying to give pleasure as much to each other as to themselves.

After, Delacour got up, pulling off her shirt, which had wadded itself in some complicated way around her neck, and padded naked across the room to get the wine. Daniel watched her easing the cork from the bottle, her thumbs with their short nails pressing the cork up into an exclamatory pop. She found two glasses and poured them each full, came back, and handed him one.

"Thank you," he said, thirsty, taking a deep swallow, which made him cough; he felt the sprinkle of wine up his nose.

Delacour smiled, lay her hand along his cheek. Her fingers were chilled from holding the wine, and they sent a tremor up the side of his face.

She left her hand there for a full minute before she drew it away. Then she lay down on the floor, propping herself on one elbow, her right breast dragging down to rest in her armpit.

"I just want you to understand," she said carefully, "that you have the right to end this. And so do I."

Daniel thought about it, looking at her on the floor, her hair squashed untidily into the cup of her hand. She seemed young and guileless.

"Yes," he said. "I understand."

"Good."

"What if neither of us want to end it?"

She took a sip from her wine, set it down on the floor beside her. "We will," she said. "Eventually."

"Why?"

"Because we'll get bored. Because we are in love with others."

Because we are in love with others. What answer could he make? He said nothing, only looked down into his glass.

Delacour sat up, reached for her shirt. She began to unbutton it to put it back on, but, impatient, finally just slipped it over her head. Daniel watched the way her breasts lifted as she raised her arms, the way her ribs showed through her skin. The shirt fell, a white curtain, around her torso.

"I have to go," she said. "I promised Bowden I'd help her with a report she's writing for Hospital."

Daniel nodded. Bowden: it was so easy for Delacour to move from one life to another, guiltless.

She slipped on her pants, reached for her coat. "Well," she

said, turning back to him.

Daniel lifted his glass. "Thanks for the wine," he said.

She stood looking at him for a moment, then she leaned over and touched her hand briefly to his cheek. "Don't worry," she said. "Everything will be all right." She pulled back, walked quickly to the door. "I'll see you."

"When?"

"Soon."

After she was gone he sat for some time, drinking more wine and thinking about the evening. Why did he feel so oddly saddened? Nothing had happened that should have surprised or distressed him, that should have changed his feelings from what they were when he met her at the door. She said he had the right to end what was between them; a few weeks ago that would have made him feverish with relief.

He got up, brushed the lightcode on the side table to black, and stalked restlessly around the dark room. His head felt fuzzy, and he evaluated the sensation: if it was intoxication, it wasn't very pleasurable.

When? Soon. She was still the one to choose.

He decided to go for a walk outside, but it was colder than he had expected, and it was starting to snow, so he came back inside and sat down in the rotunda nearest his apartment and looked out the window at the snow falling quietly into the deep-coulee. It relaxed him, and slowly his frustation with himself eased a little. His feelings for Delacour were not as simple as he would like them to be, that was all. Under the circumstances that shouldn't be too surprising. It wasn't as easy for him as it seemed to be for her to separate physical desires from emotions.

He smiled a little at his pale reflection in the window. A student who had sat down opposite him thought he was smiling at her and smiled back. They made casual conversation about the weather and school for a few minutes, and then they both got up and headed off down opposite hallways. That was what Delacour expected of him, he thought: they would pass some pleasant time together and at the end they would walk away down opposite hallways. Surely, given the alternatives, he should be relieved that was all she wanted.

It was several days later when he came home in the afternoon from his classes that he found Delacour standing outside his door.

He stared at her down the corridor, alarm freezing his body into stillness, an old instinct hoping for the luck of camouflage. What was she doing here, at this time of day, so blatantly waiting for him outside his door? He forced himself to step forward, reassuring himself that she simply wanted to see him, and the thought made him smile, quicken his step. She saw him coming then, and waved.

When he reached her, she said, "I'm sorry for loitering about here, but I thought you'd be home by now. I had to see you."

He unlocked the door. "It's all right," he said, "I'm glad you've come."

She went inside, her teacher's-robe snagging on the door; she paid it no attention, and it almost tore as it was pulled free. She sat down on the sofa, regarded him unsmilingly across the room. His alarm returned. Something was wrong.

"I need to talk to you," she said. "Sit down."

He did, in the chair facing her. "What's wrong?" he said. "What's happened?"

"Perhaps nothing." She took a deep breath, began pleating her robe between her long fingers. She lifted her hand a little toward him, let it drop again into her lap. "I may be pregnant."

"What?" He felt as though she had struck him.

"I may be pregnant. My menses should have begun by now."

"But — " He looked at her in a horror of understanding. "But weren't you monitoring yourself?"

"Monitoring? What do you mean?"

"Monitoring," he said desperately. "For your fertile days. Your mucus secretions — "

She looked at him uncomprehendingly.

"The way the — the way Shaw-Ellen does, so she doesn't, so we don't make a child until we want to — "

"Ah," she said, giving a little twitch of a smile. "You have to remember — making love and conceiving children are for us quite vastly different things; it's like thinking that washing your face will make your hair fall out. There's simply no connection."

He nodded, not looking at her. It was his fault, all his fault. How could he not have thought about it? How could he expect her to know about monitoring, when such knowledge for her had been obsolete for centuries?

"You have to stop it," he said.

"Stop it?"

"Yes. It could be a male. You have to stop it."

She hesitated. "It's not that simple," she said at last. "A person and her doctor have to go to considerable time and expense to produce ova-fusion implantation. A doctor wouldn't want to stop a healthy pregnancy."

He stared at her, not understanding. "But that's not true. A doctor will stop it whenever you want. It's always your choice."

"Where did you hear that?"

"From Doctor. In Fairview. *She'd* make it stop, even if the ones here wouldn't. She'd come down and do it, if I asked her to."

"I see." Delacour leaned her head against the back of the sofa. And then he understood.

"You did it on purpose," he whispered. "You wanted this."

His head felt like a room in which the law of gravity had suddenly disappeared, the furniture flying about, chaotic.

She lifted her head, looked at him, her blue eyes forcing themselves into his. "I didn't plan this," she said quietly. "Please believe that."

"Then you have to stop it. Can't you see that? If the child is a male — how could you explain it? Don't you see what it would mean?" He paused, but she didn't answer. "Delacour." He had never spoken her name before. *"Please."*

Still she didn't reply. He wanted to grab her, shake the right answer from her.

"Daniel," she said finally, "you have to realize that eventually people will find out. With the train up to the Peace now, you can't remain isolated any more. It has to happen sometime — "

"And you want to be the one to make it happen." His voice was thick with disgust. He didn't believe she hadn't planned it; it had been her intention all along, to conceive, from a male, another experiment, and he had only, after all, been something for her to use. He thought of the last time she had come, the things she had said, just another trick, when beneath everything must already have been her suspicion, or knowledge, of this. She had even brought a bottle of wine. To celebrate, she said.

"You mustn't assume it will be something disastrous."

"But it will! Of course it will! Before the Change — "

" — was a different time. You said yourself you're not that different from us now." She leaned forward. "Think about it for a moment, Daniel. Doesn't the idea excite you, even a little? If males became known again in the outside world, you wouldn't have to keep isolated on the farms. You could be free. Don't tell me you haven't wished for that."

He shifted in his seat. "Of course I have. But I know I sometimes have to deny my own wishes for the good of others." Even as he said it he felt guilty, knowing how much he had imperilled the good of others by his selfishness.

But to his surprise Delacour's gaze faltered, and he knew he had touched something in her.

"And the child," he pressed on, "think of the child." He did so himself, now. He had spoken of a time such as this with Bluesky, and then with Shaw-Ellen, the special joy of it when they would decide they were ready — and now it had happened, not with Bluesky or Shaw-Ellen, but with Delacour, and there could be nothing of joy here, nothing but disaster. He forced himself to continue, to imagine it. "It would be a freak, despised and feared. What do you intend for it, once you've shown it so proudly to the world? To sell it to a zoo?"

She flinched. "I'm not that evil," she said quietly. "My god."

"You're *doing* something evil. You're interfering in something you have no right to."

She only sat there, looking past him, as though at someone else standing behind his chair. It was impossible for him to tell what she was thinking, her face impassive as a plate, as a picture on the wall. She was a stranger to him, an utter stranger, whom he had deluded himself into thinking he was beginning to know, to understand.

"Of course you're concerned," she said finally. "And angry. But everything will be all right. You'll see." She stood up.

"It *won't* be all right! For god's sake — " She was getting ready to leave, to walk out his door and carry on with her mad plan, against all logic, against all entreaties. He fumbled to his feet, went over to her, and clutched her arm. She stiffened, and he made himself drop his hand. Everything had happened so quickly: just a few moments ago she had been standing outside his door, and he had gone forward to meet her, eagerly, and now —

"I suppose I should go," she said, stepping back from him.

"You promised me," he said, desperately. "Does your word mean nothing to you?"

"I didn't expect this when I promised." Her fingers twisted at her teacher's-robe. "I'm sorry." She turned and walked to the door.

"Don't you care at all about what will happen?" he cried at her back. "To the world? To the farms? To me?"

"Daniel, I do — "

"To yourself?"

She hesitated. "Myself?"

"The world will judge you the way I do. The world will despise you."

She put her hand on the doorknob, flexed her fingers, tightened them. When she turned to look at Daniel, her face had a slight, unreadable smile. "We'll see," she said. She opened the door. "Well." She hesitated, rubbing her hand on the doorknob. "Goodbye then."

He couldn't answer. *Goodbye then.* It was over, just like that. He had lost everything.

When she saw that he wasn't going to reply she stepped into the hallway. As she pulled the door closed behind her she kept her eyes down, fixed on her hand.

He stared at the closed door. *Goodbye then.* This was no dream, no nightmare on which the door of daylight would suddenly open.

He began to pace frantically about the room. How could he have trusted her? How could he have been such a fool?

What he *had* to do, he knew, was tell Highlands immediately what had happened. There was no way now to avoid his confession. If he had told her the truth right away things would never have come to this. He sat down at his desk, took out a piece of paper and pencil, and wrote down the date, in a cramped script that hardly resembled his, and then, "Dear Highlands." The pencil drooped in his fingers. What could he say? Where even to begin? The image of the farms burning, a vengeful purge, and himself holding the leading torch, what he had seen that first night he and Delacour made love, seared his mind again.

He got up and pushed his chair back so abruptly it nearly toppled over, and stumbled outside into the hall. He got onto a moveway which took him into University, and when he got off he found himself in the History sector. It made him laugh out loud, and an elderly person with a red walking stick looked at him strangely and raised her cane as though to prod him awake.

He saw a door to the outside and took it, and stood for a long time letting the cold October air scrape at his lungs.

The door beside him opened. Someone stepped out wearing a teacher's-robe. The wind billowed it out hugely in front of her.

He ran.

Twice he fell; the pillows of snow beside the path cushioned his falls, although he still scraped one knee enough to bleed. But when he stumbled, dripping with snow and perspiration, back into his apartment, he knew what he would do.

He would go home. Every moment he had stayed here had made things worse. He would go home, make his horrible confessions in person. Highlands had to be told, without any more stupid delays or excuses. If he left on the morning train he would reach her sooner than a letter.

With a feverish energy he began to pack. There wasn't much, really — a few clothes and hygiene items, but mostly books and papers, which he forced himself to take, resisting the urge to leave them all, as though they were responsible for everything. In an hour he was finished. He sat down among the four suitcases and stared around the apartment, trying to imagine himself gone, everything that had happened to him here erased.

He would have to inform University that he was going, he remembered; he couldn't just disappear without explanation. He dug through the papers left in his desk until he found an absences form and filled it in, and then he went out to the University maildrop and left it there. He scribbled a note to Mitchell-Star as well, simply saying he had to go home, and slid it under her door. He stood outside her apartment for several moments, even raised his hand to knock, but he knew it would be a mistake. His throat went tight and hard, a pain he couldn't swallow away. She had been his only friend here, his only real friend.

Back in his apartment, he was anxious to leave, but it was still several hours before the train left. He tried to sleep, but as soon as he drifted off he would jerk awake, thinking he had slept through the timer. His thoughts were full of Delacour, of what she would do. Would his leaving alarm her, make her think he had gone somewhere to plot his revenge? He didn't want her to think anything but the bitter truth, that she had won and that he was going home to hide.

He would leave her a note, he decided, as he had for Mitchell-Star. If he left it at her apartment, he could address it to Bowden, too; it would be easier then to make the message formal and to the point. He tried several versions, but the one he finally copied and slipped under their door sometime in the dark early hours, when it seemed he must be the only person in the whole complex still awake, said: *I thought I would let you know that I am going back to the farms, and that I have filed my absence papers with University. I simply find the life here too difficult. Thank you again for having me to dinner. — Daniel*

He stood outside that door for a long time, too, wrenched with memory. Delacour. He thought of their lovemaking, their conversations that seemed now to be all fragments and half-truths. He imagined her inside, curled asleep into the arms of Bowden. And inside her, growing, something she had stolen from him, something she could use to destroy them all.

A rage against her began suddenly to throb wildly at his temples. He felt like kicking, beating at the door until she opened it, then beating at her. His hand clenched the doorknob, as though he were going to rip it away, use it as a weapon.

He could kill her. Yes, he wanted to kill her. The thought was clear and strong in his mind. If she were standing in front of him right now he could solve everything so simply — he could kill her —

He shuddered, leaned against the wall, and closed his eyes. Nausea welled up into his throat; he swallowed several times, tasting it.

He had wanted to kill her. How could his mind have formed the unspeakable idea? Murder. Since the Change it was practically unknown, the act of someone deranged. It was what the males had done. He bent over, took a long, shuddering breath. *Do you find yourself wanting to hit things?* And he had answered ingenuously, *Sometimes. Don't you?*

Finally he made himself straighten and walk away. But he couldn't forget the feeling that had overwhelmed him. He thought about it as he stood waiting for the bus to take him to the train station, and all the way there, barely noticing the city passing by his window. He remembered how he had read in one of the pre-Change books a male saying that as childbirth makes a woman from a girl, killing makes a man from a boy. It sounded too barbaric, too absurd, to be serious, he had thought, explaining it away; the male must have been speaking in a metaphor. And now, he had seen the barbarism in himself.

But in a curious way, he would think later, when he was

back home, it was that incident that changed something in him, that reached inside and shook forever the boy, the child, from him.

When the train arrived he took a seat that faced forward, toward the north, and began his long trip home.

CHAPTER SIX

BOWDEN

BOWDEN LOOKED AT THE NOTE FOR SOME TIME. She remembered who Daniel was, of course, and the dinner, and how Delacour had insisted on seeing her to her apartment and didn't come back for a long time. Her leaving now had something to do with Delacour, Bowden thought angrily. The note might be just a courtesy, but she doubted it.

When Delacour got up and wandered, yawning, into the centreroom Bowden handed her the note.

"What's this?"

"It was slipped under the door."

She watched Delacour's face carefully as she read. Yes, it had clearly been a message intended for Delacour, and its literal words were only a small part of its meaning. Delacour sank down onto the sofa, folded the note back up, running her fingers several times over the crease. She stared across the room without speaking.

"You made love with her, didn't you?" Bowden's voice was tight. Delacour said nothing. "And you've done some real damage this time, haven't you?"

Still Delacour didn't answer, only stared across the room, her fingers mechanically turning the note around and around.

"All right, *don't* talk to me, then," Bowden said.

"Oh, Bowden." Delacour's voice was low, miserable. "I've — "

"You've what?" She could justify her anger this time, Bowden thought; this time Delacour had hurt someone else.

"I've gotten into something deeper than usual."

Bowden's hand tightened on her glass of juice. *Deeper than usual.* They were the words she had dreaded someday to hear, the words that meant Delacour might love someone else. She made herself walk slowly over to Delacour, sit down in a chair opposite her.

"Tell me," she said, trying to keep her voice calm.

Delacour turned her face away, closed her eyes.

"Tell me," Bowden insisted. "This Daniel. What happened between you and her?"

Finally, after a wait so long Bowden thought she would scream with impatience, Delacour turned her face to Bowden's. Her eyes ground themselves into Bowden's. "Not her," she whispered. "Him."

"What?"

"Him. Daniel is a male."

Bowden stared at her. It made no sense. "What are you talking about?" But a fear was starting to spread in her, a horrible, rummaging fear.

"You remember what we saw when we were up at the Peace. The two people. And the way one of them looked different. It was Daniel. And he's a male."

"Don't be absurd. That's not possible.It's some trick, or a joke — " She gave a feeble laugh, leaned forward a little, trying to prod a conceding smile from Delacour, yes, of course, it was a joke, how could there be males alive, how ridiculous —

"Bowden." Delacour leaned forward, dropped her hands heavily onto Bowden's knees. "It's true. Believe me."

196

Bowden was so filled with horror she could hardly breathe. It was her childhood nightmare, turned hideously real. Her heart was racing, shouting, *Run, run.*

"He's nothing to be afraid of. You met him. He's not that different from us."

"Not that *different*? A *male*? Not that different?"

"I tell you, he's nothing to be afraid of. He was just here to learn, to be educated, like any of us. All he wanted was to be — " she hesitated " — to be left alone."

"Delacour, for god's sake — You're saying they've come back, that after all this time they've come back, to take over again, to destroy us — "

"He's not like that. For heaven's sake, he was just a terrified child."

"But who knows how many of them there are, what their plans are?"

"He said there was just him and his father now. Look, he's no monster — I think there's more to fear in me than in him."

"I don't know what to believe any more," Bowden whispered.

"I got to know him, Bowden. He's no danger to us, I'm sure of it."

"And you slept with ... him. With a male." She looked at Delacour as though she were a stranger.

"It was the usual thing to do, once, you know. I was just curious, that's all."

"Curious," Bowden said dully. Around her she could feel the walls disintegrate, a blizzard wind of destruction and chaos sweeping across the world.

They talked and argued about it all morning, forgetting about going to work, about eating or getting dressed. It was only when Delacour finally shouted, "So what do want us to do? Do you want us to kill him? Do you want us to go up there and kill him? Is that what you want?" that Bowden sank down, exhausted, in her chair and sighed, "No."

But Delacour only looked at her sorrowfully, and finally knelt down beside her and put her head on Bowden's lap. Bowden ran her fingers through Delacour's hair, absently, feeling tired, defeated. She tightened her fingers in Delacour's hair, lightly, could feel her tremble in response.

"I'm sure it will be okay," Delacour said. "I'm sure I can handle it."

"Handle what?" Bowden asked.

"It'll be okay," Delacour said. "Don't worry."

Don't worry, Bowden thought bitterly. As though she could forget what she had learned, as though she could ever feel safe again.

At work in the next days she was barely able to function, and twice she found herself in a patient room with no memory of why she had come there. At lunch one day Shawna, one of the other helpers, said jokingly about a patient of theirs who had a habit of slapping at people when she spoke to them, "She's like those males you see on the vidspools — she seems to like beating you up."

The others at the table laughed. "Maybe she thinks we enjoy it," said one.

"It's not funny," Bowden said tightly.

The others stopped laughing and looked at her. "It was just a joke," said Shawna. She leaned over to glance down at her new baby sleeping in the rollbed beside her.

"We shouldn't make jokes about pre-Change times," Bowden said, picking up her glass of milk. It banged on her teeth when she lifted it to her mouth.

One of the others shrugged. "Why not?"

"We were being killed, murdered," Bowden said. "How can we laugh at what the males did to us?"

"We're not," Shawna said carefully.

In the afternoon Bowden felt foolish over the way she had behaved, but she decided if she tried to apologize it might seem even more odd. Whatever would they say if she told them the truth? She could imagine their incredulous faces.

Late in the afternoon Wayne sidled up to her, wearing her sly expression that meant she had some outrageous gossip to deliver, and said, in her shouting whisper, "Do you know what Ellis-Tom said about the dark people?"

"I don't care," Bowden snapped.

Wayne stepped back, tears beginning at her eyes.

Bowden turned, went into the bathroom, and sat there for a long time, taking deep and careful breaths. When she came out she told Wayne she was sorry, that she had been worrying about something but that worrying was pointless and she was going to stop.

And by the end of the week she had convinced herself that things might not be as terrible as she had feared. The males had been in the north for a long time, after all, and hadn't made trouble. They were isolated, separate from the rest of the world. And she had met Daniel, too — he hardly seemed like something malevolent, an instrument of disaster. And Delacour was as shrewd a person as she had ever met; surely she could not be so easily deceived. Perhaps, after all, it was possible that things could simply go on as they were.

It was Delacour who seemed to grow more and more uneasy, and several times in the next week she came to Bowden as though she wanted to tell her something, but each time when Bowden pressed her she turned away, irritated. She stopped caring about how she dressed, and sometimes, startled, Bowden would recognize in her the look of patients on her ward who, although wearing their own clothes, still looked as though someone else had dressed them, looked as though they had not participated in the process, their minds absent, elsewhere.

Once Bowden awoke at night thinking she heard Delacour cry out, but when she went to her she seemed to be asleep, her hand on the pillow twitching with dream. Bowden looked down for a long time at her, lying on the bed as though someone had thrown her there, and she was filled with a sudden sadness and longing. What she really understood about Delacour, perhaps for the first time, was that nothing Delacour did made her happy. Bowden reached over, pulled the quilt up over the hand on the pillow.

Bowden recognized the person at the door immediately — her tallness, the scar on her cheek, the greying brown hair that began high up on her forehead, something about the way she stood reminding her of Daniel.

"Hello," the person said, not smiling. "I've come to see Delacour. Is she here?"

"No, no, she's at work," Bowden faltered. "But come in, please."

Highlands stepped into the room, her eyes sweeping around it as though she were checking to see if Delacour might be there after all, camouflaged behind a piece of furniture.

"You're Highlands, aren't you?" Bowden's voice was unsteady. "I met you at the farm. When Delacour and I were up there. And got lost."

Highlands looked at her, her eyes cold, evaluating her. "Yes," she said. "I remember." She looked back into the room. "May I sit down?" she asked. "I'm a bit tired."

"Yes, of course — "

Highlands dropped herself onto the sofa, sighed. "It's a long trip, you see." She rubbed at her right eye, scooped at its corner with a grey-stained fingernail. The creases of her knuckles were engraved with earth. A farmer's hands, Bowden thought, with a pull of remembrance, the hands of her mothers.

"Are you hungry? I'll get you something to eat. Or to drink. Some water, juice — "

"I'm all right." She straightened her shoulders, reached up and pulled tight the barette that was holding her hair at the back of her neck, then folded her hands politely in her lap. "I'd just like to talk to Delacour. When will she be back?"

"Half an hour, maybe. Not long."

"Then I'll wait. If you don't mind."

"No, that's fine — " Bowden was so uncomfortable she wanted to turn and run. Why had she invited her in? Why hadn't she just told her to come back later, when Delacour would be home? She knew why Highlands must be here. Did she want to try somehow to buy Delacour's silence? Or was it something more sinister — how far would she go to protect her farm's secret?

"I know why you're here. It's about Daniel, isn't it? Delacour told me. That he's a male — " She listened to her tumbling words in dismay, unable to stop them. She stood there helplessly, guilty and afraid, as though everything were her fault. She began wiping at the kitchen counter, brushing away invisible crumbs.

"So you know." She felt Highlands's eyes snap her into focus. "Well."

Bowden dropped into the chair opposite her. "We won't tell

anyone else," she pleaded. "You don't need to worry. Delacour had no right to interfere in your lives."

"And the pregnancy? Will she stop it?"

Bowden stared at her. The pregnancy. What was she talking about?

"So you don't know about that," Highlands said drily, a grim smile for the first time nudging her lips. "Well."

"I don't know what you mean. Delacour's not pregnant."

"Yes, she is. From Daniel."

"From — " And suddenly she understood.

"It's an old-fashioned method," Highlands said, "but unfortunately it's fairly effective. I assumed you knew what had happened."

"No, no ...."

But she knew it was true. It explained so much; that was what Delacour must have been wanting to tell her. She felt suddenly dizzy, faint. The room around her shivered into unreality; edges of tables flared into jagged outline; colours leaped at her from books and ornaments and seat cushions; the hallway to the sleeprooms compressed into a narrow tunnel.

She took a deep breath. She must be calm; too much was at stake.

"I want her to stop it," Highlands said. "She has no right to do this."

Bowden nodded. "Of course she'll stop it. I'm sure she intends to."

"I don't think she does. She told Daniel she wants to have the child."

"But — No, no, she couldn't. It would be — it would be unthinkable. It could be a male, couldn't it? She wouldn't — "

Highlands smiled thinly. "Perhaps you'll help me convince her."

"Yes, of course I will."

Her thoughts flapped in her head like frantic trapped birds. How could Delacour want to keep the pregancy, risk bearing a *male* — what could she possibly be thinking of, to take such a chance? It was hard enough to know that Daniel and his father existed, on the farms, but this, this would bring males back, to the rest of the world —

Highlands reached up and pushed again at her barrette, which was dropping loosely at the nape of her neck. Her tugging only made her fine hair bunch up, so, annoyed, she pulled the barrette out entirely and set it on the end table. Her hair, thin and greying, dropped itself on her shoulders as though relieved. Aware of Bowden's staring at her, she said, her voice for the first time easing, conversational, "Silly thing. At home I use bindertwine. But for the city, well, I thought I should try to be a bit less rural."

Bowden pulled her lips back in what she hoped resembled a smile. "It's fashionable now. To use string." She forced herself to talk, as though they were two ordinary people, meeting to discuss a work schedule, a meal plan, mutual friends.

"How is this room heated?" Highlands asked. She shrugged off her cloth coat and let it squash up between her back and the sofa. Bowden noticed that the lining was worn through in places, sewn up in others with a variety of colours of thread.

"You're too warm," she said. "I'm sorry. We can't control the heat here — it's all done from Residential Central. This time of day they turn it up a little. Especially if it's been sunny. Because of the sunsavers, you see. It would be wasted otherwise." She was babbling. She realized she should have offered to hang up Highlands's coat, but it was too late now to mention it.

"On the farm we use sunsavers, too, but they're rather primitive ones. We still have to rely on wood."

Bowden nodded, her mind empty of any response. When she glanced at the time-chip she saw that only a few minutes had passed since she'd sat down. She looked at the door, willing Delacour to step through it yet terrified of that moment. Pregnant. Of course Delacour would have to stop it. There was no other choice. She simply needed to be told how. That must be why she had waited, out of confusion, uncertainty, Delacour and her dislike of Hospital, waiting for Bowden to understand and arrange it.

"We have to convince her," Highlands said, watching her.

"Yes," Bowden said. "I know." She leaned her head against the back of her chair, looked up at the ceiling the colour of pale summer clouds, and waited for Delacour to come home.

When they heard the door open they both jumped to their feet. Bowden caught a glimpse of Highlands's strained face, her eyes fixed on the door.

Delacour was several steps into the room before she saw Highlands. The arm holding two books to her chest slowly lowered until the books slid down to her fingers, which clamped on them reflexively at the last moment to keep them from falling.

"Hello," Highlands said, her voice the cold, careful one she had first brought into the apartment. "I'm Highlands, from the farms. Do you remember me?"

Delacour's face was pale, an odd, mottled colour. She sat down, so abruptly Bowden was afraid she was going to faint. Of course, she thought, if she's pregnant it's no wonder she feels ill.

"Yes," Delacour said. "I remember you."

Highlands sat down, too. For a moment they only looked at each other, hard, opaque gazes. Delacour's dropped first. She sighed, straightened the two books, and nested them tidily in her lap.

"How's Daniel?" she asked.

It was not what Bowden had expected her to say. But Delacour had made love with him, she reminded herself — she must still have *some* feelings for him.

"He's all right," Highlands said.

"I feel — " Delacour lifted the cover of the book in her lap with her thumb, let it drop closed " — sorry about the way I treated him. I wasn't very fair."

"No," Highlands said. "You weren't."

"I hope he's not being blamed. Or punished. It wasn't his fault."

"It hasn't been easy for him. He was our cleverest, our most promising. I'd hoped he would become ... that he would be able to take on more responsibility. Now it's hard for anyone to trust him again."

Delacour kept looking down at her books, her thumb rubbing the edge of the cover. Highlands's words seemed to press her back farther and farther into her seat.

For Bowden the waiting was unbearable, their inching toward the real subject. She was still standing, her muscles feeling so tensed they might not even allow her to sit down.

"Why didn't you tell me you were pregnant?" she asked abruptly.

Delacour didn't look at her. "I'm sorry," she said. "I should have. I was going to."

Highlands leaned forward, lowered her head a little, then raised it again, as though trying to prod Delacour into looking up. She didn't. "Daniel tells me," Highlands said, "that you don't want to stop it."

"That's impossible," Bowden said. "Of course you have to stop it."

Delacour didn't answer. She ran the corner of one of the book covers under her thumbnail so hard it made Bowden wince.

"You don't have the right to do this," Highlands said. "You have no right to use Daniel like that. You have no right to his child."

And then Delacour looked up. "He wanted it, too," she said. "I didn't force him."

"You threatened to tell his secret if he didn't do what you wanted."

"Only the first time. The other times were his choice as much as mine."

"That's not the question now, in any case. This goes beyond what was your choice, or his."

Highlands stood up, so tall her head brushed the lamp hanging from the ceiling, and walked over to them. Bowden took a step back. Even Delacour looked up with alarm in her eyes. But to Bowden's surprise Highlands only crouched down in front of Delacour, and set her callused hands on Delacour's knees, which Delacour instinctively pulled together.

"Listen to me," Highlands said quietly. "The males have just wanted to live their lives out in peace on the farms. They're not to blame for who they are. If you allow this pregnancy, and the child is male, can't you see what would happen? The world would know — it would cause chaos. They'd hunt us out, try to destroy us, or put Daniel and his father and the child in a cage somewhere, like animals — is that what you want?"

"No," Delacour said, her voice soft, too, but no longer defensive, the voice that made Bowden lift her hand, unconsciously, in warning to Highlands, because it was the voice of Delacour when she was determined to win, at all costs, to have her way. "Of course not." She leaned forward a little, until her face was only centimetres from Highlands. "But you're imagining the worst. Perhaps all that would happen is that the male becomes integrated again into the world — "

Highlands drew back. "You want the world to go back to how it was before the Change?"

"It doesn't have to be the way it was. You say yourself that Daniel and his father are no threat. Daniel said his father is the most kind and gentle one on his farm. There's no reason the male shouldn't be able to exist again, openly. Think of it — how exciting it would be!"

"And you want to be the one to make that decision."

"It will happen anyway, sometime. Why not now? Why not this way?"

"It's wrong," Highlands said. "It's dangerous. We know what they're capable of."

Delacour waved her hand dismissively. "Things are different now. We won't let them repeat history's mistakes."

"We can't take that chance."

Delacour stood up, so abruptly that Highlands rocked back on her heels and planted a hand quickly behind her on the floor to keep herself from falling backward. Delacour began to pace the room, throwing out her arms in extravagant gestures the way she would do when she was lecturing. "I've studied history. I *teach* history. I know what it was like before the Change. But what caused the problems were overpopulation, poor political structures, class conflicts, resource shortages, pollution — males were trapped into them just as we were. But now, we don't have those pressures; we'd be bringing them into an entirely different system."

"Which they might dominate and corrupt again."

"Or which they might contribute to and strengthen. Our world is hardly perfect now. People are still starving. Consensus doesn't always work. We're not all nice, nurturing people; we're greedy and ambitious, too, just like they were — "

"We don't make war. We don't kill each other."

"It's all in what we're taught. Males were taught to kill. If we taught each other to make war and kill, we'd do it, too."

Highlands got up from the floor and took the seat Delacour had vacated. She picked up Delacour's two books and arranged them neatly on her lap, the way Delacour had done. "No," she said. "There's ... a difference in the male. I'm not sure if it's something that can just be educated away. It's there in them already as children. As it's there in the male animals — the bulls, the rams, the stallions, the stags — "

"Animals," Delacour said. "Animals can't reason, can't learn from history."

"And suppose the males *do* learn from history. They would begin to see the time before the Change as a time when they had power. It might start to seem desirable."

Delacour frowned. Bowden knew she was annoyed to have her own argument turned and, more skillfully than she might have expected, used against her.

"On the farms," Highlands continued, "the males have always been in a limited, controlled world; we have rules and laws. But Outside — no, it's too dangerous to think of returning them to a larger society."

"It's their society, too. We know the risks. We'd be careful. We're not children who need to be protected from what's been a part of us."

"It's not up to you to decide."

"Is it up to *you?*" Delacour pointed at her.

Highlands hesitated. Finally she said, "It's been the decision of the farms. Of all of us. Not just mine."

"Is it fair for you to keep them to yourselves, like pets, making them hide themselves from the world?"

"It's not like that." Highlands said stiffly.

"Besides, if Daniel and his father are the only males left, perhaps I'm carrying their only male descendent — don't you want even one to survive?"

She didn't answer, and Delacour, in a sudden triumph, exclaimed, "Or are there others? How do we know there aren't? Perhaps *you're* a male."

Highlands stood up. The light from the window caught the scar on her cheek, a white welt. Bowden stared at her, fascinated, unable to move.

"I'm not a male," she said.

She began to unbutton her shirt. When she reached the last button, she took the shirt off, slowly, laid it across a chair, and then pulled down her denims, letting them and her underclothes puddle thickly around her ankles. She stood for several moments in front of them, waiting for their eyes to fall, and even then she made no move for her clothes.

"You didn't need to do that," Bowden said. She felt a sudden clarity in her thinking, and a welling up of anger against Delacour as she had never felt it before.

She picked up Highlands's shirt, handed it to her.

Highlands put it on, then pulled up her pants, the elastic snagging on her bony hips.

Bowden came and stood between the two of them, both so tall she felt dwarfed beside them, but she knew what she had to say. She spoke to Highlands, but she was looking at Delacour.

"I promise you," she said, coldly, "we'll stop the pregnancy."

"Bowden — " said Delacour.

"I promise you."

Highlands looked from one to the other. "Do you have that power?" she asked quietly.

"Yes," Bowden said. "I have that power."

They waited for Delacour to speak, but she only stood there, not looking at either of them. Then abruptly, she pushed past them and went into her sleeproom, closing the door behind her.

They stared after her, the sudden silence in the room like an unexpected argument.

"Well," Highlands said finally. "What does that mean?"

"I'll make her stop it," Bowden said. "It will be okay."

"Are you sure?"

"I'll make her stop it. I promise."

Highlands finished buttoning up her shirt. Bowden noticed with surprise that her fingers were trembling.

"Delacour made a promise, too. She didn't keep it."

"I'm not Delacour."

Highlands didn't answer, only looked at the closed door to Delacour's sleeproom. Then she went over to the sofa and picked up her coat, laid it over her arm and stroked it, as though in welcome.

"You know how important this is," she said.

"I know."

Highlands only stood there, stroking her coat. Finally she said, "Well. Thank you."

When she had gone, Bowden sat down on the sofa and waited for Delacour to come out of her room. She was determined not to go in to her. She poured herself a glass of wine, something she rarely did, programmed in some light music, and waited. She concentrated on her breathing, the predictable chug of her heart. After half an hour she got up and took out a shoe whose sole had come loose and which she'd been meaning to fix. She tried to glue it back on, but it was the wrong kind of glue and didn't stick, so she put the shoe away and poured herself another glass of wine and wandered distractedly around the apartment, running her hand over the backs of the furniture.

She had just sat back down, deciding that Delacour would not come out again, when she heard the door shuffle open. She forced herself not to turn around. She took another sip of wine.

Do you have that power?

Delacour had taken off her clothes and was wearing her blue sleeping-robe. She looked as though she had just woken up, her eyes stale with sleep, her hair rumpled, the right side of her face red and textured with the pattern of the decorative throw pillow on her bed. She sat down beside Bowden on the sofa, not a position from which they could easily talk to or look at each other. They sat there for a long time. I *won't* begin, Bowden told herself; it always puts me at a disadvantage.

At last Delacour spoke. "I'm sorry," she said carefully. "I should have told you. I know you're angry with me."

Bowden didn't answer.

"I want to have the child, Bowden."

Bowden got up, sat in the chair opposite Delacour. She swallowed, took a deep breath. "I know why you're doing this, Delacour," she said. "You told Highlands it would be exciting, and that's what it is for you, something exciting, with no further consequences. Highlands is the one we should listen to, the one who's lived with the males, who understands them. She knows what a horrible mistake this is. You haven't given real thought to what it all means, what a risk it is for all of us. You'd be bringing back into our world something so terrible — This is the most selfish and thoughtless and dangerous thing you've ever done, and you've got to stop it. If you don't — " Her voice wavered. "If you don't, if you have the baby, and it's a male, I'll kill it. I swear I will."

She knew it wasn't the way to do it, that it should have been a conversation, a debate, the way Highlands did it, but she didn't

211

have that skill. She sat rigid, her final words ringing in her head.

Delacour smiled. "You would kill the child, would you, Bowden? I thought not killing was what made us better than the males. Do you really think you could do it?"

"Yes."

"It would be murder." Her voice still sounded amused.

"In history, people did that. In war. If we were forced, and had children by the enemy, we would kill them. We had that right."

"Those were extreme times, Bowden."

"*This* is an extreme time."

"Well, I can't imagine you doing it, Bowden. Killing a child."

"When we were in the woods, and I shot the bear with the stunner — it wasn't hard for me to do, Delacour. Because it was necessary. And when we were riding toward the farm, and I thought, maybe there really are males there, I picked up the stunner again. I was prepared to use it. Two shots from a stunner could kill a person." She was exaggerating a little, but not a great deal.

"I see," Delacour said. She no longer sounded amused. She looked at Bowden for a long time, the easy, delicate music Bowden had programmed scrolling around them like a mockery.

"What you said about me," Delacour said at last, "it's all true, I suppose. I don't deny it. But it's more complicated than that."

"What do you mean, it's more complicated?"

"I admit I'm curious, that the idea of having a child, perhaps a male child, conceived in the old way, is exciting to me. But it's not just some experiment, some ... specimen I'm creating. It's not — " She paused. "It's not an entirely cerebral issue. I want this child. I won't believe it's some demon come to destroy us. It might not even be a male. I feel a ... protectiveness for it. It's hard to explain. Stopping it would be extremely difficult."

Bowden stared at her, nonplussed. It was the last thing she'd expected to hear Delacour say, and she tried to evaluate it coldly, as just another attempt to disarm her. It might be just the sort of argument Delacour thought would be most persuasive for Bowden.

She dropped herself down at Delacour's feet, the supplicating posture Highlands had used. "Delacour, *please*. What you're feeling is just hormonal reaction. It won't last. Of course stopping it will be difficult, but you have to think beyond that, for the good of the rest of us. In a year's time you'll agree that having such a child would have been a horrible mistake."

"I wish you could understand, Bowden."

"If it's a child you want, we can think again about having one of our own. I'll agree to it. Would that satisfy you?"

"It's not the same," Delacour said softly.

They sat in silence for a while, not looking at each other. "I'm tired," Delacour said at last. She got up, stood for a moment, indecisively. Then she reached a hand out for Bowden's head. Bowden pulled back, and Delacour's hand faltered, fell back to her side.

"Come to bed," Delacour said.

"No."

The music rose and fell around them, easy repetitions. Delacour walked to the doorway of her sleeproom. "We can talk about it more tomorrow," she said, not turning around.

Bowden didn't look at her. "I told you what I'd do," she said. "I meant it."

Delacour hesitated, half turned, then changed her mind and went into her sleeproom. After a long time, Bowden heard her get up from her bed and close her door.

I'll kill the baby. She could hear her determined voice, and she turned her head to the side, as though the words were a branch pulled forward by someone ahead of her on a path. Did she really think her threat would work, that Delacour would say, *Oh, well, in that case of course I'll stop it?* So now what would she do?

Killing: what the males had done. Would they have justified it, too, as she was doing, that it was necessary, one small death balanced against a greater good? Wasn't that sometimes how whole wars began, with one killing? The most fundamental basis of her society was nonviolence: could she really oppose it so completely? Surely there must be another way, another choice. Perhaps it would be easier if she hadn't met Daniel; she would be able to think of the child as nonhuman. She got up and paced around the room, picking things up and setting them back down. She could see the baby suddenly, lying on the sofa, its strange blue eyes watching her, its small, delicate mouth — she squeezed shut her eyes.

She had promised Highlands. Too much was at stake for her not to keep that promise.

Damn Delacour, she thought furiously. *Damn* her. It would be so easy to stop it — how dare she imagine doing anything else?

She paced about the apartment until her feet began to hurt, and finally she let herself drop wearily into the chair Highlands had last been sitting in, reaching back to pull free the two books Delacour had brought home. Her eyes caught on the title of one: *The Journal of Adam Markov, Volume 20*. At least it wasn't the Pre-Change Original this time, just a copy. She remembered reading some of the journal, it seemed like such a long time ago, before she and Delacour had gone north. She had fallen asleep and had the nightmare about the riots. All that violence: she shuddered. And Delacour would risk bringing everything back. She had liked Adam Markov, she recalled, but even in him there was the time when, watching the television, he wanted to join with the rioters, to pick up a weapon and kill, for no reason. How could any of them be trusted, ever? But then how could *she* be trusted, she, Bowden, who was thinking now of killing a child?

She opened the book, began flipping through the typed pages, which seemed stiff and uninteresting after the flow of Adam Markov's script, the words embedded by the force of his own hand into the same pages she had been holding. This journal was much later, she could see, than the one she had read before. He was old now, among the last of the males. His daughter, she remembered — Elizabeth — had been killed in the riots. Then there was Jenny, Elizabeth's mate, the one he disliked, thinking the bonding unnatural. Bowden smiled wearily. Unnatural: perhaps Delacour was right, that we learn everything, even what we call unnatural.

She decided to read a little of the journal before she went to bed. If nothing else, she thought, it would confirm the rightness of her promise to Highlands.

She flipped to the last pages, pausing at a long, detailed entry on which Delacour had put a marker, beside which she had written, "disengagement/confirmation" and "cf. 127," whatever that meant; but Bowden decided this time she wouldn't just read what Delacour had flagged, so she turned back a few pages before she began, and read all the entries to the end.

❖

THE JOURNAL OF ADAM MARKOV
Volume 20

Nov. 24, 2097:
Lovely day, sun on the snow so bright it squeezed tears out of my dry eyes. Went down to the Centre, Eleanor coming out her house at just the time I shuffled by, as though it were coincidence, but I smiled and let her think she's fooled me. Poor old thing, how long must she sit there and wait in case I come. Played cards at the Centre, me just three points away from the booby prize, but Carl got that, thank god.

Fell on my front step, a goddamned fucking sneaky piece of ice under the snow, but no damage done, I hope. Arthritis not bad today: the dry weather, maybe the B-12s kicking in. Amanda phoned, to tell me Mrs. Melnyk died — I didn't even know the woman, but I can't deprive Amanda of her little pleasure.

Nov. 26, 2097:
The damn toilet seat cracked right across this morning — good christ, surely I haven't gotten *that* obese. But it's been pinching my ass for weeks, I should have known this was coming. Mike's Plumbing: I look around for Mike, feel like a senile fool when the clerk tells me he's been dead for years, and I knew that, of course I knew that. So I look for some other man, and in the whole place, not a single man, the place is even owned by a woman now, the clerk tells me, plainly getting pissed off at the way I'm snivelling on. But she helps me pick out a new seat and I hobble home with it, noticing on the street how there's

no men younger than forty — that's how old they'd be, I guess, the last of the men, those sickly boys I remember from the sixties. Under forty it's only women. Ova-fusion women. The old order changeth.

In the paper last night: the MLA from Strathcona defeated in the by-election by a woman, and he says it's not fair — because there's so many women now their votes should count only half as much as a man's, he says. Not wanting to give it up. He's not the only one. All those big bosses still refusing to hand over to the women, the mentality of the riots, wanting to see it all in ruins rather than let them have it. And me whining about where's Mike — it's the same thing, I'm just as bad.

Oh, hell. I forgot to stop at the bank. Jesus Christ, I'm getting so feeble upstairs I might as well be brain dead.

Nov. 27:
In exactly three weeks I'll be eighty-four years old. The thought depressed me so much I just sat here and smoked up half my grass. Stupid. But what am I saving it for? I fed Mary Wanna some fish fertilizer, and she promised to make me some more. Shall we not suffer as wittily as we can?

Nov. 28:
Leslie over today, the first time in it must be a month.

It hurts me to look at her, that face with Elizabeth's delicate mouth, the funny little blip on the nose she must get from me.

"Hiya, gramps," she chirped. "How's my favourite old fart?"

I had to remind myself she's an engineer and thirty bloody years old. She looks about fifteen, and acts twelve. But once I must have been that energetic, too, that self-confident, eager for what I thought life owed me. Still, it's been hard for her — being one of the first ova-fusions in the world. (Brave new world that hath etc.) She was an experiment — it could have made her a total neurotic. I wish Elizabeth could have lived to see her.

"How's your mother?" I asked, because she expected it, because I needed to hear it myself, to remind myself that she was no orphan.

"Oh, fine." She pushed sharply at Fig, whose branches were lazing on the blue armchair she dropped herself into. At least she didn't bitch about the plants the way she used to. "Actually," she said, "I was just talking to her the other night. And she told me something about you I wanted to ask you about."

Well. Every rotten thing I ever said about Jenny leaped to my mind. I must have looked like a cornered felon.

Leslie reached over and picked up a banana and peeled it slowly. "It's about the Women's Front," she said, coyly, taking a big bite.

"Oh." So *that's* what she after, I thought. I knew I'd have to be careful how I answered those questions, too.

"Mom says that when they destroyed the Leth sperm bank you helped them." She made her voice casual, almost indifferent, but she was watching me so closely I thought she must be counting every blink.

"She says that, does she?"

"Uh-huh."

"What does she say about herself?"

"Oh, I've known for years that she was involved. But I didn't know you were."

"She shouldn't have told you anything about it. She

could get in a lot of trouble."

"Oh, I know, I know. But that's all in the past now. We all think it was the right thing to do." She took another bite of the banana, chewed it noisily.

I thought of the MLA from Strathcona: sure, everyone thinks it was the right thing to do.

"Well," she demanded. "Did you help?"

I sighed. *All in the past now.* I suppose so. Ancient history. Senile old man can boast of his revolutionary youth. "Yes," I said. "I helped. Not much. Mostly I just helped them gain access, pretending I had to pick up Elizabeth's things. I looked harmless. I watched the doors, carried some things in and out." It hurt to talk about it, to think about it.

"Ah," said Leslie. She'd stopped chewing as I was talking and now swallowed whatever was left in her mouth. She set the banana skin on the coffee table like a large, freckled yellow flower. I stared at it, blinking hard, not wanting to remember.

"It must have been difficult, deciding to do that, to destroy, well, the future of your own kind?"

"They'd killed my daugher, for christ's sake!" I shouted. I was suddenly so furious at her.

She sat back. Fig jabbed her in the neck. "Oh," she said, in a little-kid voice. "I'm sorry."

"She was your mother. Jesus."

She was quiet for a long time, then finally she said, a mollifying voice, the voice they use on me at the Centre when I'm being crabby, "I never knew her, Gramps. I suppose I don't feel the loss like you do."

And I guess somewhere around there she must have gone home. I can't remember her leaving. I remember sitting there and crying for a while, and then I went and gave Mary Wanna some more fertilizer, although now that I think of it I just gave her a big dose yesterday, no wonder the house smells fishy, I thought it was my armpits, and then I sat down and began to write, and here I still am, here I am, still, my body turning into one huge cramp. It's so hard to get to sleep. In youth the days are short and years are long;/ in age the years are short and days are long.

Nov. 29:
Cloudy today, windy, a chinook maybe, blowing a little rain around with the snow. Felt too achy to go out. These damn leg cramps. I should use the cane but I hate the merdy thing.

I had a dream about what happened. Talking to Leslie jarred it loose, I suppose, a black bat memory flapping around my subconscious.

Thinking back to that time is so painful. Which is why I never do it. Elizabeth, it's all connected to Elizabeth. Would I have helped them if she hadn't been killed? Probably not. I don't want to think about it. The political is always personal, etc.

So what should I have said to Leslie? Respect me, for what noble thing I did? Pity me, for I acted out of rage and despair? Forgive me, for the grouchy old fart I art?

Introspection makes me constipated.

Nov. 30:
I look at what I wrote yesterday. Love me, that's what I could have said to Leslie. Love is all you need etc. Not that simple. The people I want it from have all preceded me down death's dark corridor [sic]. That bleak hotel never

short a room. I dug out Linda's photograph this afternoon, set it back on my desk. Forty-five years gone, now. Funny how I suddenly remembered the day we drove out to Drumheller, what she said, exactly, every word, and the funny frilly shirt she wore; but I didn't remember Emily Mandel's name today at the Centre, and for god's sake I've been playing cards with her now for two years. I am old, Father William, I am old. I shall wear the bottoms of my trousers rolled. At my back I always hear. Our sons inherit us. Ha.

My leg cramps are getting worse, moving up into my thighs. I have to make myself walk more.

Dec. 2:
So cold today. Minus thirty. My parsley in the window got frostbite overnight, poor dear, I had to amputate. I can't find my corduroy pants, and I've looked everywhere. I got so frustrated I started to cry. Amanda phoned to tell me someone else I don't know died.

Dec. 3:
Don't know why, but I phoned Jenny today. Not letting myself think about it at all, just punching in the numbers, Jenny, I thought, I'm going to call Jenny.

Of course she was surprised. It must be more than a year since we talked, and then only because of some business about Leslie.

"How's the weather there?" When you call long distance you should always ask about the weather.

"Cool," she said. "But I'm driving to SanDiego

tomorrow and it's warmer there. How's Leslie?"

"Fine, you know her. She came to see me the other day. She said you'd told her about the ... you know, when we destroyed the sperm bank."

There was silence on the line, just dead static snapping in my ear. "I suppose I shouldn't have," she said carefully. "But I thought she'd be discreet."

"Jenny." And then I didn't know how to continue, my throat sealing shut like a goddamned lid on a jar.

"Yes?"

"I'm glad Elizabeth had you. You made her happy. I'm sorry I acted like such an asshole about it."

There was silence, just the static, and I felt stupid, why did I say that, she'll think I've gone soft in the head, all that.

"Thank you," she said.

So that was all, her voice so neutral, just two words, over all those miles, pulses through a wire, just *thank you*, and what did I expect, after all, that she would start to cry in gratitude, forget all those times I treated her like merde?

So I don't know. I'm glad I called, anyway. I suppose I did it for me as much as anything. Nothing is altruism. Do unto others so you can feel magnanimous about yourself.

But, oh, Elizabeth, my sweet little girl: you could have done worse than Jenny, that's the truth, and I'm sorry I didn't understand that. If you were alive now I'd —

No, not the *if you were alive I'd* crap. Therein lies madness, if you're lucky.

My stomach feels strange, heavy, wobbling around inside its ageing cage when I walk, time a knife sliding down the walls of the cake pan, loosening, detaching.

I still haven't found my goddamned corduroy pants.

Dec. 4:

Started yelling at the TV today, some boring program on agriculture, and they're talking about the big pheremone-resistance breakthrough of fifty years ago. I'm not even really listening, but then suddenly I'm sitting up saying, "Wait a goddamned minute! That was Robert Pendowski's discovery — he won the Nobel for it." And what they're doing is showing this woman, Christa somebody, and saying *she* discovered it, as though Pendowski never goddamned existed.

It's not the first time I've seen it happen. They find some woman who was in the lab or wherever at the same time and give her the credit. It's what they did with the polio vaccine thing, and the discovery of one of the moons of Jupiter — now they're even doing it with events in my lifetime.

I went raving on to Leslie about it once, something in one of her textbooks, and she just gave me her lizard-eye stare and said, "How do you know this isn't the truth? Now that we're doing the research and writing the books maybe we can finally tell it the real way, our way."

And, oh, maybe she's right. What finally does it matter? Revisionism: we did it, too. History is only the version of the winners. And so much was destroyed in the riots — how can we blame them for replacing what was lost with their own truth?

I must be mellowing in my old age. The soul's dark cottage, battered and decayed,/ Lets in new light through chinks that time has made. Lets out light, too, that's the trouble.

Sigh. And so to bed. The pencil fell from his nerveless fingers.

Dec. 5:
My legs have gone so numb. I should go to the doctor.
Want me to cut them off? she'll say, as though that's fun-
ny. It's like walking around on two pieces of wood.
 And so it goes.

*Editor's note: At this point there is an interruption in the
entries, and it is likely that Adam Markov suffered a stroke.
The remaining two entries are undated, and written in a barely legible script. The word "sunburn" in the first entry could
also be "return", and the line "She brought Ivy to visit" has
also been transcribed as "She thought I was sick". On the last
page is printed, possibly by Jenny herself, the words: "Adam
Markov died February 12, 2098".*

 my mother with the pails full of raspberries and our
fingernails all red, and what a sunburn.

 some pain, and the drugs. Linda came to see me today
but it was Jenny. She looked nice. She brought Ivy to visit.
It's hard to remember exactly.

❖

Bowden sat for a long time holding the journal, feeling an unexpected sadness settle over her. That's where it all ends, she
thought, in death.
 Finally she forced herself to get up, and she went into the
kitchen and poured herself a glass of milk. She walked to the

window and stood looking out at the snow coming down quietly, small, repetitive flakes. They clung to the wire sculpture of the buffalo, that oldcreature hunted into extinction, that she could see outlined against the darkening sky across the deepcoulee.

She had a habit, when she was upset, of reading everything as though it would offer her some direction in her own life, but in Adam Markov's journal now she found only further complexities, ambiguities. She had expected it to confirm her promise to Highlands, but this part of the journal was so unlike what she had read before. The males here seemed more pathetic than dangerous. And she had forgotten that Adam Markov had been a part of the Women's Front, although she must have learned that in school, and reading it now disconcerted her. He was a male, yet, as his granddaughter said, he turned against his own kind, to make possible this future.

As Delacour, she thought suddenly, was turning against *her* own kind, to make possible another future. And would males three hundred years from now be applauding her courage, too? She shuddered, turned abruptly from the window. She felt cold, cold, but when she checked the heat it was normal, so she pushed the opaquer on the window so she wouldn't have to see the snow and reached for another sweater from the hall closet. Her arm brushed the battery lamp on the shelf beside her sweater and it clattered down.

"Merde." She reached over and picked it up, put it back on the shelf.

"What's happened?"

Bowden jumped, nearly knocking the battery lamp down again. Delacour was standing beside her, sleepily rubbing her chest. She was wearing the blue cottonweave pyjamas Bowden had given her last Christmas, which Bowden hadn't seen her wear for months.

"Nothing," Bowden said. "I'm sorry I woke you. I just dropped the battery lamp."

"I wasn't sleeping very well, anyway," Delacour said. "I think I'll warm some milk for myself. Would you like some?"

"No, I have a glass." She went and sat on the sofa, watching Delacour in the kitchen pour the milk and program it warm. A detached part of her mind was making a dutiful note that the jug would be almost empty now and that she would have to order a delivery for tomorrow. "I've just been reading the Adam Markov journal," she said.

"Have you?" Delacour came over to her, sat beside her. "Tell me what you think about it."

They were behaving as though this were any ordinary evening, as though nothing were wrong. Still, if Delacour wanted to talk to her, about anything, it was better than silence, Bowden decided. She picked up her glass of milk, sorry now she hadn't had Delacour warm it, too.

"I'd forgotten that Adam Markov was part of the Women's Front," she said. "I was just thinking about the ... courage it must have taken to do that."

"Yes," Delacour said. "Of course his part was pretty minor. And he admits he was acting only out of personal rage."

"Still — I think he must have had a greater vision than that. Considering he was a male — "

Delacour sipped her milk. "Yes, he was a rather special one." She yawned, set her milk down on the end table.

"It's interesting," Bowden said cautiously, "that even one of the better males thought they should be destroyed."

Delacour shrugged. "It was just a choice he made, that's all. We don't know what a future with males would have been like."

"Yes, we do! It's there in the history you teach every day!

226

It would have been full of wars and violence and destruction."

Delacour sighed. "Not necessarily."

Bowden banged her glass down on the end table beside Delacour's. Their rims touched, gave a sharp cry, *ping,* of contact. "Don't you have any doubts at all about what you're doing?" she demanded.

Delacour didn't answer. She reached over and pushed the two glasses absently a few centimetres apart. Suddenly she said, "Did you look at the appendices at the end of Adam Markov's journal?"

"No. Why?"

Delacour picked up the journal, turned to a section at the end, and leafed through it until she found the page she wanted. She handed the book to Bowden. "The right-hand page," she said.

Bowden took the journal. On the right-hand page was a geneological table, in fine print, covering about a dozen generations. Her eyes slid down the thickening column.

And so on. Bowden glanced up at Delacour, not understanding. "Why do you want me to look at this?"

"The bottom. One of the names. On the right-hand side."

Bowden looked down to the bottom of the page, where about

ten branches were represented. What was she supposed to be looking for?

Her hands clenched on the page.

Jesse-Lee — Rhea

|

Delacour

"You're a direct descendent," she whispered, "of Adam Markov." Her eyes moved again up the column. There seemed to be so few names, suddenly, less than a dozen, so little time, separating Delacour's name from Adam Markov's.

"Yes. Funny, isn't it?"

"Why didn't you ever tell me?"

"It's not important."

"But ... it's interesting. You must feel some special connection."

"Not really."

"Then why did you show this to me? Why now?"

Delacour reached over to take the book from Bowden's hands, but Bowden pulled away. Annoyed, Delacour said, "You were reading the book. This is just a part of it. I thought you'd find it amusing, that's all."

Bowden put her finger lightly under Delacour's name. "And what will the next edition write here?" she asked. "Is that what you're waiting for, to add the name that will bring it all full circle somehow?"

Delacour snatched the journal away, slapped it shut, and tossed it on the end table. "For heaven's sake," she said. "I'm not interested in any kind of a dynasty. And I really don't care who my personal ancestors were."

"All right," Bowden said. "I believe you." But she kept looking at the book lying on the end table. *The Journal of Adam*

228

Markov. And in it was Delacour's name, like some eerie prophecy.

Delacour put her arm around Bowden's shoulders, tried to pull her closer. "What *will* be in the next edition, though," she said softly, "is your name, beside mine."

"Are you sure? I thought that if there are children the names of the mothers appear. They'll write Daniel's name beside yours. The mother and the ... father."

She felt Delacour's arm tense on her shoulders, and she knew she had been right and that the idea had unsettled Delacour. She had to press any advantage she could. "*Please*, Delacour, you have to believe me, that I want what's best for you — "

Delacour leaned back against the sofa, dropping her head against the headrest. Her arm slid away from Bowden's shoulder, fell limply into the space between them. She sighed. "Look, Bowden — I know you're only trying to help, but — "

Something in the words, the voice, the way it sounded querulous at the same time as it alleged the opposite, tugged at Bowden's memory, and suddenly she began to laugh. She pulled back, shook her head, dismayed, not believing this outburst, laughter at a time when nothing was funny.

"I'm sorry," she said, swallowing, forcing herself to stop. "How stupid. It's because of what you said: *I know you're only trying to help*. It's what Jesse-Lee said when I last saw her, and, I suppose because I saw her name in the journal just now, well, she said those exact words, and it triggered Central, and when they came on she shouted at the communicator to shut up. I don't know why I thought of that. I'm sorry. It's not funny."

As she spoke, Delacour looked at her impassively, and then she pulled her brows down and closer to each other the way she did when she was angry, so that it looked as if her forehead had grown a ridge of muscle. She opened her mouth, but what came out was not words at all, but a strange sobbing, hard pieces

229

of sound that dropped into the silence. She sat there with her mouth open as though her jaw were refusing to close, and she cried.

Bowden stared at her. She reached forward, her hand trembling, and stroked Delacour's knee, but Delacour flinched away from her touch and stood up, turning her back. It seemed to take a long time before she stopped crying. At last Bowden heard her take a deep, shuddery breath, and then she said, her voice struggling and angry with itself, "I'm sorry."

"It's all right — "

"It's stupid. I hate crying." She turned abruptly to look down at Bowden. Her eyes were red, raw-looking, her cheeks blotchy. "I know I didn't deal very well with Jesse-Lee's death," she said, her voice still rough and uneven. "Or her life, either, for that matter. I never felt she loved me. When Rhea died, I was just a reminder to her of what she'd lost. You know what she said to me once? She said, 'You were Rhea's idea, you know. Not mine.' "

"But that doesn't mean she didn't care about you. I know she did." But Bowden could almost hear Jesse-Lee's caustic voice saying it: *You were Rhea's idea, not mine.* What would it have been like for Delacour, growing up with those denying words whispering always in her head?

Delacour snorted. "Care about. I care about the books I read, the, the — " she waved her hand in the air, gesturing vaguely across the room " — the water-reflector I made, the teacher's-robe I wear. It's not the same as love." She picked up her glass of milk, finished what was in it, then spun the glass between her palms, looking into it. "Jesse-Lee had a birth-child of her own, you know," she said abruptly. "She died when she was a baby. I only found out by accident, snooping through some records-papers. I suppose that was the child she really loved."

Bowden struggled to find an answer, the right words. What she did say, finally, was what she would say to the old people who still brooded about an unkindness, an injustice, done to them long ago by a mother, a friend, a mate, a daughter: "You have to forgive her."

Delacour only frowned, peered more deeply into her glass.

Perhaps, Bowden thought, she should tell Delacour that Jesse-Lee had told her about her birth-child, how Jesse-Lee might have told Delacour about it, too, if Delacour had gone to see her one last time. But she decided it would be a mistake. She wondered suddenly why the child hadn't been listed in the geneological chart. If a baby died that young, it must not have to be recorded. If a baby died that young — she winced, flooded with the memory of another baby, of her promise to Highlands.

"Oh, well," Delacour said, sighing, setting the glass down. "I wasn't an easy child, either. Maybe we get the mothers we deserve."

"And the child you're carrying — will it get the mother it deserves?"

Delacour didn't answer, but she turned her eyes now on Bowden. They were still red and painful-looking. "I wish you understood, Bowden," she said at last, softly, sadly. "I wish you wouldn't be afraid."

"But I am," Bowden said. "I am."

Delacour stood looking at her for a long time, and then she sat down again beside her. "You shouldn't be," she said. "Oh, Bowden — " She paused. "I've been thinking a lot about us in the past few weeks. And if you still want a monogamy-bond, then I'll agree."

"What?" Bowden looked at her, amazed.

"I know it seems like an odd time to bring it up, but, well, it's true. I've been thinking about it. You deserve better from me than what I've given you."

"This is a ... a bribe, isn't it? If I don't oppose you in this pregnancy you'll offer me a monogamy-bond." Her harsh assessment surprised and dismayed her. A few months ago Delacour's words would have delighted her. Now she looked at them coldly, cynically — perhaps because she had offered Delacour an even crueler bargain herself. What has become of us? she wanted to cry. But she only sat there, rigidly, waiting for Delacour to speak.

Delacour didn't answer for a long time. Finally, she stood up and, half-turned away from Bowden, she said, in a low voice, "I'm sorry you think that."

Bowden looked at her, all her arguments, all the things she wanted to say, suddenly seeming futile and repetitive. It would be only later, much later, that she would realize that Delacour had probably been sincere in her offer. Now the only thought left circling in her head, madly, desperately, was: *I'll kill the baby.*

CHAPTER SEVEN

DANIEL

Daniel stood up, stretched his arms high above his head, then pressed his open hands into the small of his back, hard, trying to squeeze away the aching. A noose of stiffness circled his neck, and the back of his legs felt as though the muscles had been stretched taut and fastened down, like barbed wire pulled tight on fenceposts and stapled there. He rubbed at his thighs and calves, but it only made them hurt more.

Shaw-Ellen, who was picking the beans along the other side of his row, stood up, too. "It's so hot," she said.

Daniel nodded, reached over, and picked off the thin green stem that was stuck like an ornament to her cheek.

"Thank you," she said, taking it from his fingers as though he had given her a gift.

"Let's take a rest," he said. "We'll get heat-stroke if we're not careful."

"I just want to finish this row," she said. "I think I've only done half what you have today. Here, you can take these back." She reached for his pail, poured the contents of her bucket into his, which did indeed contain about twice as much as hers. He was a faster picker than she was, and the only reason she kept parallel with him on the row was that he picked so many beans that were really on her side.

He knew why she was giving him her beans now to take back — because Highlands had finished with the washing and had come out to help Huallen cut up the beans. Shaw-Ellen wanted Highlands to be impressed with his industriousness, even if it meant that he took credit for her work. He smiled, decided not to tell her he understood her motives.

"Why don't you come, too?" he said.

She shook her head. "Let me finish this row," she said.

She bent back down and began picking, her fingers in the plants going snap, snap, the beans rattling into her empty container.

He swung the pail to his side and began walking to the houses. Sweat ran down his forehead and dripped off the end of his nose; his shirt stuck to him. He thought this was probably the hottest day of the year.

He approached Travers, who was picking on the next row, and she squinted up at him. Travers was from East Farm, and she had mated with Johnson-Dene six months ago, which improved Johnson-Dene's disposition considerably, but Travers herself was a strange and unpredictable person, and Kit at East Farm had told him they were glad to have her go.

"Are you quitting?" she demanded.

He made himself smile. "No. Just taking a rest. It's so hot."

She wiped the back of her hand across her cheek. "It's not so bad. Hurry up and come back."

"I will," he said. He resisted the urge to say something sarcastic to her about the hour-long break she and Montney had taken in the morning.

As he neared the houses he could see Highlands and Huallen sitting out on Highlands's porch, cutting up the beans. His step faltered, but he made himself continue.

It had never been the same between Highlands and himself since what had happened at Leth, and how could he expect it to be? He knew how much he had disappointed her. She had had such faith in him, that he would do well and come back laden with learning, and instead he had done the worst thing of all. The others had been shocked and angry with him, too, of course, but, because Highlands had been able to resolve things in Leth, they had, except perhaps for Johnson-Dene and Travers, eventually forgiven him. But it was different with Highlands. He had exposed a lack of judgement not just in himself, but in her.

When they talked with each other now they were stiff and uncomfortable, and so mostly they avoided each other. Around her, Daniel thought, he would always feel like a failure, an undisciplined child who ran away from the damage he had done, expecting her to follow behind and mend it. When she had returned from Leth and told them that it had been settled, that she trusted Bowden to see that the pregnancy was stopped, he tried to thank her, but she had said, coldly, "You were luckier than you deserved."

And then she'd said, "I had hoped you could be the next Leader, Daniel. But now I'm sure you can see it's not possible."

He'd stared down at his feet. Of course he could see. No one would select him, would trust him. He wouldn't even select himself. It would have been difficult enough, being a male, but after what he'd done — He wouldn't blame them if they forbade his even coming to Meetings.

"I can see now being Leader would have been too difficult for a male," Highlands continued. "There's too much responsibility."

His fingers tightened on the wire handle as he remembered standing before her, knowing he had no defense, seeing everything changed. His very name now would become a warning to other males, an example of their untrustworthiness, a reason to restrict them.

He set the pail down in front of Huallen. "Well, aren't you fast!" she exclaimed. "You just brought us a pail."

"These are Shaw-Ellen's, too," he said. "I just wanted to come back for a break. I feel like I'm getting sunstroke out there."

Highlands squinted out at the fields, where Shaw-Ellen and Travers and Montney looked like dark buds attached to the thick, long stems of rows. "Aren't the others coming in, too?" she asked.

"No," he said. "I guess I'm the only one weakening."

Highlands glanced at him but didn't answer. She took another handful of beans and began cutting off the ends. She was, Daniel couldn't help noticing, much less efficient at it than Huallen.

"It's so hot," Huallen said. "I feel guilty sitting out here in the shade doing the cutting. The kichen is almost unbearable. Christoph says he feels like the beans he's cooking. When he comes out he does look like he's been boiled."

Highlands laughed. "Tell him that," she said.

Daniel shifted uncomfortably, "I'm going down to the stream for a minute," he said. "I won't be long." He turned and walked away.

When he reached the woods he immediately felt cooler, the slight breeze pulling up from the creek drying the sweat on his face and back. He stumbled down the incline to the water. Pulling off his shirt, he lay down with his face and torso in the stream. He opened his mouth, let the water run in, swallowed. He spread his arms out in it, felt it bounce lightly against his armpits, his shoulders, run over his forearms and wrists and hands as though they were simply branches fallen from the trees.

It was the way his father found him, and, alarmed, he stumbled down the bank and pulled at his arm. "Daniel!" he shouted. "Are you all right?"

Daniel sat up, flinching from the sudden light, his father's disturbed face. "Yes, of course." He smiled. "Did you think I was trying to drown myself?"

His father sat back, laughed nervously. "Well," he said. "I thought you might have fallen."

Daniel dried himself with his shirt, shook it out, and put it back on. "Did they tell you to come and get me?" he asked.

"No, of course not. They just said you'd come down here. It sounded like a good idea." He picked up a pebble, threw it, underhand, a few feet into the stream.

"Well, I suppose I should get back. I don't want anyone to think I'm shirking."

"Why would they think that? Good heavens, Daniel, you've been working twice as hard as anyone. You always take extra workloads."

"I have a lot to make up for." He picked up a pebble and tossed it, the same way his father had, into the stream.

His father sighed, didn't answer. They had had this conversation before.

Daniel watched him, pretending he was looking at something in the fir trees across the stream. In the past year his father had lost half his hair, and even though he laughed about it Daniel knew it made him feel ugly and anxious, worrying about sickness, unsure whether to believe Doctor, who said it was normal for males to lose their hair. He thought of his own thick hair, the way Delacour's hands would clench in it when — The unexpected image startled him, and he stood up abruptly. It was a year since he'd been in Leth — he shouldn't be having such vivid memory flashes any more.

"I had a nice talk with Shaw-Ellen last night," Daniel's father said. "She's a good person. You're lucky to mate with her."

237

"I know."

"She has a more agreeable nature than Bluesky," his father said, then stopped, sliding a quick, uneasy look at Daniel. It almost made him laugh. It seemed like such a long time since he had felt so strongly about Bluesky. She had moved to North Farm two months ago, and, now that he didn't see her every day, he rarely thought about her at all.

"Yes," he said, "I'm lucky Shaw-Ellen will have me. I don't deserve her." He stared across the stream, at a blue jay hopping from branch to branch on a poplar tree, getting lower and lower until it was on the bottom one, and then it lifted its wings in a flare of blue and flew away.

"You're different," his father said abruptly, "since you came back. You seem more ... calm, perhaps. But you're also ..." He lifted his hand, moved it sideways as though to stir the term he wanted from the air.

Daniel tensed himself for the word.

But the one his father found surprised him. "You're unhappy."

Daniel smiled. "Unhappy," he said. Was he? Since he had come back he had immersed himself so deeply in the work of the farm — building the new barn, digging another dug-out, in the winter doing almost all the teaching — he hadn't allowed himself to think much about his own feelings, to remember. *More calm*, his father had said, too. Well, he was that, he supposed. But *unhappy*? Wasn't being unhappy just another emotional indulgence of the kind he thought he had put behind him?

"Why should I be?" he asked, trying to make his voice light.

"Perhaps you miss Leth. Perhaps you miss Highlands."

For one awful moment he thought his father had been going to say *Delacour* instead of *Highlands*, and he went rigid with denial. But what his father did say was just as uncomfortable to face. "I suppose I miss some things about Leth," he said carefully. "But my life is here. I don't yearn to go back. And High-lands .... Well, things are different between us. I try to accept that. She has every reason to distance herself from me."

His father nodded, didn't answer, and they sat for a while in silence. A fish twisted out of the water downstream. They saw it flash like polished silver in the light, and then they kept watching the point where it fell back into the water as though they expected it to resurface.

"Are *you* happy, Father?" Daniel asked.

His father looked at him, startled. "Why do you ask?"

"I've always taken your happiness for granted, I suppose."

His father looked down at his hands. "I don't really think about it," he said. "I suppose that means I'm happy enough."

Daniel smiled. It was the kind of answer he should have expected.

"You know," his father said, "it's time you called me by my given name."

Daniel shifted uncomfortably. He wondered when his father would mention that. It was something he could have started doing when he turned eighteen. Perhaps he had resisted it, not just because of habit but because he was reluctant to see his father as simply another person, a friend instead of a parent and protector. And he should be calling his mother Cambria, by now, too, although that might be easier, since he was ac-customed to hearing the children with two mothers using their parents' given names right from the beginning.

"Christoph," he said, trying it out.

"That wasn't so hard."

Daniel laughed. "It will take getting used to. Christoph."

They sat for a while longer, and then Daniel said, "Well, I guess I should go back."

"I'll stay a bit longer. If I'm not back by nightfall tell them to hitch up one of the horses and drag me back."

The sun hit at Daniel like a hammer as he stepped out of the trees and headed for Highlands's house, past the land he and Shaw-Ellen had cleared last month for their new house, which they would start building after the harvest if the weather held. They would be formally mated next month.

He turned the corner of Highlands's house and was relieved to see Huallen there alone cutting the beans. He smiled at her, picked up his empty pail, and headed out to the field.

He saw that Shaw-Ellen had picked his side of the row, too, so he came even with her and set his pail down. She looked up, her face pebbled with sweat, and smiled. "You're all wet," she said.

"I went and lay down in the stream," he answered, bending down. "I wish you'd have come, too." He began picking, his fingers stiff, having to relearn the motions.

By the time they finished, the sun was brushing the tops of the trees. They plodded wearily back to the houses with their full pails and left them with Huallen, and then Shaw-Ellen followed him to his house to wash for supper.

Daniel was soaked with sweat; even his shoes felt full of it. When he pulled off his socks they looked like drowned mice curled up beside his shoes. He stripped himself naked, ran the cold, wet washcloth heavily over his body, the cold shocking his skin into goose bumps.

Shaw-Ellen had taken off her shirt, too, and was leaning over the basin; she cupped and lifted her breasts, one after the other, to wash underneath them. Soapy water dripped from her nipples. She saw Daniel watching and smiled. "You're lucky you don't have these things," she said. "They're a nuisance."

"Lucky!" he exclaimed. "Would you rather have mine, empty and useless?"

"They're not as heavy, at least," Shaw-Ellen said, laughing, cupping her hand under his flat right breast. They towelled themselves dry and got dressed and went in to supper.

Shaw-Ellen seated herself where she usually did, beside her mothers, Cayley and Sara-Berwyn, and Daniel followed her and sat on her other side. He watched for his father — Christoph, he made himself think — to come in, hoping he would sit with them, but it was Travers who slid into the empty seat, offering him her odd smile that always made him uncomfortable.

Then Highlands came in, with Daniel's sister, and they sat at the end of the table, intent on a conversation they had begun outside. Daniel watched them, trying not to let himself remember that it was he who had so often been there beside Highlands. It was likely Highlands would recommend Mitchell as Leader now. Well, he thought, pulling his eyes away and focussing them on the blue wall opposite him, Mitchell would make a good Leader. Although she still had an unwise devotion to her brother. He smiled wryly at the wall.

The others had all come in by now, everyone talking excitedly about how the grain harvesters from East Farm had just arrived at North Farm, which meant they would be here in less than two weeks. A lot needed to be done before then — the food had to be prepared, the tents put up, and, most importantly, the roads to the fields, many of which had only been travelled on horseback since last year, needed to be cleared and widened for the machines. Only Daniel and Cayley had learned how to drive the farm's tractor, so when the harvesters brought them their fall gas quota they would take turns working with the harvesters in the fields. It was hard and dusty work, going late into the night, leaving no time to visit or talk. Meanwhile, there were still the garden crops to finish. It exhausted him just thinking about it. Johnson-Dene and Montney, who were serving the food, brought it in then, and they all began to eat, hungrily, asking for second helpings.

Travers poked at his forearm with the blunt end of her knife. When he looked at her, she leaned over and said, loud enough for the others to hear, "I was reading one of those books you brought back from Leth. It was talking about how before the Change the males would force people to have babies they didn't want. Is that true? Is that really what males could do?"

Daniel made himself swallow his mouthful of potato-beef. He was aware of the others listening, of Highlands's eyes on him.

He made himself think carefully before he replied, not because Travers really cared about the answer, or because of the others who were listening, but because he needed to explain it to himself. He thought of how he had once said he wished he'd lived before the Change so that Bluesky wouldn't have rejected him then; of how he had explained away, even run away from, such questions when he was at Leth; then of the murderous impulse that had shaken him so badly outside Delacour's door. And of how his whole relationship with Delacour had begun — *she* had forced *him*, in a way. He remembered the shame, the anger, the fear he had felt. Yet he had not been physically compelled: how much worse it would have been to have lost that final, crucial choice. He remembered hurting her, how he had had and wanted that power, even then.

Power-over — that's where it all came from, he thought, all the exploiting and hurting of others: wanting power-over, envying or fearing it in others, using it to make oneself feel strong and capable, when all it would do is make one weaker, more pitiful, more of a child. The seeds of it were in all of them — he had seen it in Delacour as much as in himself — but the pre-Change males had nurtured it, valued it, taught it to their male children. He could see that now.

"Yes," he said evenly to Travers. "It was called rape. And the doctors were often even forbidden to stop such a pregnancy."

"Merde," Travers said. "Monsters."

Daniel pushed his fork into a cube of tomato. "Yes," he said. "I suppose those who did that were. It was one of the ugliest kinds of power-over."

"Merde," Travers said, shaking her head. "Merde."

They continued to eat, the other conversations picking themselves up around the table. Shaw-Ellen put a hand on his thigh, squeezed. When he looked at her, she smiled. He smiled back, put his own hand on her thigh.

They made love later, outside, on the edge of the clearing, where their new house would be built next spring, in the hot summer grasses, the foxtail that was turning its silkiness brittle, preparing for the long voyage into winter.

It was two days later, when they were digging the potatoes, that the bell rang, twice, the danger signal. Daniel straightened, pressed the garden fork automatically into the ground with his foot, and looked over to the houses, but all he could see that was unusual was Highlands outside her house, ringing the bell.

Shaw-Ellen stood up, holding two potatoes in her left hand. "Strangers!" she exclaimed. "It must be." She dropped the potatoes into her pail, rubbed her dirty hands lightly together, and squinted toward the houses.

"Can't see anyone yet," she said.

"Well, I suppose I should go," Daniel said.

"I'll come wait in the longhouse with you."

"I don't think you should. The more people out working the more natural it looks."

"All right." She sounded disappointed.

"This is all just an excuse," he said, "so the males won't have to work as much as you do."

She laughed and kicked at his ankle. She looked toward the houses again, and waved; Highlands must have signalled to her.

"I better go," he said. He turned and walked down the row to the longhouse.

Highlands was standing by her house where she had rung the bell, watching him approach. He quickened his step.

"Who's coming?" he asked.

"We don't know. They're still up the trail. Cayley saw them from the hill."

"How many?"

"I don't know, Daniel," Highlands said, glancing to her right, at the main road into the farm. "Now please just hurry."

He turned and trotted toward the longhouse. Christoph was holding open the door for him. "Come on," he said. "Montney's already inside."

They went in and closed the door behind them. Montney glanced up at them from across the room. He was almost as tall as Daniel now. "I'm tired of doing this," he said. "This hiding. I don't think it's necessary."

"It's a precaution," Christoph said. "We can't be too careful. It's what we've always done."

"What we've always done. Times change. If we were doing what we've always done, males wouldn't be hiding from visitors in the longhouse.

Christoph picked up a book lying open on the floor, brushed his hand across the pages, twice, then closed the book and set it on the shelf. "Montney, First Law has let us survive all these years. You've no right to challenge it."

Daniel leaned back against the wall, pressed his head against the logs. It both amused and saddened him, hearing Montney's complaints: it must have been how he had sounded once. He stared across the room at the pictures of flowers the children had drawn. A piece of bark began to cut into his scalp.

He could feel both Christoph and Montney looking at him now, each expecting his support.

"First Law isn't so bad, Montney," he said. "It's there to protect us. We should be grateful it no longer says, 'Males must Live in Shame.' "

"What?" Montney said. "That isn't part of First Law."

"It was once. Your mother told me so." He had actually forgotten about it, until now. "Wasn't it?" He turned to his father.

Christoph looked at him uneasily, hesitated. "Yes. That used to be part of First Law. You can be glad it's not any more."

"Did you have to learn it that way?" Montney asked.

"It changed when I was young."

"But you *did* learn it that way."

"Yes, but it was changed."

"And did you obey it? Until it was changed? Did you live in shame?"

Christoph shifted uncomfortably on the seat he had taken. "No, I didn't," he said. Before Montney could answer he continued, his voice sharp. "And I know what you're going to say. You're going to say that if I disobeyed that part of First Law, then why shouldn't we disobey the rest of First Law? How do we know any of it is true and demands our obedience? But the old First Law changed because attitudes had changed; people realized it no longer served a purpose for males to feel shame."

His forceful defense surprised Daniel. The argument, he realized, was one Christoph must have had within himself. Intrigued now, Daniel walked over to him while Montney, growing restless and bored with the discussion, wandered over to the window and kept watch.

"So if First Law can change when attitudes change," Daniel said, "then First Law might change again. Someday it might no longer say 'Male must be Hidden.' Someday it might even no longer say, 'Before the Change was Chaos, and it was Male.' "

"No," his father said firmly. "The first part is history. It will never change."

"I suppose so," Daniel said. His father looked relieved.

But Daniel couldn't stop his mind from returning to the argument: for a moment all of First Law had seemed vulnerable, no longer absolute, and he felt himself stand back from it as though it were a building whose bottom boards had begun to crack. If First Law were simply rules of behaviour, to be discarded when they no longer suited the times —

He stopped himself from finishing the thought, the terrible *then* waiting at the conclusion of *if*. He had tasted the freedom outside of First Law, and what had it been but a deceitful fruit, skin over stone? Christoph had been right to refuse that temptation. First Law was necessary. Males could not live Outside. Daniel's own life, surely, was a testament to that.

"Come sit down," his father said.

Daniel nodded. Yes. He would listen to his father, his friend, and sit down.

"They're coming," Montney said suddenly. "Two of them. On horses." He dropped himself quickly to the floor, pulled out the loose piece of plaster, and peered through.

It took Daniel a minute to realize what he was talking about, to remember why they were here. Then he followed Christoph to where Montney was crouching and knelt beside them, their faces squashing together as they squinted through the crack.

It was Bowden Daniel recognized first, her red hair like fire in the sun. A wave of dizziness swept over him. He clenched his hand, hard, on the log he was leaning against.

"It's them," he whispered. *Delacour*. Fear tightened his ribs like a tourniquet.

"Who?" Christoph and Montney demanded together, their breaths pushing at his face.

"The ones from University," Daniel said, his voice still a harsh whisper. "Delacour. And Bowden."

He watched them ride closer. His heart had begun to pound wildly. What had they come for, what awful message did they bring? He had thought it was over, that they were safe, that Highlands had settled everything — Christoph's hand clamped on his shoulder, whether to reassure or restrain him Daniel didn't know.

Highlands had come out to meet them. It was, Daniel realized, the exact scene he had, breathless and sweaty and frightened, witnessed here before; it was how everything had begun, with them seeing him in the woods with Shaw-Ellen and following him here. And now they were back.

"I can't watch," he said, rolling himself to the side and facing the back of the longhouse. "Tell me what they do." He raised his hands to his face, pressed so hard against his cheeks and temples his fingers hurt. His eyes were squeezed shut, but he could still see them clearly, burned onto his retina, Bowden with her circle of brilliant hair, and Delacour, sitting tall and straight on her horse, with her hard blue eyes like rubstones that could cut through the logs, see him crouched here, cowering, at her mercy, again.

"They're dismounting," Montney said. "Now they're just standing and talking to Highlands. Now ... the red-haired one is tying her horse to the poplar. And the other one is just standing there, talking to Highlands. The red-haired one is taking the other horse and tying it."

"You should look," Christoph said. "It might be important. You should be prepared."

Daniel took a deep breath, nodded.

"Huallen's come out now," Montney said. "And the four of them are talking ...." Suddenly he gasped. "Mother's pointing to the longhouse! She's pointing to us!" His voice cracked with terror. "To us! She's giving us to them!" He pushed himself back from the wall, from what he saw, as though that would change it, and he looked wildly around the room, a cornered animal in a den with one entrance, and that one discovered.

"It's all right," Christoph said, but his voice was afraid, too. "Highlands knows what she's doing." He turned to look through the crack again.

"They'll find us," Montney cried. "They'll find us!"

"She's sending Huallen," Christoph said. "It's all right. It's only Huallen."

They sat, afraid to move, waiting for the door to open. The fear-smell of their sweat filled the room. Daniel tried to fix his eyes on the wall across from him, but his vision kept blurring and losing its focus. He closed his eyes, forced his breath in, out, in, out.

At last there was a knock at the door, and then Huallen, not waiting for an answer, opened it and stuck her head inside.

"What do they want?" Christoph demanded.

"Why did Mother tell them we were here?" Montney whispered, pressing himself against the wall.

"I don't know," Huallen said. "She just told me to come and get Daniel."

"Just Daniel," Montney breathed. He looked over at his cousin, guilty relief on his face. "Just you," he said.

Daniel stood up. "Just me," he said numbly.

"What do they want with him?" Christoph asked, standing

up, too.

"I don't know," Huallen said. "Highlands only said for me to bring him."

Daniel walked to the door. He fixed his eyes on the trees, on the distant horizon.

"Daniel — " Christoph stepped to the door, put his hand on Daniel's arm. "This isn't your fault," he said quietly.

Daniel set his hand on his father's, turned to face him. "Of course it is," he said, just as quietly.

He took the two steps to the ground, feeling the way the second board gave a little, as though he would need to remember it.

"You look so pale," Huallen said. "Don't be afraid."

He nodded. "I'll be all right," he said.

He could see them now in front of him, Delacour with her back to him talking to Highlands, Bowden bending down to brush at something on her leg. As she straightened up she saw him, and she lifted her hand in a hesitant wave. She looked nervous, tired.

He made himself lift his arm, limply, to acknowledge her. She reached out to Delacour, touched her on the arm, and she turned toward him.

She was smiling. *Daniel* — he could see her lips making the sound of his name. She reached her hand out toward him.

It was all he could do to make himself keep walking, toward that outstretched hand, the smile. The farm seemed to be gathering itself around him like a snare, every step pulling the wire tighter.

It wasn't until he was only a few metres from her that he saw the child, held against her chest in a tight holder the same colour as her shirt.

"Daniel," she said. She stepped forward until she stood in

front of him, close enough to touch. "How have you been?

He couldn't speak, only stared at the tiny white head, the tiny white legs that hung from the holder.

"Yes," she said softly. "It's your child."

Your child.

Finally he pulled his eyes away, forced himself to look up at Delacour. Her face was blurry, distorted, as though there were pieces missing.

"Is it a male?" he whispered.

"Yes," said Delacour. She reached her hand up, laid it on the child's back.

"I thought ... " His tongue felt too large and clumsy to form words, to translate the emotions twisting through him. "I thought you were going to stop it."

Delacour rubbed her hand up and down the child's back. Its legs responded in two sharp convulsive kicks, a beached swimmer still dreaming of water.

"I didn't," she said.

She reached to the sides of the holder and began unbuttoning it. When the flap fell forward she cradled the child in one hand and lowered it slowly from her chest. "See?" she said.

He looked at the baby's face, small and winced with sleep, the tiny fist of mouth, the eyes, which he was suddenly terrified to see open, blue and accusatory. His child, a male child, born into the world outside of the farms, an innocent monster. He lay there in the air between them.

Daniel felt such an unexpected surge of yearning and protectiveness that his breath caught painfully in his throat. He wanted to reach out for the child, but he could only stand there, his arms hanging like heavy weights at his side.

"Daniel." Highlands stepped forward, stood in front of him. He took a step back. Her face was blotted out by the sun.

"Delacour wants to talk to you alone. I think you should." Her voice was uninflected, every syllable hitting his ear with equal weight, nothing betraying what she was feeling.

He nodded. What did it matter, whether he talked to Delacour or not? The worst that could happen had already happened.

Unexpectedly, Highlands reached up and put her hand on his shoulder. She didn't smile, her face still impassive, but the gesture felt to Daniel like a reconnection to the real world. He took a deep breath.

"All right," he said, looking past Highlands at Delacour, who had pulled the child toward her again and was buttoning him into her holder. "We can go down to the stream."

He turned and began walking, fast, past the houses, to the woods, feeling on his back the eyes of the others. Behind him he heard Delacour almost trotting to keep up, but he didn't slow down or look behind him. As he passed the woodpile, Mitchell, who was chopping today, let the axe fall with an ineffectual thunk into her log as she stared at them, but he wouldn't meet her eyes.

When he was behind the woodpile and screened from the houses he made himself slow his pace. What was the point of trying to evade Delacour now? He had to face what she had done, what he had done.

She panted up alongside him.

"I'm still here," she said cheerfuly.

"I know," he said.

They reached the woods and made their way down toward the stream. A rabbit suddenly bolted in front of them, and Delacour stepped back, startled. "What was that?" she said.

"Just a rabbit." Her fright gave him a grim nudge of satisfaction. This was his land; here, at least, was a place where he knew more than she did.

She rubbed her hand up and down the baby's back. "Just a rabbit," she told the child.

They came to the bank, and Daniel led her down the easiest incline. He felt obliged to offer her his hand, since the baby affected her balance, but when she didn't take it he was relieved.

"Ah," she said, when she got to the bottom, "it *is* lovely here." She thrust her arms out from her sides, took a deep breath. The child dangling in its holder gave a loud hiccup.

Daniel walked over to the water, seated himself on a large, flat rock, and looked out over the rattling water. Delacour came and sat beside him. She was a tug of blue in the corner of his vision, but he fixed his gaze on a rock in the stream around which the water opened, a split seam. The shadows of the trees on the ground and water moved and shifted, like pieces of rotting cloth.

"You wanted to talk to me," he said at last, trying to keep his voice neutral. It occurred to him that for the first time since he'd known her they were truly equal, nothing any more between them of fear or coercion. It was a kind of freedom, he thought wryly, kicking with the flat of his foot at a large root imbedded in the creek bed in front of him.

"I've thought about you," she said, her voice light, casual. "I've wondered how you were."

"You thought about me." He gave a harsh laugh. "Do you expect me to be pleased? That you come here to show me the baby as though it's something to celebrate, to prove you could deceive us after all? You know what it means for all of us. You know what kind of a life you're dooming this child to. My god, what kind of game is this for you?"

A slight, impervious smile set on her lips as she listened. She might as well have been the rock in the stream against which his words spilled, broke. "It's no game. I just wanted to see you. And bring the baby. You've the right to see him."

"How generous of you." He picked up a small rock, sent it skimming across the water. His wrist hurt from the twist of the throw. "How many other people know about him in Leth?"

"Only Bowden."

It surprised him. "You birthed him yourself?"

"Yes. It felt as though it took weeks. Bowden was almost going to give up and take me to Hospital. Fortunately, it didn't come to that."

"How could you keep it a secret from the others? Couldn't they see you were pregnant?"

"A teacher's-robe is a perfect garment in which to conceal oneself. I could probably have continued to work until the very end and no one would have noticed. You know yourself that unless you give someone a reason to be suspicious she will assume things are as they seem. But I took a study-leave for the last two months, anyway."

"A study-leave. Very appropriate. And the child is the product of your studies. Do you plan to present him to the others like some exciting new discovery you've made? They'll obviously have to know about him eventually."

Delacour looked across the water, rocking the baby lightly. She didn't answer for several moments. "You can't keep isolated here forever," she said at last. "You know that."

"We were doing so for centuries before you came." He picked up another stone, pressed it between his palms. He wished he could harden himself into a stone on the creek bed, with no thoughts, no feelings, no memories.

The baby whimpered and circled his fists in the air, and Delacour stroked his back, cooing, "There, there, it's all right, there, there," and he wound down again into sleep, the tiny fingers of one hand hooked into the buttonhole of Delacour's shirt. Through his thin hair his scalp gleamed as though it had been oiled.

"What have you named him?" Daniel asked. He tried to make his voice casual, disinterested, fighting his attraction to the child, knowing that such caring would only make the knowledge of him a greater grief. He was helpless to save him from the future Delacour had planned; all he could hope was that she felt enough mother-bond to protect him from the most obvious cruelties. He watched the way her hand was stroking the baby's back: she could have been any mother, caressing her child.

"Bowden wanted to call him Adam-Markov — you know, after the writer of the journals — but that's, well, a bit much to burden him with."

"Considering what else his life will be burdened with." He threw the stone he'd been holding, hard, so that it crossed the stream and landed on the other side, startling a small, rock-coloured bird into flight.

She ignored his remark. "I suppose we should have named him by now. He's three months old, after all. He must have been conceived the first time we made love. Which ... surprised me."

"Why?"

"Well, it seemed the least pleasant of the times. The most ... violent."

He winced, remembering it, the way he had thought he had hurt her, and been glad. And from that hurting this child had come.

"History tells us children were often conceived by violence," he made himself say. "You should know that."

"Yes, I know that."

"So you know what you might be bringing back to the world."

She didn't answer, her eyes narrowing against the sun, which splashed into her eyes as a wind tugged away the shade above her. Her face went from dark to light, dark to light, a pattern of leaves.

The baby stirred again, and began a muffled wailing against Delacour's chest, pumping at the air with its legs.

"You poor thing," Delacour said, "I bet you're hungry." She unbuttoned the child from its holder and reached in her pocket for a tissue to wipe his face, but as she pulled it free something else fell out, a small metal clasp that clicked into a crevice between two rocks. She bent over to retrieve it.

"I almost forgot about this. It's Highlands's barette. She left it in our apartment." She held it out to Daniel, who took it reluctantly. "She may not even want it, but give it to her, will you?" She turned back to the baby, wiped at his wet, straining face.

Daniel looked at the object in his hand. A barrette in the shape of a butterfly, its blue paint half chipped away, the elastic on it stretched and loose. It was like some cruel reminder of Highlands's trip and its failure. He could imagine giving it to Highlands, her derisive snort for the vanities imposed by cities. Perhaps she had even left it behind on purpose.

He remembered, suddenly, her hand on his shoulder before he came down here, and it gave him a surge of comfort, that even in his worst moment, the collapse of everything, she had reached out to him, her hand on his shoulder, absolution. She hadn't touched him like that since before he'd gone away. He slipped the barrette into his pants pocket.

The baby was wailing louder, beating at the air. Delacour began to undo her shirt, letting her breasts, heavy with milk, slip free. She pulled the child to her, and he took the nipple hungrily. Milk trickled from the corners of his mouth.

Daniel watched them, the sight of her nakedness wrenching him with memory. He forced himself to look away, not remember making love with her, angry at himself for feeling anything at all. Was he still the same fool he had been in Leth?

Across the stream a deer suddenly stepped from the trees, stood gazing at them. "Look," Delacour breathed.

Daniel picked up a stone, threw it in the direction of the deer. The sudden gesture of his arm was enough to startle the animal, and in one leap it was gone, back into the forest, before the stone even landed.

"Why did you do that?" Delacour demanded.

"I was saving its life." He knew the remark didn't make much sense, but she didn't ask him to explain. They looked at the spot where the deer had vanished. A breeze pushed around them from the west, smelling faintly of coolness, a distant rain.

"Daniel," Delacour said suddenly. "If you could choose to stay here, or to live in the city, which would you do?"

He glanced at her, without moving his head. "Why do you ask?"

She shrugged. "Just curious."

"It doesn't matter what I'd choose. I've forfeited my right to make such choices. Once the world finds out about the baby it's the world that will make those decisions."

"It's just a hypothetical question. Imagine there were no baby. Tell me where you'd rather live."

"Hypothetical. I see." It was just another of her games. Yet he felt his thoughts engage the question, felt, in spite of himself, his mind begin to arrange the idea in his head into two logical columns. If he could freely choose. On the one hand, his life here on the farm, isolated, bound to the repetitive seasons; on the other hand, the life in the city, University, the excitement of books and ideas — and Delacour.

No. He closed his eyes, set the columns up again. On the one hand, his life in the city, hiding, always afraid, his very self a constant, shameful wrongness, bound to Delacour and able to live only as she allowed it. On the other hand, his life here on the farm, the freedom of the land, people who loved him, people he loved, Shaw-Ellen —

Shaw-Ellen. And, yes, he did love her. Perhaps he hadn't really understood that until this moment. He had learned to love her. He wanted to live his life with her.

"I'd stay here," he said.

"Are you sure?"

"Yes."

"You don't feel yourself a prisoner here?"

Daniel looked at the trees across the creek. "No. Not now. I was more a prisoner in the city."

"I see." The baby had finished nursing, his head lolling back against Delacour's arm. His eyes were half closed, like those of a doll whose lids were weighted. Delacour pulled him slowly away from her and laid him on his stomach on a rock at her feet, rubbing his back. "So you're happy here? You're satisfied?"

Am I? He remembered the conversation he had had with Christoph, the answers they had given each other. He thought for a while before he replied.

"None of us is ever completely satisfied. There are always things we desire and can't have. It becomes a question of appreciating what we do have."

"What a wholesome philosophy." She was probably, he thought, being sarcastic.

But then, he remembered, this was just a game she was playing, a game he was playing. It was easy for him to see everything so clearly now that choice was no longer possible. "Of course," he said, "this is all just hypothetical. I can't choose.

Soon there will be nowhere I can belong."

"Nowhere. Or everywhere."

Daniel shrugged. It was useless to argue with her. The child had been born, and nothing could undo that. Their lives would all be changed, beyond imagining. She had forced her will on all of them, impervious to any argument, and now she would follow her perverse plan to its end. What Delacour wanted was to recreate the world. This one bored her; she would change it into one that might be more interesting. *Before the Change was Chaos, and it was Male* — Perhaps that was really what she wanted, chaos. She had asked him if he would be satisfied here. He should ask her if *she* could ever be satisfied.

To his surprise, he felt a sudden pity for her, for what in her was like him, the restlessness. But he had a place he belonged, at least for now, a family, a home. And things wouldn't work out the way she wanted them to. If she thought the world would revere her for what she had done, she was wrong, he was sure of that; people would see her as freakish and as dangerous as her child. Of course, ultimately it would depend on who was left to judge.

She stood up abruptly, took a step back, as though she felt his thoughts, his pity. "Well. I think I'll go back up." She turned, began to walk away, her feet grinding on the rocks.

"The baby — "

She stopped, didn't turn around. "I'm leaving him with you."

"What?"

"I'm leaving him here. On the farm."

Daniel scrambled clumsily to his feet. He looked, confused, from her to the baby lying on the rock. "What do you mean?"

She turned then, faced him. The flap of the holder hung down over her stomach, making her suddenly seem flat and thin, a blue cut-out pasted on a green background. "I mean what I said." Her voice was flat, too, like words printed on a page.

"I don't understand." His heart was galloping against his ribs. It must be another trick, another one of her cruel games. "Are you making a joke?"

"I'm not making a joke. I've decided. The baby will stay here. It's where he belongs. I assume that will be agreeable with you."

"Stay here," he repeated. He wouldn't let himself believe her. Why would she have changed her mind? "But — if you refused to stop the pregnancy you must have wanted the child. And now you're willing to give him up? It doesn't make any sense."

She stared past him and over the squirming child, across the stream, as though something in the distant trees had snared her gaze. She rubbed her right hand up and down her left arm, the gesture of someone getting cold. "Perhaps not."

Perhaps not: her words had the tone he had heard in his own voice when he'd asked the child's name, too deliberately casual and dismissive, the tone that feigned uncaring, that was hardening itself against loss, against pain.

So he began to let himself think it was true. That she was actually intending to leave the child here. The breath he had been holding broke from his mouth, almost a laugh. What she said made no sense, no sense at all, yet why would she lie?

But she must have a reason. He had to understand it, what would make her come to this decision, against everything she had professed she wanted. She must have other motives, conditions she would set. He ran through their conversation in his mind, looking for clues, but nothing betrayed her intentions, nothing until —

"Is it because of what I said about choosing the farm? Would you be doing this if I'd chosen the city?"

She dropped her eyes to him, looked at him for several

moments. "It makes it easier," she said.

"But it wasn't what made you decide," he said, feeling foolish. Of course she must have made up her mind before she came. "What *did* make you decide?"

Again she was silent for several moments. At last she said, "Bowden."

"Bowden? What do you mean?"

"I mean I wouldn't be giving him up if it weren't for her."

"Bowden promised Highlands she'd make you stop it. If she couldn't do that, how could she make you give him up now?"

"Well, first she said she would kill the child."

"What?" Daniel glanced quickly at the baby, then back at Delacour, in disbelief, the memory of his own murderous impulse outside her door that night flooding over him. But he was a male — he thought that was why — How could Bowden, placid Bowden, have such thoughts, even imagine such a thing?

"Of course I couldn't really believe she would do it, but, still, it was ... unsettling. That she would even make such a threat. That perhaps she thought herself capable of such an act. That others might feel the same."

"Did she? Think herself capable?"

Delacour hesitated. "She might have," she said finally. "But when the baby was born, and I saw her holding him, so ... tenderly, well, then I was sure she couldn't. In fact" — she brushed a fly from her leg " — I think he convinced her that she wants a child of her own. Our own."

But Daniel was still trying to push from his mind the image of Bowden, threatening to kill, to kill a child. It was no reassurance to him to think that people, especially people like Bowden, could have such thoughts, ones as ugly as his own had been as he stood outside Delacour's door. They were thoughts that belonged to pre-Change times, to pre-Change males. He remembered how he had explained to Travers about the way males had forced people, the way it came from the desire for power-over and that the seeds of it were in all of them, but that the pre-Change males had nurtured and valued and taught it to their male children. The same, then, he thought, could be true for killing, the ultimate power-over.

He made himself concentrate on what Delacour had just said. Bowden had held the child tenderly. Yes. Thought was not action.

"So how could she make you give him up, then?"

Delacour shifted her gaze down the stream to where it disappeared in a thick white braid around a bend. "She'd leave me," she said quietly.

Daniel nodded, not looking at her. There was only the noise of the stream, a blackbird calling in the distance.

Bowden would leave her. Why should that explanation press in him some small nerve of disappointment? What did it matter that it was Bowden who had made the decision, Bowden, not Delacour herself caring enough about the future of all of them to do what was right? The important thing was not the reasons, or the person who made them, but the result.

And the result was that the child would stay here. The farms would not be revealed. They were safe. He felt like laughing, like shouting into the air.

And suddenly he realized Delacour was walking away.

"Wait," he said desperately. "Don't go."

She stopped, turned, but not completely, so that she stood in profile, facing the bank, waiting. But Daniel could find no words in the churning of his mind, everything he wanted to say to her suddenly impossible, beyond language, and he only stood helplessly looking at her, already so far away. He would think about her in the years to come standing just that way, in seeming ambiguity, facing half away from and half toward him, still, like a photograph thumbtacked to his memory.

The baby was whimpering and kicking small bits of gravel onto himself. Daniel bent, his hands trembling, to pick him up, and the child, feeling a stranger's hands on his back, began to shriek. "It's okay," Daniel said. "It's okay."

When he straightened with the child to look back at Delacour he saw she was at the incline and pulling herself up it in large, clumsy steps. At the top she paused, as though she were not sure of the way, but she didn't turn around, and after a few seconds she began walking in the direction of the farm. Daniel could see her blue shirt flash in the trees and then she was gone, leaving a swirl of birds behind her in the air.

"It's okay," Daniel said to the baby. "It's okay." He began to cry, pressing the child to his chest. The tears ran down his cheeks, fell on the white hair of the child. He rocked himself lightly from side to side until finally both of them quieted. It's over, he told himself, it's over. He had been given another chance. It was more than he deserved. He put his hand on the back of the child's head and tipped him to look into his face. He was overcome again by such a surge of feeling for him that he could hardly breathe.

His child. His son. A male to whom he would have to explain the world. He was the father now. Would he be as patient as his own father had been? Would he be able to teach the boy contentment here?

Or would he — Delacour's predictions spilled into his mind — have to prepare him for discovery, for the inevitability of the outside world? For a time without First Law. *If First Law can be changed* — the sentence he had refused in the longhouse completed itself without his willing it — *then life will become as it was before the Change.*

Frightened, he clutched the baby to him again, his heart pounding as though he had just saved him from danger.

"No," he whispered into the child's damp neck, "no." There would be other ways to complete the sentence. There had to be. They were safe, he had thought a few moments ago: but *they* had to mean more than himself, or the other males, or the farms. They had to mean everyone, the world. If the males ever returned to the Outside they could not become as *they* once had been. They would have to nurture and value and teach each other different things than they had then.

At last, the baby squirming in his arms, he turned and walked back to the farm.

CHAPTER EIGHT

BOWDEN

Sᴴᴇ ᴋɴᴇᴡ Dᴇʟᴀᴄᴏᴜʀ ᴡᴀs ᴄʀʏɪɴɢ, so, even though there was room to ride two abreast, Bowden pulled her horse back, let her be alone. It wasn't until they had gone several kilometres that Delacour slowed her horse and waited for Bowden to come up beside her. They rode on for a while without speaking, the morning sun dabbing at them through the trees.

"I didn't think I'd feel this damned awful," Delacour said.

Bowden knew what she meant, could feel the loss herself. In a way, the time after the baby's birth, once they had resolved its future, had been the happiest she and Delacour had spent together. The child had, except for its one physical difference, been like any normal infant, and she had been drawn to it in spite of herself, had enjoyed taking care of it when Delacour was out. When she thought of her vow to kill it, she almost wept. Perhaps she had known all along she could never do it. Or was that just what she wanted to believe, now? If Delacour hadn't agreed to give him up, she didn't know what she would have finally done. Gone mad, perhaps.

Delacour had told her of her decision the day, less than a week after the baby's birth, that Delacour had asked her to come with her and the child to the cemetery. Surprised, Bowden had

265

agreed: Delacour had never asked her to come with her before. She was even more surprised when it was to Jesse-Lee's grave Delacour went first, not to Rhea's beside it. Delacour knelt down, pressed her right palm into the soft soil of the grave, then took the child and pressed his tiny right palm, too, into the soil beside her own handprint. It was the old gesture of farewell, and of love, the one she had not made the day Jesse-Lee was buried. When she stood up, pressing the baby to her chest with both hands, she said, her voice so low Bowden could hardly hear it, "We have to give him back to the farm, Bowden."

Bowden nodded. She was not totally surprised. For the past few days she had seen Delacour looking at the child with such sadness, once with tears running down her cheeks, that she had begun to hope Delacour might be moving toward such a decision. She had said nothing, only waited, hoped.

She took Delacour's hand, the one that she had pressed into the soil, and held it to her cheek, and they stood there for a long time, looking down at Jesse-Lee's grave.

"It will get better," she said now, gently, to Delacour.

"I hope so," Delacour said, her old querulous voice. "I hate feeling this way." She batted angrily at a horsefly that was circling her head.

"At least you know he's where he belongs, with people who love him."

"*I* love him."

They rode on again in silence. A partridge flew suddenly up beside Delacour's horse, and it shied, but Delacour quickly tightened her hold on the reins and got the horse under control. She had, Bowden observed, become quite a good rider.

"Daniel asked me why I decided to give up the baby," Delacour said suddenly. "And you know what I said? I said, 'Because Bowden would leave me.' "

"What?" Bowden was more startled by Delacour's words than she had been by the partridge. "I never said I'd leave you."

"But you would have, in a way. You'd never have forgiven me." She slowed her horse. "I'd intended to tell Daniel it was because I hadn't the right or because the child's not mine to keep, something noble like that, which would have been the truth, after all, I suppose, but — oh, I don't know. Maybe it was just as well, to leave Daniel thinking I was still as selfish and untrustworthy as always."

Bowden smiled. "And you're not?"

Delacour snorted. A twig was caught in her hair and stuck out above her ear at a comical angle. "We'll just have to wait and see, I guess," she said.

Bowden laughed. Yes, she was willing to wait and see.

OTHER BOOKS BY LEONA GOM:

NOVELS:
Zero Avenue (Douglas & McIntyre Ltd., 1989)
Housebroken (NeWest Publishers Ltd., 1986; Distican, 1990)

POETRY:
Private Properties (Sono Nis Press, 1986)
NorthBound (Thistledown Press Ltd., 1984)
Land of the Peace (Thistledown Press Ltd., 1980)
The Singletree (Sono Nis Press, 1975)
Kindling (Fiddlehead, 1972)